THE SHAM

CONVENIENCE BOOK ONE

STELLA GRAY

Copyright © 2020 by Stella Gray

All rights reserved.

No part of this book may be reproduced in any form or by any electronic or mechanical means, including information storage and retrieval systems, without written permission from the author, except for the use of brief quotations in a book review.

❈ Created with Vellum

ABOUT THIS BOOK

Our marriage is a sham. I'm the first to admit it. Only privately, of course.

Notorious playboy Luka Zoric needs a wife, and the good PR it brings.

I just need the career boost being his top model will give me.

It's a win-win--on paper. But since when has real life been simple?

His jealousy makes me crazy.

The control he maintains over my body is unacceptable.

I really shouldn't be so turned on by it.

But there's more to both me and my husband than meets the eye.

ABOUT THIS BOOK

And it isn't long before I'm wondering--which of us has made the bigger mistake?

ALSO BY STELLA GRAY

∼

Arranged Series

The Deal

The Secret

The Choice

Convenience Series

The Sham

The Contract

The Ruin

PROLOGUE

LUKA

My brother is hiding something.

I look across the dining table just in time to catch him exchange yet another covert glance with his wife Tori and can't help feeling like another huge bombshell is about to drop. Maybe it's the recent scandal hanging over my family, but I've had this nagging sensation of impending disaster for months now.

Finding out your father was the mastermind behind an elicit, multimillion-dollar prostitution ring will do that, I guess.

Still, this isn't just paranoia. I knew something was up from the moment Stefan and Tori invited me over—family dinners are my brother's usual M.O. when he has something serious to discuss. I've noticed more than one thoughtful pause from him tonight, but each time he opens his mouth, it's nothing but small talk, punctuated here and there by Tori's typical rambling about her linguistics classes at UChicago.

So now here we are, finishing up the last of the world's most perfect duck in red wine sauce, and I'm still waiting for them to tell me the real reason behind this whole evening.

"Best meal I've ever had," I say, setting my cloth napkin over my plate. "Please tell Gretna that whenever she's ready to accept my shameless bribery, I'll be happy to welcome her into my service."

"Don't hold your breath," Stefan says.

He knows I've tried countless times to woo his personal chef, but so far, I haven't been successful. Seems like my charms are more effective on women in the 18–35 age bracket. Not that I'm complaining.

"We're so glad you liked it," Tori says sweetly. "And I know Stefan appreciates seeing you outside the office. But there's actually another reason we invited you over."

And there it is.

"We'll discuss it shortly in the living room," Stefan says. It's more of a command than an invitation. Typical. My brother is what you might call a control freak.

"Sounds great," I say, trying my best to mean it. "I'll meet you in there."

Tori flashes a little smile as she and Stefan rise and begin gathering up the dishes.

My sister-in-law and I had friction when we first met—which I admit was mostly on me. I was too caught up in my manwhoring ways to respect Stefan's arranged marriage, and I crossed the line with Tori more than once, figuring I'd have a taste of her just like any other woman I set my sights on. In hindsight, I regret how I acted. Tori isn't just good for my brother, she's great.

While they clear the table, I move to the couch and mull over the last few months. What could Stefan have to talk to me about? Ever since our father went to jail and Stefan took over KZ Modeling—now renamed Danica Rose Management, in memory of our mother—I've shown up every day at the agency, on time and with a can-do attitude, quote unquote.

I still go out to the clubs, but after a brief stint at AA—where I realized that as much as I was using alcohol as a crutch, I didn't actually need it to survive—my drinking is under control. Hell, I haven't even been sleeping with that many women. The fact is, the more energy I've put into my job, the less I've been able to put into all my former bad habits. I'm practically a new man—and it's been pretty fucking boring.

But I know it's for the best.

In my new executive role, I audition, sign, and manage talent. On top of that, I also unofficially maintain our client roster, aka schmooze my ass off. Phone calls, dinners, drinks, networking events—I've been there every step of the way, reassuring everyone of DRM's commitment to integrity and transparency, making sure our models keep getting booked.

After a very public fall from grace, I've fought tooth and nail to get the agency—and myself—back on track. So if Stefan thinks he's about to fire me or demote me so he can fill my executive position with someone more experienced, he's got another thing coming.

He and Tori suddenly bustle back out with overly toothy smiles, Tori carrying a black and gold inlaid tray that holds a glass carafe of coffee, sugar and cream, and three mugs.

"Should we have an after-dinner coffee?" she chirps. "It's decaf Ospina, ground fresh. Stefan said it's your favorite."

"Three-hundred-dollar coffee beans?" I say. "Now I know you two are up to no good."

"It's not a bribe," Stefan says, but judging by the clench

of his jaw and the stress lines on his forehead, it isn't safe for me to relax just yet.

I savor the aroma after Tori passes me a cup and then take a long, satisfying sip. To be honest, I'd prefer the standard after-dinner brandy, but I appreciate them respecting my new limit of two drinks per week—and I'd rather be 100% sober if this conversation goes sour.

"All right, out with it," I say, eyeing them as they sit across from me in their matching leather chairs. "I've been expecting the worst since you two invited me over. Just say it."

They exchange another glance, and Tori gives my brother a slight nod.

"Fair enough." Stefan leans forward, clears his throat, and says, "The truth is, the business is...frankly, in an unstable position."

"I'm aware," I say coolly. "Dad's in jail for trafficking, half our models will be testifying against him, and the whole world knows he used the agency as a cover to pimp them out. That's why I've been putting in so much overtime to right the ship. I assume you've noticed—"

"You've done amazing work for DRM," he says, cutting me off. "That's not the issue."

I frown. "Then what is it?"

"I'll just give it to you straight, Luka. Our first quarter P&L was ugly, and this quarter looks worse. We're in the red. I've been paying employee salaries out of my own pocket."

"What?" I sputter.

"I'm trying to tell you, the business isn't sustainable," Stefan goes on. "If the company can't improve its reputation —and fast—we're going to sink."

I let out a breath, my mind blown. This job was

supposed to be the start of my new life. A chance to finally prove myself. And now it's all about to crumble.

Finally, I say, "How do we keep Danica Rose from shutting down?"

By now, Stefan has calmed himself. He's back in his chair with Tori holding his hand.

"It's going to take a huge act of goodwill to convince the public we're not monsters," he muses. "We can't erase the past."

It's no secret that the reason the press and social media have condemned us is because of what our father did. I've done my best to combat that, but even with all my schmoozing and my fancy MBA, rescuing a business from a major public downfall is a huge mountain to climb—and I'm still learning as I go. I'd never been involved in running the agency like Stefan was.

But after Dad's arrest, I told my brother I was committed to the family business. Since then, Stefan has made it clear that co-CEO is in my future if I roll up my sleeves and work hard, quit drinking, and stop fucking around. So that's what I've done. Apparently, it wasn't enough.

"So what's our move?" I ask. My coffee tastes bitter now. It's growing cool in my cup.

"We're going to take control of the narrative," Tori says confidently.

"Control the narrative," I repeat, nodding. "Okay. So we give the media a new story to chew on. Something to redirect their attention and make us look human again. I'm all in."

"We're so glad to hear that," Tori says, giving me an encouraging smile.

Like I said, I wasn't so sure about her when she'd first

come into my older brother's life via arranged marriage. Who even did that kind of thing anymore? I almost shudder.

Admittedly, though, it seems to be working for him. He's changed, and I can't even say anything bad about it. Tori has made him a more level-headed, calmer version of himself. Still, there's no way in hell you'd catch me shacking up with an arranged wife. Or any wife, for that matter. I enjoy a variety of pussy too much to settle down.

"Okay. A new story. Let me think." I spread my hands. "How about a few social media ads with our models, talking about how we launched their careers? Maybe I can organize a photo shoot with some of our new diverse models cuddling pets from the local animal shelter. Everyone loves puppies. Or get our employees to do some publicized community service?"

Stefan shakes his head. "No. We need to focus on *you*."

"Me? Why?"

He glances at Tori, and she sets her cup down and clasps her hands.

"It isn't just the agency's reputation that's the problem..." She offers a gentle smile. "It's yours. The media's been crucifying you lately—"

"They're assholes," I can't help myself from interjecting. "I can't walk out the door without a camera in my face, and half the time they're slapping made-up headlines over photos of me getting blackout drunk from a year ago—"

"They hate you," Stefan agrees. "We've all done our best to rebrand, but you seem hell-bent on keeping the Zoric image in the gutter."

"That's not fair." I lean forward, my anger rising. "I can't be the only twenty-five-year-old who likes to visit the occasional strip club on the weekends or bring a couple women home from the club to f—" Stefan clears his throat. "To entertain," I finish.

"But you're the only one who works for a company formerly run by a sex trafficker. And it's public knowledge that you slept with half the models. It's not a good look," he points out harshly. "The last headline I saw called you a sex- and money-hungry monster, following in the footsteps of the fallen Zoric patriarch—"

"So what, then? Are you trying to fire me?" I say, tapping my finger impatiently against my coffee cup. "Look, I do what I want. The media doesn't like it? That's their problem."

Stefan practically jumps to his feet. "It's not, though, Luka. It's *our problem*."

There's nothing I can say because I know he's right. I throw back the rest of my lukewarm coffee as if it's the drink I so desperately want right now.

"Luka," Tori interjects softly. "You're the most notorious playboy in Chicago. *We* know you've changed, but the public needs to see a bigger effort."

I lean back, my voice dripping with sarcasm. "I didn't realize I was the agency's poster boy. How nice to suddenly realize that *I alone* am the entire face of our family business."

"You're the Executive VP of Talent, and a *Zoric* who's unfortunately grown up in the public eye. Of course you're a face of this business," Stefan says. "Take this seriously. Please."

Suddenly, it hits me like a physical blow: he's disappointed in me. Until our father's criminal activity blew up, no one in the family had taken much time to be disappointed, or anything else, in me. Their approval never really mattered.

Until now.

My mother died when I was only four, and my father was such a textbook workaholic that my siblings and I were raised by a series of nannies. Even as a kid Stefan was defiant and ill-behaved, and our little sister Emzee was the baby, but our nannies always said I was a perfect angel—I learned pretty early on how to get what I wanted from a woman. They spoiled me rotten. As a result, I grew up doing whatever the hell I wanted, with few consequences.

By the time I hit my teenage years, I had realized that there wasn't a screw-up horrible enough to make my father notice me. Didn't matter if I slept with Emzee's babysitters, crashed one of Dad's Porsches into a hedge, or drained the entire contents of the liquor cabinet. I was invisible. So the way things are now—going from being mostly ignored, to suddenly being weighed down by expectations and responsibilities—has been an uncomfortable transition. I'm not opposed to doing what's right for my family, but they could cut me a fucking break.

My shoulders sag a little, and I rest my forearms on my knees. "I'm barely drinking, but if you want, I'll quit dating so much. Won't be seen with as many random women."

I've cut back on my one-night stands, and certainly none of the women I've been out with recently have been connected to our modeling agency in any way. Even I had the sense to realize I couldn't keep fucking the models after what my father did.

Tori takes a sip of her coffee and catches my eye. "We need to seem family-oriented. A clean, stable corporation."

Relief washes over me. That's easy. "Fine, then you two have a baby. The public loves babies. See if you can shoot for twins or triplets, yeah? Problem solved. We done here?"

I start to rise, but my brother's voice stops me cold. "Sit down."

Stefan looks to the ceiling, his jaw tensing, and Tori frowns and says, "We're not going to have a kid just to fix the agency's PR status. Besides, we still have our hands full adjusting to Max and Anya's role in our lives."

Finding out she had a seven-year-old half sibling was a shock for Tori, and she's been slowly integrating Max and his mother (Stefan's ex-girlfriend, if you can believe that) into her life. She puts up a hand to give me pause as if she knows what I might say next. "*And* we've already exploited as much positive PR as we can from that. We don't want overkill."

"I understand what you're saying," I say. "But you're both looking at me like you want me to do something. You're crazy if you think I'm having a baby. And don't even suggest I get a dog, or I'll know you've both gone off the deep end."

Tori and Stefan look at each other and I get the sudden feeling like I'd better hang on tight to something.

"We had something a little more demonstrative in mind," Tori says sweetly.

"Like what?"

Tori clears her throat, then shoots my brother a pointed look.

Stefan looks me square in the eye. "You need to get married."

BROOKLYN

CHAPTER 1

I never thought I'd get this chance again.

My black stilettos clip loudly on the floor as I stride into Danica Rose Management, formerly known as KZ Modeling. It feels surreal that I made it to these offices. I had a chance to audition with them three years ago, but that opportunity quickly turned into a disaster and I never went through with it. So when a friend told me about this latest call, I booked an immediate flight from LA to Chicago. No way am I missing another stab at making my dreams come true.

Despite all the bad PR lately, this agency didn't get to the top without knowing all the ins and outs of the business, how to launch huge careers, how to stay relevant. Maybe the bad press will even work in my favor, if it means fewer models are coming to these auditions.

I briefly wonder if *he's* going to be here. My stomach does a little flip at the thought, even though I remember him telling me that menial tasks like auditions were beneath him. He only worked with already-established supermodels, he'd said. Looking back, I should have recognized right away that that kind of arrogance wasn't going to end well for me. Still, a little chill goes down my spine as I imagine him here. This is his domain, after all.

"Are you here for the audition?" The pleasant voice of a woman behind the gleaming black reception desk grabs my attention.

I head toward her and glance at the clipboard lying there. Guess I was wrong about the bad PR. The page is covered top to bottom with names.

"Yes," I say, keeping my voice confident despite my anxiety at being here. "Brooklyn Moss, signing in."

I sign my name, then head toward the waiting area she indicates. The office is exactly how I imagined it: gorgeous, modern, and spacious, with lots of chrome and glass and black leather. There are also huge framed photos on the walls—not of models, but of breathtaking landscapes and architecture, like something out of *National Geographic*. I can see the city of Chicago spreading for miles out the floor-to-ceiling windows.

The open seating area where the rest of the models are waiting is packed. All I see are glossy lips and perfect, shining hair, long legs, and arched brows. I expected no less. I might stand out in most crowds, but at a casting call for models, I'm just another pretty face.

When I was just starting out, I was sure my eagerness and determination to work hard and "give it my all" would get me to the top. That if I just wanted it badly enough, I could make it happen. Now? I'll be the first to admit I was incredibly naïve. The older me has learned through experience that this is a brutal profession I've chosen, that competition is dog eat dog.

Booking jobs is hard, even with a face like mine. I'm not conceited about it; I simply know I have a remarkable face—

THE SHAM

people have been telling me I should go into modeling since my teenage years. I guess it was easy to stand out in the Midwest with my father's height and strong jawline, my gorgeous Italian mother's olive skin and incredible cheekbones. The icing on the cake is the beauty mark set just above my pouty lips—I basically won the genetic lottery. But even with the gift of beauty, I haven't launched into the supermodel stratosphere. Not yet.

Maybe today will be my big break.

I force myself to look nonchalant as I sweep past a few couches crammed with hopeful young women, all of them pretending they aren't measuring me up. There's nowhere to sit, so I lean against the wall and try not to slouch. Then I glance around at everyone else, my expression as warm and open as possible. I might be ambitious, and of course I'm competitive, but I'm not the mercenary type. After all, 99% of us aren't going to make it. There's no reason not to be friendly. We're all in this together.

Unfortunately, most other models don't see it that way.

I estimate there are about fifty girls here, and I study their faces to see if I recognize any of them. I was relatively successful in the Chicago scene during high school, modeling for local companies, doing print ads, and gaining traction in the tri-state area. Auditions were a breeze for me back then; scouts took one look at my "exotic" face, snapped a few pictures, and threw me jobs so fast it made my head spin. But eventually things stalled, and I realized that I needed representation. Steady gigs and national exposure required an agency like KZ Modeling.

I've had KZM in my sights for as long as I can remember, as I suspect most of these women have, but could never get an appointment...until now.

I have a hunch the company's recent rebranding efforts

go a lot further than simply changing their name to Danica Rose Management—that they're looking for brand new, undiscovered talent to act as the new face of the company. That means they'll be promoting the hell out of whomever they sign next. Booking huge international campaigns. Maybe even flying them out for fashion events, or to walk the red carpets in Hollywood. My mind spins with all the possibilities. I want this. I'm ready.

The scent of spicy male cologne piques my memory, but when I look around, I don't see anyone except the rest of these hopefuls, all of them female. Even so, my pulse jacks up, ticking hard inside my chest as my lips begin to tingle. That kiss...those lips on mine...

Shit, Brooklyn, quit this. I give myself a mental shake. I can't allow the indiscretions of my past ruin my future. I screwed up my chance with this agency once—I won't do it again.

"Want to sit?" A blonde uncrosses her legs and shifts to the edge of the ottoman she's perched on, giving it a little pat. She's in a knee-length black leather skirt and a tight white blouse, her outfit teetering between professional and sexy, and her fresh, dewy complexion screams youth. She can't be much older than eighteen.

I blink, suddenly feeling old at twenty-two. But I smile anyway.

"Sure, thank you." I take the seat and keep my posture aligned but relaxed.

"I'm Marin." She flips through a magazine, while absently handing me one. "You might as well browse. It takes the edge off."

"I'm Brooklyn," I say. I accept the media, but don't open it. Her hand trembles slightly as she flips the pages too fast to be absorbing anything. I don't tell her I've auditioned enough that nerves no longer apply. There is no edge for me anymore. Just steely determination and hope.

I subtly watch her, noticing her profile as she cocks her head and tucks her hair behind her ear. She's got a classic beauty, a symmetrical face with full lips, rounded cheeks, a perfect brow. I imagine her in a white dress, walking the streets of Bellagio with a gelato in hand. I'd capture her just as the streetlamps come on to soften the already muted golds and yellows of the buildings, the softness of Lake Como behind her as she grins directly into the camera.

What an Instagram photo that would be.

She glances up and catches me staring. Smiles and returns to her ardent page flipping. "Are you new? I'd remember your face if I'd seen you around before."

I want to laugh. New? Chicago is my hometown. I haven't lived here in over three years, but my face still graces a few advertisements around the city.

"I live in LA now, but I grew up here."

That gets her attention. "Really? I'd think this place would have snatched you up already. I mean, just look at that face." She waves a hand in a circular motion around my head. "You definitely don't look like anybody else. I actually expected you to have an accent."

I get another flash of that mysterious cologne scent. Nope, not going there. I'm over it.

"I had kind of a hard time breaking out in Chicago." It's true enough. No need to get into the details of my humiliating flop with KZM, the subsequent career nosedive, or the fact that I'd been desperate for a fresh start and a place to lick my wounds.

"What made you decide to try LA?" She closes her magazine and rests her hands, palms down, on top of it. Her expression is eager, as if I might have some wisdom to impart.

"I think I was just ready for something completely different," I say, "and the opportunity presented itself at just the right moment. I have a pretty big social media network, so—"

"You're like, an influencer or something?" she interrupted.

I shrug. "You could call it that. I promote modeling, some products, my photography. Over the years I've gained a lot of followers and eventually made some friends. People I chat with every day and share personal things with. This cute guy Mateo kept telling me I should fly out to LA for a visit. So, I went. And I've been there ever since."

"*Aww*, how romantic." The girl's eyes light up. "So you fell for each other?"

I laugh. "Not in the way you mean. Mateo is more like... the best friend I never knew I had. We spent the weekend watching 80s movies, eating Mexican food, and drinking champagne out of plastic cups on the beach. When my Uber pulled up to take me to LAX, I realized I couldn't bear the thought of going back to face another Chicago winter."

"I hear you on that." Marin nods sympathetically. "So you stayed."

"Yeah. We found this French Normandy-style apartment building in West Hollywood, and it's kind of falling apart, but...it's just so beautiful there. People say LA is a city of cars, but where we live you can walk anywhere you'd want to go. And it's always warm."

"Sounds dreamy," she says. "Do you book a lot of jobs there?"

I shrug. "Some. Not enough for rent though, so I waitress at a luxury supper club. But then I miss all the go-sees, since I can't just call out every time something promising pops up."

"Yeah," Marin coos sympathetically. "I'm lucky I live at home and work part-time."

"I just don't want to waste my prime years hustling for tips when I should be focusing on my big break, you know? Mateo is a model too, and he does great, but I'm ready for it to be my turn. I'm glad I took the leap, and it's been a ride, but I'm ready for what's next. So here I am."

Thinking of Mateo, I fight back a tiny pang of jealousy. He and I used to go to auditions together, and then one serendipitous job modeling for Lady Gaga's makeup line tossed his career into overdrive. He's in high demand now, with so many jobs on offer that he actually has to *turn them down*. I'm proud of his success, but it's left me wondering if my own ship has sailed.

It's also forced me to realize that I need to make a choice. I either go all in on modeling, do everything I can to break through, commit myself fully to this career path, or I need to suck up my failure and go to college, maybe apply to an art school for photography. Either way, I need to find something else to do with my life besides waitressing.

Luckily, I have some time to figure it out. Mateo decided to come to Chicago with me and leased an apartment here in Wicker Park. Hopefully, I can make something happen.

I'm curious about something. "How did you find out about this audition today?" I ask.

"My friend's agent told me," Marin says. "She said it wasn't a standard casting call, but she couldn't provide a lot of details. It's KZ—I mean Danica Rose—so of course I came, details or not." She lowers her voice. "Word on the street is, they're hungry for new faces."

"Right. I figured as much. Though I don't see any men here."

Marin shrugs. "They probably do the calls for the guys separately."

"Hmm. I guess that makes sense."

The friend who'd tipped me off mentioned there was some secrecy around the contract it involved. Which only made me more excited. Whatever this is, it's big. And I *need* big, before my dreams slip through my fingers—though that'd certainly make my parents happy.

They'd never been thrilled with my career choice. Even in high school, when I was making real money from modeling, they'd tried to convince me to pursue something else. They had signed permissions for my underage contracts, sure, but it had always been reluctantly.

I always thought that if I could just land one huge national gig, they'd finally see that all my hard work had paid off. That I'd made something of myself. They'd finally be proud.

At the far end of the hall, the frosted glass doors sporting the Danica Rose logo open and a curvy brunette in a navy pantsuit strides out. Her walk is confident, but her expression is definitely not. Everyone looks at her, and low whispers go around the room. I'm sure they're all wondering what went on behind those doors. I know I am.

The brunette goes to the refreshment table and pours a cup of cucumber water from a carafe. She takes a small sip, then clutches the paper cup to her chest as if she's lost in thought.

"Okay, I'm dying to know." Marin bursts from her seat and approaches the brunette. Luckily, I'm close enough that I can hear them talk. Everyone else rubbernecks to do the same.

"What happened in there?" Marin asks gently. "Are you okay?"

The brunette takes another sip and tosses the cup in the trash. "I'm fine. I had a couple pictures taken and got asked a bunch of weird questions and...that was it. Time was up."

"What kind of questions? Like your vital stats, or your experience?"

"No." She shrugs. "Like...do I own any pets, what do I think about downtown living, do I have any bad habits? Just, *weird* stuff. Not the usual. I don't even know who the client is."

Marin's face screws up in confusion.

"Brooklyn Moss."

My attention snaps to those glass doors, where a woman waves me over, a tablet in her hand. I make eye contact with Marin as I rise and smooth my hands down my skinny jeans.

"Good luck," she whispers before turning back to the brunette.

I shoot her a smile as I straighten my posture and toss back my hair. It's game on, and I get myself into the zone where I always go when I'm in front of a lens. I feel confident. Prepared. The adrenaline pumping through me is a good thing, a strong thing. I've so got this.

I silently chant those words all the way down the hall. The tablet woman nods at me as she pushes the door open, gesturing me through, and I step inside.

And come up short.

What the hell?

The room is empty save for a dark-suited man sitting behind a large black desk across the room. His head is down as he writes on something, but my heart beats with familiarity.

No, it can't be.

He glances up, and my heart skids to a stop.

It's him. The man who promised me the moon and then ghosted me after we slept together. The man who ruined my first chance with this company, my first chance at breaking out and skyrocketing my career.

Luka Zoric.

BROOKLYN

CHAPTER 2

Three Years Ago

It was the biggest fashion show I'd done so far.

A bunch of up-and-coming designers had descended on Chicago to debut their new lines in front of the local fashion media, and it had caused a frenzy. The new manager I'd recently signed with had really come through for me by booking me for the show. I mean, I'd have preferred to be walking the runway in Milan but having some of the country's top designers fit me with their clothes just so I could be photographed strutting around in them was a huge win for my career. Plus, national agencies like KZ Modeling were going to be there and I'd been trying to catch their eyes for a while. I was nineteen and working my way up. I figured it was just a matter of time before they noticed me—I hoped—but it couldn't hurt to give them a little push.

I tried to focus on my strut, my eyes fixed in the

distance, my trademark Mona Lisa smile on my face. But still, it took every ounce of self-control I had not to look into the crowd with a triumphant grin while I was on the catwalk. Just knowing all those agents were out there, looking at *me*, was everything.

Now, it's all over. I'm euphoric and high on adrenaline, still wearing one of the designs from the show. A black satin dress with a low-cut bodice, thin straps of fabric interwoven across my chest and down my hips, with a flouncy skirt that barely covers my ass. It sort of resembles a sexy bondage fairy costume, but I like it. The designer asked me to wear it to the afterparty and I had readily agreed. Looking around at the fashionable bodies around me, I'm glad I did.

I've never been to a party like this, and simply being invited to attend after the show is messing with my head. I feel giddy, and a little out of myself. Some of the faces are familiar, but I don't really know anyone here. Mingling will change that. Networking is something I've never been great at, but I've made it a goal to be more outgoing. You have to be, in this industry. There's plenty of beauty and talent to go around. Who you know is everything.

The rooftop terrace has been decorated to perfection with strings of softly glowing overhead lights, thick velvet curtains, and exotic potted flowers and tropical shrubs creating a magical backdrop that's dotted with tiny lights in the shapes of stars. A full bar wraps around one side of the terrace, and a band plays on a stage on the other side. Plush furniture is scattered in clusters, allowing people to sit and mingle. There are even a few private spaces tucked into dimly lit corners. I only know this because the people inhabiting them don't seem to realize there's more lighting than they think.

After adjusting the camera settings on my phone for the

duality of dark and light, I snap a few test images of the décor. Subtly moving to the edges of the crowd, I find my muses and take a few more shots until I'm happy with the results. The floral and greenery backdrop is stunning in my photos, like something from a fairy tale. My social media followers will love it.

They'll love all of these pics.

My follower base is in the thousands, and it's growing every day. It might be because of what I do for a living, but I like to think it's also my photography skills. I'm drawn to more than how things look, but how they *feel*, and the more I practice getting angles and arrangements and lighting just right, the better I get at capturing those feelings. See, anyone can take a picture of a melting ice cream cone at Navy Pier in July—but *my* goal is to get the picture that makes you feel the pure, childlike joy of devouring that ice cream cone on a perfect summer's day.

"Excuse me."

I do a double take at the rude voice, suddenly realizing I'm blocking the people trying to use the photo backdrop. As usual, I've lost myself in taking pictures. My face heats as I apologize and move out of the way. A stunning couple poses stiffly while a professional photog takes their picture.

I peek at the digital snap with a critical eye—I'd move the woman slightly to the left to show off the dazzle of her sparkled bodice, adjust my own position until I caught the flash of the diamond necklace resting in the hollow of her throat, instruct her partner to gaze at her. Then I'd mess with the depth of field to achieve that slightly blurry, dreamy quality for the background—

"Champagne, miss?"

A smiling waiter gestures with one hand while holding a tray of elegant flutes in the other. I nod and grab one before he realizes that I'm not of age. But he walks away without question, and I figure he couldn't care less how old I am. He's paid to pass the alcohol, not worry about who's drinking it.

The excitement is back as I take a covert sip of the champagne. It bursts full and sweet on my tongue, the effervescence tickling my palate. If this is what afterparties are like, sign me up.

"Don't tell anyone," a masculine voice whispers conspiratorially into my ear, the close heat of the man's mouth and the spice of his cologne sending shivers down my spine, "but they're serving two-hundred-dollar bottles of Louis Roederer in *fake* crystal flutes. How gauche."

I grin and turn toward the source of that sexy voice, only to come face to face with a pair of green eyes, slicked-back dark hair, and a body that's perfectly made for a tux... or maybe it's the other way around. I can't ponder it, though, because I've apparently lost my ability to think.

Or breathe.

Luka Zoric flashes his dimples at me as if he's just spilled a dirty little secret. I've never met him, but I know exactly who he is. Everyone in this industry knows who he is. He's the playboy second son of Konstantin Zoric, owner of KZ Modeling. I've seen all the Zorics in the tabloids and on social media more than I want to admit. I follow their pages, of course, and with the face of a god, Luka makes for some nice eye candy when you have idle time to browse.

"Well," I finally manage. "That's...a shame."

Oh, God. Is that the best I could come up with?

"It really is," he goes on, "considering the host of this thing rakes in fifty-mil a year."

My eyebrows lift and I take another sip, because I'm not sure what else to do. Suddenly, he's thrusting one perfectly broad and strong-looking hand my way. And I take it, feeling a frisson of electricity as I slide my palm against his, praying I don't say anything else too lame.

"Luka Zoric. It's a pleasure to meet you..." He leaves space for me to introduce myself. My mouth is so dry that I have to take yet another sip of the bubbly before I finally feel like I can offer a genuine smile, instead of one born from awkwardness.

"Brooklyn Moss," I say, narrowing my eyes at him, as if I'm thinking hard. "You know, I think I *may* have heard of you."

Oh, so now I'm flirting.

He laughs, open and unaffected, turning him even more impossibly handsome. He drinks from his flute and I do the same, barely realizing mine is almost empty now.

"You looked stunning out there earlier, Brooklyn Moss. Like you were actually having fun. Most of the models put on the sour face when they're on the catwalk. Not you."

My chest tightens as I weigh what he just said. A bigwig at KZ Modeling noticed me on the runway! Don't panic. Do. Not. Panic. "Thank you. To be honest, it *was* a lot of fun."

"You're a natural," he says smoothly. "I've been doing this long enough to spot those who are made for this industry, and those who aren't. You're definitely in the first category."

"Is that so?" I say with a smirk, my body language indicating how confident I already am.

"It is," Luka says, his sly grin matching my own.

He licks his bottom lip for a fraction of a second. Just enough to make me notice his lips and how perfect they are. Everything about him is perfection. Right down to the cut of his midnight blue tux and the Hermès pocket square expertly tucked near his lapel.

I'm young, but I'm not naïve. I know a line when I hear one. A man like this, especially with a reputation like his, says anything to get pussy. It's the one thing my parents repeatedly warned me about. So yeah, I know the game. Any woman in this industry knows the game. You learn early which moves to play and which to pass.

Draining my flute, I set it on the tray of a passing waiter and snag another. I can play my hand one of two ways. I can let him seduce me and use it to arm my way into an audition at KZ Modeling—and finally get the chance with them that I've been working toward. Or I can keep my dignity and wait for them to notice me for the strength of my work, not who I slept with.

My parents disapprove of my modeling career, and the least I can do for my mama is keep my dignity. Even if I want to climb Luka Zoric like a tree. Even if merely standing next to him is intoxicating.

"Look," I say, making up my mind. "I know how this works. And I can't go to bed with you. So if that's all you're after, then it's only fair you know it upfront." I raise my champagne to him and smile, hoping to take the edge off my rejection.

"Ouch." He puts an unconvincing hand over his heart, but the glint in his eye tells me that sex is, in fact, exactly what he's after. "You mistake my intentions, milady."

"Do I?" I cock an eyebrow, wishing I wasn't so turned on by this sexy scoundrel.

"Indeed," he says, and then tips back the last of his champagne. "Just to sate my curiosity though, why can't you sleep with me?"

"Because I want to get signed by your agency, and I'm

planning to audition at the next open call. Sleeping with you before that would only make things messy. Besides, I'm not here to screw my way into a contract. I'm a hard-working professional and I handle myself accordingly." I lift my chin and gaze fiercely at him.

The left corner of his mouth twitches up right before he catches my eyes. "You're an honorable woman, Brooklyn Moss. I can respect that."

With the barest of a nod, he sets his empty flute on a table, turns his back to me, and walks away. My stomach lurches a little as I watch him go. Did I just drop a huge opportunity? I almost want to call him back or hurry after him.

Sex. With Luka Zoric. *God.* I can't even begin to imagine what that would be like. If only I could keep my professional aspirations out of it.

Trying to put the encounter behind me, I start to make my way through the crowd. I barely get across the roof when I feel a light touch on my elbow. I turn and find Luka there, his eyes searching my face.

"A word?"

"Sure," I say with a nod.

He draws me away from the crowd with a hand on my lower back, and I let him lead me, trying to ignore the hot pulse between my legs.

Then his finger is lifting my chin as he stares greedily at me. "Look, since you were honest, I'll be honest too. I want to fuck you. That alone is a good indicator that you're KZM material, but since I have a feeling you want to do this the right way, how about a private audition, right now?"

I'm incredibly turned on by him saying he wants to fuck me, but I force myself to focus on the opportunity he's just offered me. "Right now?"

"Yes."

There's something in his eyes that draws me in and steals my rational thought. Minutes later I find myself in his Bugatti, speeding down the highway and back to the event center that held the fashion show. It feels like a dream, or maybe it's the two glasses of champagne in fake crystal flutes that I consumed. But this whole thing feels as if it's happening to someone else. He flips on a few lights in the auditorium, then holds my hand while I step up onto the runway...and stand there, waiting for his instructions and trying not to pinch myself to see if this is real.

I'm doubly glad I'm still in the designer dress, because never in my life did I expect to have an immediate audition with my dream agency.

Luka takes a seat right next to the stage and sets his cellphone on his lap, gazing up at me with a serious expression.

"Let's have you walk to the main stage and then back to me, please."

I swallow hard, hoping like hell that I don't wobble in my heels, and then do as he asks. I make a tight spin when I turn back toward him, one hand on my hip, my other arm moving just right as I strut. I clear my mind, stare into the distance, get in the zone. Even with the champagne making my movements a little loose and languid, I know I'm on point. My heels are loud in the empty room.

"Good. Good." He pauses and I hope he can't hear how hard I'm breathing. "Do one more turn for me right here."

I turn, knowing full well that he's getting a front row view of my ass from where he's sitting, but too caught up in the audition to worry about it. He snaps a picture. "That's perfect. How about both hands on your hips?"

I do as he asks, and he takes more pictures. As he waves me back down the runway, I get little direction, so I help him out—pausing at intervals for photos and flashing my subtly amused half-smile, my sultry scowl, my look of otherworldly distraction. I've been doing this for years, and I have all my looks down pat.

Even so, I'm getting the impression that he's not well-versed in auditions. At least, I've never been bumbled through one quite like this before. When I stop before him again, he runs a hand through his hair and looks up at me.

There's a pause that makes me nervous. Is this real, or was he simply baiting me to get what he wants?

"Do you want my vitals?" I suggest. When he hesitates, I clarify, "My measurements."

His face lights up. "I do. Yes."

I give them to him as he types the numbers into his phone. "Anything else you want to know? My resume, where I live?"

He circles a hand in the air. "All of it. Yes. Of course."

I give him the rundown and cross my arms as I speak. My hopes are getting dashed by the second—it's obvious I know more about the business than he does, and that says a lot, considering that he's a *Zoric*. But then he comes up on the stage and takes my hands in his, a confident smile robbing my breath. His cologne smells amazing and I imagine myself pressed up against that hard chest, running my hands inside his tux.

"Brooklyn Moss, there is no doubt in my mind—everyone is going to know your face. And your name. If you sign an exclusive contract with KZM, I'll make your career." His voice is strong and even and he sounds sincere. "I'm not just saying that to get in your pants, either."

Holy shit, he's giving me a contract! I touch his chest, lay my palm flat against it as if I'm compelled. "So you're saying you don't want to get into my pants?" I say.

He grips my wrist gently and my body breaks out in shivers. "Oh no, I definitely want to have sex with you. But that's absolutely beside the point."

"Well then, Luka Zoric," I say, our eyes locking. "I think you'd better take me home."

BROOKLYN

CHAPTER 3

Three Years Ago

Luka takes me to his million-dollar penthouse in River North and all I can think of is how nervous I am.

I'm no innocent, but the truth is, I've never had a man of his prestige and stature interested in me. Sure, I attract men. Some older, some wealthy. Some young and dirt poor. But I've never felt such an enigmatic pull to any man the way I do to Luka Zoric. Maybe it's because he's going to launch my career—finally! Maybe it's because he's pure masculine perfection, or because of the way he's had my pulse racing since the very first words that came out of his mouth. I don't know. All I know for sure is, I don't want to overthink this or talk myself out of it.

I want this. Even though I've never gone to bed with a man I've just met, and certainly not after I've been drinking. There's no denying the sparks flying between us, the way he can't keep his hands off me, how wet I am thanks to him squeezing my thigh the whole drive here.

I barely get a decent glance at the upscale building before he zings the car into his private underground garage. Lights pop on as we enter, illuminating a pristine space with a polished concrete floor and stark white walls, three bays housing three different candy-colored sports cars. I'm awed for about two seconds before he whisks me through a door and into an elevator.

Luka spins me as the elevator begins to rise, pushing me against the mirrored wall and taking my lips with his. He's a little rough with me, and I like it. I gasp into his mouth as he fists my hair, tugging and then relaxing, over and over as he kisses me, sending tingles from my scalp to my toes. I've never had my hair pulled like this before, and the line between pleasure and pain has me breathless. I slide my hands across his delicious pecs as he meshes his mouth perfectly to mine, hungrier than before, and I can feel my nipples going hard and achy against the fabric of my dress. I reach for his belt, wondering how much longer we'll be in this elevator, my mouth already watering in anticipation, but then he's pulling away from me as the car comes to a stop.

A whimper escapes my throat, making Luka laugh.

"There's no need to rush, Brooklyn," he says. "We have all night."

He taps a code on the keypad and the doors open to reveal a short hallway that spills into an airy room with a wall made of windows overlooking the city. It takes me a second to realize that he has an elevator opening directly into a hallway in his home.

His own elevator. Silly, I know. I'm sure there's much, much more to wealth like this.

"Welcome to my home."

He unbuttons his tux jacket and leads the way. My mouth drops as I take in the space. It's magnificent and so far beyond any luxury I could've imagined. Reclaimed wood floors contrast beautifully with stark white walls, and the black casings and trim of the expansive windows. Equally dark crown molding graces where walls meet ceiling, and a massive cast iron light fixture hangs from the center of the room, giving off a soft white glow. To the left, an open kitchen hints at expanses of polished granite and fixtures of modern stainless steel. But I don't get that far. Luka reaches for my purse and shawl and sets them on the side of the L-shaped black leather couch in the center of the room.

Then he rests a hand against my lower back and walks me over to the view.

"What do you think?"

I think that I want to frame up some amazing shots of the city lights to share with my Insta followers. It's a passing thought as I peer out the window at the beautiful illumination below. The lights are amazing against the night sky.

"I think you're a lucky man to have a view like this. I've never seen Chicago at night from so high up before. It's magic."

His fingers trail over my shoulder to the nape of my neck, where he moves my long hair aside to bare the skin. He's smiling, his eyes intensely focused as he holds my gaze. "I definitely could not imagine a better view."

My cheeks warm and I look away as a rush goes through me. This is happening so fast. He seems to sense my anxiety as he lightly takes my hand. "How about a tour?"

"I'd love one."

He starts by opening a set of French doors that lead to a

double balcony, one a few steps below, one slightly higher and up a staircase. A variety of succulents grow in glazed pots and an infinity waterfall appears to spill from the roof, splashing into a small pool that's maybe large enough for two or three people.

"Can you swim in that?" I ask.

"It isn't very deep, but you're welcome to try," he says teasingly. "No suit required."

"I'll have to take you up on that next time," I laugh.

I take his arm. Honestly, if he had just told me to strip and get in, I would have. Just like that. Instead, we head back inside where he shows me a second lounge room, a little smaller than the main living room. It boasts a flagstone wall with a rectangular fireplace cut in the center, with cream-colored recliners, a carved Balinese coffee table, and a leather sofa arranged around it. Floor-to-ceiling bookcases line two walls, and a mini bar is tucked into the back.

"After a dip in the pool, I find there's nothing better than a sherry by the fire," he says. "Naked, of course."

Even though I know he's just trying to get a rise out of me now, I can't help but shiver at the mental image I'm getting. Luka Zoric. Naked by the fire. Of course.

We turn down a hall and come up to the backside of the kitchen. Just as I suspected, it's completely professional, decked to the hilt with high-end everything. Dark cabinets offset the shine of the stainless steel. A large granite island in the middle has a sink on one end, and chairs around one side. There's even a small electric fireplace peeking out from the far wall near the breakfast nook. Opposite is another recessed area with a Murano glass chandelier, long formal dining table, and chairs to seat ten.

I run my hand along the smooth surface of the granite, leaning against the island.

"Do you entertain a lot?"

Luka watches me run my fingers over the polished stone. "Not really. I prefer to keep things pretty quiet around here."

I grin. "Makes sense. You don't strike me as the kind who does a lot of family dinners."

A sound comes out of him, a cross between a scoff and a laugh. He looks at the long table and shrugs. "Definitely not. I didn't really grow up with them. My dad wasn't around much."

He looks away, and my heart immediately goes out to him. "I'm sorry."

"Don't be." Luka grins, back to the smooth-talking sex-god persona. "It was for the best."

God, I would so love to photograph this penthouse. How does it feel to be so accustomed to having luxury like this, that it doesn't faze you anymore?

"Do you get lonely?" I ask.

He laughs. "No. I'm out and around people all the time. Kinda comes with the Zoric territory. This place is my sanctuary."

"I get it," I say with a nod. "But if this was my place, I definitely wouldn't let it sit empty all the time. I'd want to share it—have people over as much as possible. It'd be so nice to have my friends and family all together in a space like this. I mean, look at this gorgeous table. It's a shame you don't use it."

I walk over to the long table, admiring the gleam of the wood.

When I turn around, he steps into me, our hips touching. Our eyes lock and his hands slide over my bare shoulders and up my neck to cup my face between them. My heart is beating fast in my chest, the tabletop cutting into the back of my thighs.

"Oh, I definitely use it," he says. "Let me show you how."

He kisses me, his mouth hard and demanding, and my whole body goes hot and liquid, aching for him. I've never been consumed like this. Letting out a soft moan, I open my mouth wider and lose myself in the deep stroke of his tongue. His hands slip down to cup my breasts, and then he lifts me onto the table, stepping between my open legs. I brace my hands behind me for support, tilting my head back as he trails kisses down my neck, making me gasp with every little suck and nip. Then he tugs the straps of my dress down, exposing my breasts.

We're both panting. Even though he's stepped back to take in the view of my body, he's already eye-fucking me. When his mouth closes over my bare nipple I cry out, arching against his tongue. I can feel my pulse between my legs, my pussy clenching with need.

I should be scared, but I'm not.

I should stop this, but I won't.

I don't want to.

The things he said earlier...he's going to give me an exclusive contract. He was serious. I know he was. Luka's the kind of man who sets his sights on something and then conquers it, so if he says he's going to make my career, I know he means it. The way he's making me feel right now just proves it.

I moan in encouragement as he hikes up the hem of my skirt and pulls off my G-string, letting my heels fall to the floor. He roughly pushes my thighs apart, exposing my glistening cunt to him, before catching my gaze with complete greed in his eyes. I swear my heart stops, but I don't get time to catch my breath before he dips his head and feasts on my pussy.

Crying out, I dig my fingers into his thick hair, holding him to me as his lips suckle and his tongue laps at my clit. Jesus, this man knows what he's doing.

"Luka," I moan. "So good. So fucking good."

I'm drowning in sensation as he fucks me with his mouth, licking in tight swirls and sucking my nub into his mouth, pressing his teeth against the sensitive skin there. A zing of pain is followed by the swirl of deep pleasure as he repeats this over and over, until I'm right on the edge of the fastest-building orgasm I've ever had in my life.

"Fuck, I'm going to come," I pant, trying to catch my breath.

Luka pulls my hips down until my ass is nearly hanging off the table. Then he loops my legs over his shoulders, and my thighs clench around his head as he continues to tongue-fuck me with everything he's got. I moan louder and louder, grinding against his mouth, losing myself in the ecstasy of this. Just when I'm sure I'm about to shatter, he slips his fingers inside me, curling them against that sensitive spot just inside my walls.

I see sparks as white-hot heat radiates through me. He finger-fucks me harder, deeper, stroking his fingers against my G-spot until I'm almost crying for release, caught right at the edge. Abruptly he withdraws, and I moan in protest. Catching my eyes, he suddenly slaps my pussy, soft yet firm, the brunt of contact over my clit. I yelp in shock, then moan as the sting is followed by the headiest flow of pleasure I've ever experienced.

"Oh my God," I breathe. "What are you doing to me?"

"Again?" he asks.

I nod.

He does it again and I can't look away from him. My orgasm builds, so fast, so deep.

So hard.

Slap.

Fuck. I fly over the edge, crying out my pleasure with throaty moans as I lose myself in the sensation washing over me. I've never had sex like this before.

God, this man lives up to every word of his reputation.

Still panting, I come back to myself. Luka has stepped back and he's holding his hand out to me. "Are you ready for more?"

"Yes," I say, my voice rasping.

"Then get up." His firm voice sends a shiver down my spine. I can barely function, but I take his hand as he helps me off the table, then down the hall to his master suite.

Luka pulls my dress the rest of the way off, tossing it in a wad on the floor. I have the barest thought that it costs a lot and I should hang it over the back of a chair, but he's unbuttoning his shirt and I can barely draw a breath. I help him, our fingers working in tandem until I peel the shirt off him. His chest is magnificent, so perfectly sculpted, his arms bound in bands of muscle that I can't wait to feel around me.

He leads me over to the bed and I sit down and slide back as he crawls over my naked body, taking my wrists and forcing my arms above my head. He's so dominant. I fucking love it.

"Beautiful Brooklyn. You're a goddess."

Any reservations I had about him melt away as he kisses me, his free hand grazing lightly up and down my body, giving me goosebumps.

Eager and needy, I try to spread my legs, but his knees block me on either side. He chuckles low as he slowly works his belt free, then the button and zipper on his pants. All I can do is stare as he gets up to remove the last of his clothes.

Jesus. Christ.

His perfect cock springs free, bobbing long and thick as he comes back to the bed. He takes himself in one hand and gives it a few strokes. Without meaning to, I lick my lips. I'm not sure what's written on my face, but Luka seems amused by it. "You like what you see?"

"Yes," I murmur, my heart racing.

I've never been with anyone as big as him, but I've never been afraid of a challenge. He grins and climbs back onto the bed and suddenly that huge cock is over me, lowering down to my mouth until I have to take the tip between my lips. I suck softly and then harder, making him groan, opening up so he can push in farther. The velvet of his skin glides against my tongue and I take him into my mouth deeper, my jaw screaming as I push the limit and open all the way.

Luka's breathing picks up as he begins to lightly thrust into my mouth. I suck and swirl my tongue around him. Each pump of his shaft makes me hungrier for him, until I'm aching so hard, I have to reach between my legs and cup my pussy to relieve the pressure.

"Oh, no, sweetheart. That's all mine. You want my cock so badly you can't wait?"

I try to nod, but he just thrusts harder, deeper, gagging me. I love it.

Finally he pulls out, rubbing his head back and forth over my wet, open mouth.

"You know what? I'm going to give that greedy pussy exactly what it wants."

He turns away, leaving me gasping as he grabs a condom from the bedside table. He slips it on, and I barely spread my legs before he's pressing into me with the tip of his cock. Raising my hips, I meet his slow thrust until he's all the way inside me up to his balls, my pussy stretching deliciously from his size.

I. Can't. Get. Enough.

"Fuck me, Luka." I'm begging and I don't care.

"Say please." He smirks, starting to ease out of me.

"Please!" I say obediently. "Please, give it to me. I need you to fuck me."

His eyes search mine, as if he needs to see the desperation there, how badly I want him.

"Please," I whisper one more time.

"That's a good girl."

With that, Luka slams back into my pussy, his face a mix of pleasure and concentration as he pulls my wrists up over my head again and thrusts deep and steady, finding a rhythm. I look up at him, taking in the lust in his eyes, the parting of his lips, the flush in his cheeks, the way he groans as he pumps into me, his abs flexing with every movement. He's not just fucking me, he's throwing himself into this like it's an Olympic sport.

"Yes, yes, yes," I moan, wrapping my legs around his waist so he can thrust even deeper.

It feels like he's splitting me open, every stroke jolting through me. My orgasm builds, but it's different this time—it's so deep it's almost like it's coming from the inside out. I want to fight it, but I can't. I can only surrender to the sensations overtaking me.

My cries start to come faster and louder, and it must be obvious I'm about to climax because Luka suddenly rolls onto his back and pulls me on top of him, his hands on my hips, never breaking our rhythm as he forces me to ride him.

"Come on my cock, Brooklyn," he growls. "Let me see you come."

I lean back and spread my thighs as wide as I can, grinding faster and faster. I'm watching him enjoying the sight of me, licking his lips as he watches my breasts bounce, as his gaze drops to the view of my split-open pussy getting pounded by his cock. I can feel him grow even harder inside me, and I close my eyes and let the waves of pleasure wash over me.

The orgasm hits, taking my breath away.

"Luka, yes, yes," I moan desperately, leaning forward over him to grab onto his shoulders for support. I'm so wet and he feels so good.

Without warning his mouth clamps over my nipple and he sucks it so hard I cry out, groaning as his thrusts go jerky and erratic.

He's about to come, I can feel it, and I'm still not done yet. Jesus, it keeps going, wave after wave, even as his body tenses and he pulses his release into me with a final, deep groan.

I'm shuddering through the final throes as Luka gently rolls me back onto the bed, both of us looking up at the dark ceiling as we struggle to catch our breath. I must doze off, because the next time I open my eyes, he's gone to the bathroom—I think—and it's a while before he comes back. When he does, I'm just barely aware of him pulling the blankets up and over me.

I wake to sunlight streaming over my face.

I sit up with a start, the night before slowly returning to me. Did Luka ever come back to bed? I glance over and see the covers on his side look untouched. There's no sign he'd slept next to me. Maybe he spent the night on the couch in some backwards show of chivalry, or maybe he's just a light sleeper and prefers his space. Either way, there's no note on the nightstand, and it strikes me that we'd never exchanged numbers—so he couldn't have texted me even if he'd wanted to.

My belly flips.

Maybe he got called in to work.

Maybe he went to get us breakfast. Maybe he's *making* us breakfast.

I smile, rub my hands over my face, and find the restroom, then clean up a little and get dressed. My cellphone says it's almost nine. Shit! My parents are going to notice that I didn't come home last night. I'm an adult, but my mom has a hard time remembering that.

Looking for my heels, I find my way back to the kitchen. The scent of fresh coffee hits me in a glorious wave. Sounds are coming from there, like someone is moving around. My heart leaps. A leisurely breakfast with Luka? Yes, please. I smooth my hair as I step into the kitchen.

"Hey, I—"

An older woman in a maid's uniform gives me the barest glance as she wipes down the counter near the espresso machine.

I pull up short. "Oh, hello."

She replies with a noncommittal grunt. The air seems thicker, and it's clear how much I'm not wanted here. On top of that, my brain is starting to catch up with what my heart already knows. Nausea rises in my throat, my pulse picking up. "Um, is Luka here?"

The look the maid gives me is no-nonsense. "Let me guess. He didn't leave a note. You don't have his number. And you woke up alone. You're a model, right? He offer you a contract?"

I feel myself nod slowly, dread curling in my belly.

"I shoo girls like you outta here seven days a week," she explains.

The nausea burns now. Threatening to choke me. "Are they…always models?"

"Not always." She shrugs. "My advice? Walk it off. If he's interested, he'll find you."

Suddenly it's like the wind just got knocked out of me, and I'm struggling for air.

"Okay," I say, but my voice wobbles and I'm shaky on my feet.

The maid sighs, seeming to soften. "Let me pour you a coffee, hon. Have a seat there. I'll call you a cab. You know where you're going?"

My brow furrows.

I don't know anything.

Except that I'm the worst kind of naïve.

BROOKLYN

CHAPTER 4

I blink a couple times and try to clear my head, but it's hard to forget the past when I'm staring it right in the eye.

Luka coolly rifles through the papers in front of him and glances down, writing something on a page. There was no recognition in his expression when he saw me. The best sex of my life, and the guy I'd had it with couldn't even spare me a second look or tell me I seem familiar.

It's like we're meeting for the first time here, and I'm incredibly embarrassed—and angry. He's apparently erased me from his memory. I wish I could do that so easily. Forget how I'd checked my cellphone a thousand times just in case he'd gotten hold of my number and tried to get in touch. How I'd obsessed over my social media to see if each new follower was possibly him. I wish I could forget how humiliating it was to realize—after three agonizing months—that Luka Zoric wasn't going to call. That he probably hadn't thought of me even once since we'd slept together.

Even still, I continued hanging on to the hope that he was eventually going to reach out to me on a strictly professional basis, give me the contract that he promised. But at the six-month mark, I had to face the facts. During the entire "audition" I'd done with him, there had been zero paperwork involved. He may have taken down my stats, but there was no contract besides the promise he'd made verbally—no request for official headshots, no exchange of contact information, nothing. The entire thing had been off the books.

He'd used the "private audition" to get laid. I'd bet anything it was his standard method of banging pretty girls.

I guess, in a twisted way, it worked out in my favor that I'd been too embarrassed to follow up with the agency about my audition and Luka's empty promises, considering everything that's come out about the place now. I may have been naïve, but at least I didn't end up getting linked to the prostitution ring the elder Zoric got busted over. I'm confident that mess is behind the agency now, though, and I'm willing to give them a legitimate shot. I just need to suck up my humiliation, be a grown-up about the whole thing.

"Good morning. I'm Luka Zoric, VP of Talent Acquisition and Management," he says. "Please, take a seat."

His voice rings out with that gravelly, sexy edge that I remember. My body immediately comes to life. He'd seduced me with that velvet tone, whispering in my ear.

Never again.

Pulling my shoulders back, I stand straighter and project a confidence I don't totally feel. Then I take the chair across from him and cross my legs. His eyes follow the movement before dropping back to his papers, and I can't help looking him over while he's not paying attention.

His dark hair is finger-combed back, lacking the slick professional style he wore before. The top few buttons of his dress shirt are undone and he's not wearing a tie. His sleeves are rolled up, and his entire persona is far from the designer-clad socialite that I remember. He's more relaxed today, as if he's digging in deep to this project.

I'll be damned if he isn't even sexier now.

"Let's get started. Please state your name."

"Brooklyn Moss." I watch him, waiting for any sign of recognition, but he doesn't even look up. The muscles in his forearm flex as he writes on the paper and a hot pang of desire hits between my legs. How can I still want him after everything that's happened? I press my thighs tighter together. No way in hell will he see a lick of want in my eyes.

"Is this address on your resume current? Los Angeles?" he asks, glancing at it.

"I have a lease here in Chicago, actually," I tell him, and when I give him the address in Wicker Park, he writes that down before looking up at me again.

"Ms. Moss, I need to inform you that you are required to answer each question in its entirety, or you will not be considered for this...opportunity. Do you understand and agree?"

What do I have to lose? "I do."

That gets his attention for some reason. His head snaps up, his eyes searching mine for a beat before he clears his throat and looks back at the page. I realize then that he's following a script that dictates exactly what he's supposed to say. Odd.

"Great. Okay. Ms. Moss, have you had any recent or past health conditions which required medication or hospitalization?"

This is unusual, but thanks to the heads-up from the brunette in the waiting room, I'm not that surprised. I roll with it. "I had my tonsils out when I was twelve, my wisdom teeth out last year. I was on painkillers, but obviously it was temporary. Not currently taking any drugs, prescription or otherwise."

"You're currently healthy?" he prods.

"As a horse. Do you need me to fax over the results of my last yearly physical?"

He glances up, and the brief moment of eye contact makes my pulse ratchet up another notch. "Ah, that won't be necessary."

He seems tense, or maybe just a little embarrassed about all these questions, and it's hard not to smirk at the effect I'm clearly having on him with my attitude. Serves him right.

"Would you say you follow a healthy dietary and exercise regimen?" he goes on.

I shrug. "I work out most days, take classes with friends. Cardio, cycling, kickboxing. So yeah. I'm mostly vegetarian, but I never turn down bacon. Or dessert. You only live once."

The corners of his mouth turn up, but he seems to hold back from actually smiling as he scribbles a few things down. I can't help wishing he'd look at me, like full-on look at me. I want him to remember who I am. I'd love to see the discomfort on his face when he remembers I'm the girl he fucked and ghosted all those years ago. Well, one of them.

"Are you involved in any charities, philanthropy, or other charitable work? Clubs, missionary work, volunteering programs?"

I smile. "Not sure missionary is my thing, to be honest."

He clears his throat. "If you wouldn't mind just answering."

I'm kind of loving this, but I cut him a break.

"Actually, I've been part of Heart and Home Chicago

since high school, and even though I've been in LA for a few years, I'm still active on the committee. We raise funds for area homeless shelters to provide maintenance, expansion, help with the food budget, that kind of thing."

"Hmm." His jaw works back and forth. "How active are you, exactly?"

"Very. I took over as the committee co-chair of fundraising last year. My face and bio are on the homepage, if that helps. I also founded a new program for domestic abuse survivors who've had to flee their homes and need a place to go and figure out their next steps," I say, relaxing as I warm to this topic that's so close to my heart. "Beyond meals and shelter, we offer specialized counseling, daycare, connect them with services. It's been amazing."

Luka scribbles furiously, nodding as he does so. I hope it's a good sign.

"Are you currently using birth control?"

I'm thrown, and I can't make an immediate answer pop out of my mouth. "Excuse me? What does that have to do with—"

"It's a standard part of the medical questionnaire," he says, spreading his hands.

"Fine. Yes, I am using birth control, not that it's anyone's business." I fold my arms, trying to push back my annoyance. "Does that meet with your approval, Mr. Zoric?"

"As I said, it's just a medical question, Ms. Moss. No judgement implied or intended." He clears his throat again and moves his pen down the paper. I see he's checking off boxes for each question. "Just a few more things, now. Do you have an arrest record?"

"No."

"Any past or current narcotic addictions? History of mental illness?"

"*No.*"

He looks up then, searching my gaze, and my heart flips. Silence blossoms between us. That's right, Luka. *See* me. But he goes back to his papers and I feel the loss like a snapped wire.

I need to get it together. Let this go. I mean, I thought I already had. I haven't felt angry or resentful over our one-nighter in years. I put that bitch to bed. Seeing him has stirred up those emotions, though, and I'm not quite sure what to do with them.

"Can you tell me about your family? Mother, father? Siblings?"

Perfect. Nothing like talking about my parents to make me feel even worse. "I'm an only child. My parents live here in Chicago. We're pretty close."

"Do you drink alcohol, and how often?"

"Socially, mostly. I don't know…maybe one or two drinks per week?"

"Perfect," he murmurs, seeming to ponder something before he writes on the paper. This checklist seems suspiciously family-friendly. Maybe this gig is for someone big with a strict morality clause, like the Disney Channel or American Girl. I can play the girl next door if I have to. I don't care if it's not my preferred type of gig; I just want to go national.

"How do you feel about living in the city?"

"Born and raised in Chicago. I currently reside in LA. That should be answer enough."

He smiles. "Indeed. Do you rent or own your place in LA?"

"Rent, but the lease is up next month, and as I said, I have an apartment here for a while."

"Great. And how do you feel about pets?"

There's something about the way he says, "pets" that signals I'd better say that I don't have any. I don't, but I'm not opposed to having one in the future. Luka's mouth pulls into a line and I go with the cues.

"No pets. No desire for any."

He sets down his pen, then rises, his long, hard body stretching out before me, his shirt going tight over his sculpted torso. My pussy aches, just like that. He might as well have snapped his fingers and told me to come because I could. I seriously could, just from looking at him and remembering in vivid detail how loud he made me scream—

"Ms. Moss? Can you stand please?"

My cheeks heat as I realize he'd probably already asked that, and I'd been totally lost in the memory of fucking him. I get up and set my bag on the chair. Then Luka comes around the desk to me and holds out his hand. I have a flash of déjà vu, taking his hand and letting him lead me. My palm slides against his and his fingers curl around my hand, but I don't grip him back. He can hold on to me, but I'm going to hold on to myself.

He takes me to the center of the room and positions me, then moves to stand beside me. Even though our arms are barely touching, I can feel his body heat and the firmness of his biceps, and being this close to him makes goosebumps break out all over my body. Damn him.

"What is this?" I ask.

"Just seeing how you fit next to me," he answers breezily.

Weird. But okay.

"And now if you'll just turn toward me," he says.

I do as he asks so we're now face to face. I find myself looking up at him because I can't not. Those sexy eyes slanted a touch at the corners, his lips parted just so. I know how he looks when he's fucking, when he's close to orgasm, when he comes. A shiver runs through me.

Just when I'm about to lose my willpower from the intoxicating scent of his damn spicy cologne, he steps back and gestures that I should return to my chair. Taking out his cellphone, he types something into it and then puts it away. Then he leans against the desk and puts on a Prince Charming smile.

"Ms. Moss, one more question."

I sit, already wondering what kind of nonsense he's going to ask next. "Go ahead."

"How do you feel about marriage?"

BROOKLYN

CHAPTER 5

How do I even respond to that?
My mind goes blank.
"M-marriage?" I stutter. "I mean, my focus is on modeling. Is this for some kind of reality show or something? Because I'm not really interested in that kind of thing."

"It's not for television. It's for me." Luka spreads his hands and I feel my jaw drop. He just smirks. "Not what you were expecting when you came here today, was it?"

That's an understatement. I had no idea I'd run into him again, despite half hoping I would, and I certainly never imagined he'd be more or less proposing we get hitched.

"You're right," I stammer. "I was expecting to audition for a job. Or a contract."

He clears his throat. "It is a job, if you want to look at it that way."

I blink at him, still not quite comprehending what he's offering.

"I know this is a lot to take in," he says. "But you may

find the arrangement to be to your benefit. Perhaps we should discuss it in more detail over dinner. At my penthouse."

His cheeky smile throws me off-center. It's the same self-confident, alluring grin that shattered all my defenses three years ago—and the lust that's been teasing me since I walked in here comes at me full force. It's awake and alive. If I'm not careful, I'm going to give it free rein.

I'm so torn, but I'm also so intrigued. Plus, I can't help feeling like I owe it to myself to explore exactly what he's offering. "I'll do dinner, but not at your penthouse."

His eyes drop to my lips. "Fair enough. Meet at Luciana's at eight?"

It's a small Italian restaurant, popular with locals and fiercely guarded from tourists. Though the food is incredible, it's not a five-star restaurant—but still fancy enough to be labeled a date-night destination.

This isn't a date, I remind myself. *It's a business meeting.*

And I am definitely, for sure, one hundred percent not going home with Luka Zoric.

"Sure," I say.

I'm not going down that road again. This time, my interactions with him will be purely professional. I know better than to accept private auditions, and then offer up my body in exchange for some sweetly placed false words. I'm older now. Stronger and wiser, and come hell or high water, I'm not giving in to the extreme need for Luka's touch. Even if it kills me.

The only thing I need is to get signed by Danica Rose so I can step into the next phase of my life.

There. I've already decided how this evening is going to go. I stand and slip the strap of my bag over my shoulder.

Then I extend my hand to where he's still standing beside the desk. He takes it with a raise of his brows.

"Thank you so much. I'll see you tonight at eight."

I turn on my heel and leave, not giving him a chance to reply, forcing myself to walk confidently even though I want to race out of there and rush home to figure out the perfect outfit. I walk into the waiting area only to find it empty. I look around, as if the other models might be hiding behind potted plants or in one of the glass-walled conference rooms, but I see nobody.

The receptionist is still here, typing away on her computer. I consider asking what happened to the others, but I decide not to.

I don't really care.

As I ride the elevator back down to the lobby, my mind starts racing all over again. I have a non-date with the ex-one-time-lover who ghosted me. No, scratch that way of thinking. I have a *business meeting* with an *agency professional* who can make my career.

But he said marriage. He can't possibly mean like marriage-marriage, can he? I'm both incredibly nervous and curious to find out—but the most nerve-wracking thing of all is being alone with Luka.

I take an Uber to Wicker Park and resist calling Mateo as soon as I step inside the apartment and find that he's gone. I know he'll want all the details, and I'm too nervous to talk about it right now. Besides, tonight is the real substance of this whole thing. I'll call him after my dinner with Luka so he can talk me off a ledge if need be.

After I change into yoga pants and a hoodie, I stop by Heart and Home's main operations center to help sort donations and then make a Starbucks run for the admins who work so hard in the office. They're used to seeing me pop in at random hours, especially since I've moved back to Chicago, and I'm happy for the distraction...although Luka is never far from my thoughts. Still a mix of giddy and anxious, I grab a quick lunch and then take a long walk in Humboldt Park to burn off some adrenaline, soaking up the weather and the dog-watching along the way. Then I head back home. Mateo's still out. Time to get ready.

Even though I showered this morning, I've had the longest day ever, so I pull my hair up into a bun and take another. The hot water relaxes me and helps me center myself. Then I take my time doing my makeup and styling my hair. It probably doesn't really matter what I look like for this meeting, but I can't help fussing—it's just my nature.

In the end, I opt for a nude look with a little bronzer on my already golden skin, some pale pink cheek tint, and a kiss of clear gloss on my lips. After getting frustrated with my inability to pull off a sexy-messy French twist, I decide to just let my hair fall however it wants, adding some Argon oil for shine, and then slip into a simple navy blue wrap dress. It shows just a little cleavage, but the hem falls past the knee, so it's both sexy and professional—exactly what I'm going for. As much as I'd love to have Luka desire me so I can turn him down, I don't want to give off a "sleep with me" vibe, either.

He's already at Luciana's when I arrive. The hostess leads me past a roped-off doorway to a private table on the patio, tucked into a corner with a green wrought iron fence behind it, towering hibiscus flowers blooming between the rails. I wonder if he paid the restaurant extra to keep the patio blocked off just for us tonight, or if they did it for him as a favor.

He stands as I approach, a gentlemanly touch I'm not expecting, and his smile is warm. Kind, even.

"Brooklyn Moss," he says. "Glad you could make it."

"Me too." As if there was any chance I'd cop out.

Still, it doesn't escape me the way he sweeps my body with a heated look that makes my nipples perk. I smile and sit quickly.

"Can I get you something to drink?" the hostess asks. "A waiter will be right with you."

Spying a glass of something clear and fizzy with a lime twist in front of Luka, I ask for the same and settle into my seat.

God is he breathtaking. He skipped the suit jacket again and I'm glad that he did. He's in a dark green dress shirt that complements his eyes, top buttons undone again, and dark, expensive-looking jeans. I love the no-tie look he's got going on and the messy thing he does with his hair. It's hard not to reach over and just run my fingers through it.

"Thank you for meeting me," he says. "You look amazing, by the way."

"Thanks." I don't compliment him in return. No matter what, I'm staying in control of this meeting. If he really, really wants me for this assignment, or whatever it is, he's going to have to work a little for it. "Though something tells me you don't seriously worry about people standing you up."

His eyebrows lift and he shrugs nonchalantly, rather than reverting to "preening peacock" mode. Huh. This Luka really is different than the one I remember. He's still intense and carries that air of self-aware, wealthy sex appeal, but this time around he seems calmer, quieter. More focused. Maybe the downfall of KZ Modeling has forced him to grow up in a big way.

"You might be surprised," he says. "People don't always

react to me the way you'd think they would. Especially lately."

He searches my face, maybe to see if I'll acknowledge the elephant in the room. I will.

"Look," I say, "I'm well aware that your family's business has been through hell the last few months. Guilty or not, I don't pretend to know all the details of whatever went down, but...as far as I'm concerned, you have a clean slate with me." It's only partially a lie.

I can see him visibly relax, some of the tension going out of his shoulders and a smile playing at his lips. "I appreciate that."

"No problem. And for what it's worth, I think this will work best if we're both as open and upfront as possible, yeah?"

"Agreed."

As gratifying as I thought it would be to make him squirm, I can't help the warm fuzzies I'm getting now that I've established some good will between us. Maybe it'll even give me the upper hand.

Our server arrives and sets down a breadbasket, a dish of olive oil and Italian herbs, and my drink. I take a sip and realize it isn't a cocktail at all, but sparkling water. I hold back a grimace. I hate that stuff. I figured Luka would be having a drink-drink, but I guess not. We both order pasta, which I know will be fantastic since they make it in-house—carbonara for me, alfredo for him—and then we're alone again.

"Shall we get down to business, or are we still trying for small talk?" I ask. "You know everything about me thanks to my 'audition' this morning, but I don't know much about you." *Except that you're a manwhore.* I take a sip of my drink and force myself to swallow it.

He shrugs. "There's not much to tell. If you don't live in a cave, you've probably gotten some kind of impression of me from the media. Though I'd say it's largely inaccurate."

I half-snort without meaning to. "Inaccurate? I thought we were going to be honest with each other."

Luka laughs, and his grin is sheepish. "Fair enough. I'll admit I lived a privileged life of excess and hedonism for... well, a while. But like you said, there's been a lot of turmoil in my family over the past few months, and it shook us all up. Watching your dad go to prison for sex trafficking kind of takes the flavor out of things. So, I don't know. I've changed."

"I'll believe it when I see it," I say, ripping a hot piece of crusty bread apart and letting it soak up some oil and herbs before popping it into my mouth. I close my eyes and stifle a moan. It's perfection.

"You're making that innocent bread look downright sinful," Luka says, his eyes glued to me.

"Sin with me, then," I say, pushing the basket toward him. "It's that good. And then go ahead and try to convince me that I have any interest at all in a sham marriage."

"That's a tall order," he says, digging into the bread. "Especially considering that I don't have the gift of negotiation and persuasion quite like my brother and...father seem to."

He says the word *father* like it's distasteful, and I'm quick to smooth over it.

"I imagine that you're very persuasive," I say carefully, trying to keep any hint of accusation out of my voice. "But if I didn't know any better, I'd almost think you feel inferior to them in some way."

My voice is light and teasing and he takes it that way, grinning as he crosses his arms on the table and leans over them. "You got me. The truth is, I'm the black sheep of the Zoric family. It's easy to prove. Just look at my profile."

He turns his head to the side, and I laugh, not at all sure what he's up to.

"It's a very nice profile."

Scoffing, he turns the other way. "Look at this side. Do you see it now?"

"Again, very nice." Very, very nice.

"You flatter me—but I'll have you know that I'm the least photogenic of the family, by far. Which is ironic, isn't it, considering what our family business is?"

"That's a terrible shame."

"It is. I mean it's tough, having to walk around with a paper bag over your head during the holidays and family functions, trying not to mess up any group photos."

The mental image is so ridiculous I have to laugh. I can't believe we're flirting like this, and that it feels so easy and natural.

"But you know," I tell him, "everyone takes a bad photo once in a while."

He reaches over to tuck a strand of my hair behind my ear, his fingers brushing my cheek for a split second. *Don't react*, I tell myself. *Just, don't.*

"I highly doubt that you've ever taken a bad photo, Brooklyn."

There he goes again, saying exactly the right thing. Charming me. Making me *want*. I shake my head and pull away to grab my wallet from my purse. "Oh, yeah? Be prepared to be proven wrong." I tug out my driver's license and hold it against my chest. "Come on, yours too. Fair is fair."

He fake groans and makes a big deal of pulling his out of his wallet. Then he tosses it across the table and plucks mine from my fingers. I pick his up and let out a laugh. He's hot as hell, but that picture is something else.

"This is like a straight-up mug shot," I say, before realizing I've just said the most awkward thing in the world to someone who did indeed get arrested a few months back.

But when I look up at him to gauge his reaction, he's got the biggest smile on his face. "To be honest, my mug shot looks way better than my driver's license," he says. "Google it."

Now we're both laughing, and I have to remind myself that this is the same man who lied to me, who used me, who doesn't even have the decency now to remember my face.

He hands my license back. "Okay, I was wrong. This *is* a terrible photo of you."

Just then, the waitress appears with our meals. By the time she leaves, I've composed that part of myself that wants to just run away with the superficial lust between us. Setting my napkin on my lap, I press my palms into my thighs.

"Tell me what the point of this whole marriage thing is," I say, cutting to the chase.

He gives a slight nod. "Sure. Got a little distracted there."

My stomach tightens in expectation of what he might say. The pasta smells amazing, but I'm not sure I can take a bite right now. Luka, on the other hand, digs right in. He notices that I haven't touched my food, sets his fork aside, and clears his throat.

"So basically, the reason for all of this is that my reputation needs work in light of my father's recent arrest. The disgrace he brought down on the business and our family name is no secret, and with him in jail, I've been the media's scapegoat."

I nod. "Makes sense. People are angry. They need someone to take it out on. Not that it's fair to you." I finally start on my spaghetti as he leans back, seeming to gather his words.

"Even with every other member of our family being cleared of any wrongdoing, and the fact that my older brother pretty much handed my father over to the feds on a silver platter, we're still struggling to regain the public's confidence in us. As a business and as humans."

"Sure," I say, pausing to blot my mouth with my napkin before continuing. "I mean, I was floored when I heard about it. It made me think twice about going to the audition today, and whether I wanted to be associated with the Zorics at all."

It comes out sounding harsher than I meant, but Luka takes it in stride.

"I'm sure you're not the only one who feels that way," he says. "All the KZ models were released from their contracts after the scandal broke, and not all of them signed back on with Danica Rose. We lost some great talent. Not that I pity us. A lot of people got hurt, taken advantage of. Lives were ruined. Something like that rips people's trust away pretty deeply."

He looks off, thinking hard, and I finish chewing and set my fork down.

"So things are royally fucked right now," I say matter-of-factly. "Not to salt the wound. And it's your job to sway public opinion back into a positive light."

"Yes. My brother and I agreed to use our collective influences to make over the Zoric empire's image. But since I'm the resident bad boy and he's happily married and settled down, I'm the one who needs to change my lifestyle in a big and very public way. And fast."

I pause for him to go into detail of said lifestyle, but he resumes eating. I feel a little smug, though, because I know exactly what he's talking about. His online presence is flooded with images of him clearly intoxicated, out with a different woman every night, sometimes more than one. He parties hard. He fucks hard. He spends money hard.

Luka Zoric has always been a diehard playboy.

It hits me just then, what's different about him. He's shed some of that old skin. And now he seems contemplative, and a little bit lost, like he's not sure what to do next.

I might have a few ideas.

He takes a long drink and then gives me a pointed look. All signs of flirting are suddenly gone. "Here's the deal. It'll be a two-year commitment, maybe three, depending on public response. After that, a very amicable and quiet divorce and you'll be free to live your life."

My mind is already racing with the "what do I get out of it" portion of this conversation. The part where I use him in return for using me. I've never been that kind of a person. But here? Now? With Luka Zoric? I just might be.

"You're the ideal candidate," he adds. "You're well spoken, accomplished, and you have a good background. And not to be a dick, but you'll look amazing on my arm—which in this business really matters. Plus, your philanthropy work is great PR for both of us."

"And what do I get out of it?" I reply without missing a beat.

He starts talking more animatedly, really getting into it. "You want a contract with us, right? I'll sign you right away and send you out on the most prestigious calls, get you in all the major campaigns and runway shows. You act as my wife, and we'll do everything in our power to make you a supermodel." He pushes his plate to the side and leans toward me. "Plus, if my image is cleaned up and the rep of the agency bounces back as planned, that will help you out as well. It's a win-win all around."

I let out a long breath.

"I really just want to be a model," I tell him. "Taking part in a marriage—even a fake one—is a huge thing to ask of someone. My life won't be my own."

"Come on, Brooklyn. Do you know the kind of press and attention you'll get just from being married to me? You'll have professional power like no one else. Every photographer and designer that matters will be bombarding you with opportunities."

I shift in my chair, my jaw going tense. These pie-in-the-sky promises are sounding eerily familiar. And after the shit he pulled three years ago, there's no way I can trust him.

"Thank you for dinner, Luka, but I'm leaving."

I stand and grab my purse. It's satisfying, looking down at him and seeing how intently he's watching me.

"The answer is no. Thanks again for the opportunity."

I spin on my heel and leave. That's right—I'm the one leaving him this time. And it feels almost as good as it would have if we'd gone to his penthouse.

On second thought, nope.

This feels much better.

BROOKLYN

CHAPTER 6

"Obviously I can't take the offer."

I scoot back onto the overstuffed chaise and hug my knees. Mateo is lounging on the plush ivory rug on the floor, a wine glass in one hand as he lies on his side and studies me.

I'm so glad he decided to come to Chicago with me, and extra grateful that I didn't have to move back in with my parents while I chase this next phase of my career. Mateo is making bank, thanks to the way his modeling career has soared—and extra props to him for being one of the first openly bisexual male models to get this big—so he's got the money to live wherever he wants now. And while I do enjoy the perks of being his bestie, like this posh little apartment in Wicker Park, what I love even more is that we've got each other's backs.

No matter what happens in our lives, I hope our friendship never changes.

"Why the hell not? I mean, how can you not even consider it?" He sips and grins and sips some more. "Normally, I'd frown on this sort of thing, but *think about it*,

Brookie. You'll be Luka Zoric's *wife*. You get to *bang* him. Repeatedly. As often as you want. Hell, I'd even go monogamous for that man."

I chuckle. Mateo monogamous? That will be a cold day in hell. When he's not dating two or three at a time, which is never, he's on the prowl for replacements.

In the very scarce in-between of those moments, he's tried to convince me we should be friends with benefits. I've always shut that kind of talk down, not really knowing if he was serious—and honestly, I don't want to know. He's my absolute favorite person in the world and I never want our relationship to change. Plus, I'm too jealous to get involved with someone who only has open relationships, and as his platonic friend I'm free to cheer on his flavor of the week.

He rolls onto his back, balancing his wine glass on his abs, and looks to the ceiling.

"Tell me everything, one more time."

"Ugh. Mateo." I pretend to be annoyed. I've already gone through the entire story with him twice. Honestly, I think he's using my narrative to role-play himself into my place, with a different ending that results in him and Luka fucking behind the restaurant in some bushes.

He knows I slept with Luka three years ago, and I've lost count of how many times he begged me to retell the story of that doomed escapade. He was ridiculously disappointed tonight when I got home and told him there'd been no sex.

"No sex" is Mateo's most hated phrase.

"We went to dinner. We ordered pasta and sparkling water."

"Eww. The water. Seriously." His face scrunches up.

"*I know*. Anyway, he said he needs to clean up his reputation and get married to jack up his image. In return, he'd give me a contract to model for DRM."

Mateo starts to speak, but I cut him off. "Do you think I should try to get another appointment, maybe with Stefan or something? I mean, this wasn't even a real audition."

He sits up and shrugs. "They hold two open calls a year, and this was number two."

"It wasn't an open call, though! It was a...spouse screening." My heart sinks at the thought that I've missed my chance, again, to get a legit contract with the agency.

"Sorry, hon. Look on the bright side, though. You can totally wait around until next year to go crawling back and hope to God they like you enough to offer you a contract that won't hold a candle to the *insane deal* Luka just tried to make you...*or* you can say yes *right now*, become Zoric royalty, and get famous by association so the next time the lease is up on this place, you can pay to keep it." He looks at me pointedly and then says, "Your call."

Then he looks away, pretending to inspect his nails nonchalantly, but it's obvious which course of action he thinks I should choose.

"Funny. But it's not like I don't have other options. I had that audition for Maxilene cosmetics before I left LA, remember? I should be hearing from them soon."

When the second largest cosmetics company in the world hosts an open call for models, you don't run, you go super-sonic and get your ass there. I was the third in line and breezed through the audition, batting my lashes and smiling like a maniac while flourishing the tube of mascara they'd given me as a prop. Now if only they'd call me back.

Mateo's got a curious look on his face, but maybe it's the wine. He's on his third glass.

"I'm telling you," he insists, "there is nothing negative in the offer Luka made you. It's all positive. All of it."

"No, it's not. He lied to me. He ghosted me. How can I trust him now? And why should I even want to help him after what he did to me?"

"He gave you the best fuck of your tender little life, you ungrateful wench. You could have that every day. Every. Day."

I lie back dramatically and toss an arm over my eyes. "You don't understand, Mat. I'm aging out. I don't have much longer to make something of myself. You had your break and look at you now. I'm nearly out of chances."

"Don't be silly. You're barely twenty-two. You have a bright, successful future ahead of you. And plenty of time to get there."

"You don't know that," I say, my voice hitching with emotion.

There's rustling beside me, and then the cushion sinks near my hip. I peek and see a wine glass thrust at me. Mateo holds it out impatiently. I sit and have a sip, and he looks pleased.

"It's true that I have smoother, younger looking skin than you, Brookie. And I don't have as much trouble staying in shape." I roll my eyes as we bump shoulders good-naturedly. "But you have an amazing face and an incredible personality and a feisty attitude that has gotten you plastered all over this beautiful city. You're a fighter, and believe me, you ain't done fighting yet. Luka Zoric would be damn-ass lucky to have you."

Slipping an arm around him, we side-hug, and I hand him back his wine. He settles onto the floor again, swirling his merlot and looking thoughtful. "Let's just say—for the sake of argument—that getting married *is* your best option for breaking out right now."

He side-eyes me and I groan. That's his guilty face, which I don't see often because Mateo rarely feels guilty about anything. "Why are you saying this?"

Mateo hangs his head in shame. "Okay, look. I wanted to hold off on saying anything until I knew more, but...I have good intel that Monica Shore had a private meeting with the head of Elite Image. Like, really good intel."

"Dammit." I put my face in my hands and silently scream into them. Once again, it's just not going to go my way. "Do you think they're looking at her for the Maxilene campaign?"

"I'm compelled to think so, considering that every other Maxilene model just so happens to have been an Elite girl."

"Yeah. Everyone knows that." I let out a big sigh.

Monica Shore is kind of a big deal. At one time, she had the new-age face that everyone talked about—huge, wide, otherworldly eyes, a delicate heart-shaped face, lips that would give Steven Tyler a run for his money. All she has to do is bat her baby blues and she gets signed every time. Rumor has it that she'll stop at nothing to book the jobs that she wants, and from her impressive resume, I have to believe there's some truth to that. She walked into Elite after a recent, messy split from her longtime former agent and I'm sure she walked out with a brand-new contract and the Maxilene gig to boot. No wonder I haven't gotten a call back yet.

I shift my weight and look at the floor. The truth is, Elite Image *is* interested in me, more than I've let on to Mateo. He doesn't know about the recent conversation I had with them...and what the results of that conversation were.

A pang of guilt goes through me. Sometimes I feel like I'm turning into the person I said I would never be. The one who does anything to get a contract.

The thought makes me feel a little sick.

It's not like me to cry over my career. I learned early on that it left you with undereye bags for days and no resolutions. So I'm surprised when tears threaten. Holding them back is easy, but it bothers me that I'm now stressed to the point where tears are my only option.

Well, not my only option.

Maybe I *should* consider Luka's arrangement. It's just... I've never cheated my way into a job, and I've always been firmly against it. Sleeping your way to the top is commonplace in this profession, but it's something I've avoided at all costs. Until now.

Brooklyn Zoric, supermodel.

It has a nice ring to it. A very nice ring.

I catch Mateo's eyes. He looks smug, as if he's reading my mind. "Just make sure the prenup includes a clause that says getting laid all the time is a requirement. Oh, and a guest room clause for your bestie."

I huff a laugh. Yeah, right...like I'd actually go through with this. Although I can't deny how hard my nipples get when I think about sliding into bed with Luka every night.

Reality slinks back in and I shake off these ridiculous notions.

I can't marry Luka Zoric.

So why the hell are my panties wet just thinking about it?

LUKA

CHAPTER 7

After my epic failure with Brooklyn, I decide I need to blow off some steam. I text my workout buddy Diego and then meet him at the gym to do a few hardcore weight circuits. But even benching three hundred pounds of iron with the latest Nas album blasting in my AirPods can't distract me from replaying the dinner date over and over in my mind, trying to figure out where I made that fatal wrong turn.

If I had the conscience to feel guilty about things, I'd feel guilty about fucking her three years ago and then ghosting her. But of all the women in the world who could've shown up to my wife auditions, I never in a million years expected Brooklyn Moss to walk through that door.

It took all of my willpower not to react when I saw her. My cock remembered her before my brain did, a flash of heat and lust coursing through me—and then I remembered why. Those sultry, smoky eyes, those legs that go on for miles. That mouth wrapped around my dick. The dirty talk. How hard she came, as if I was some kind of sex god. I've never been the type to need an ego boost, but hearing her scream my name like that sure hadn't hurt.

Diego and I trade off machines for an hour or so, and then I head back home, my muscles burning pleasantly as I drive through the nighttime lights of the city.

I've been with a lot of beautiful women, but Brooklyn is the kind that a man doesn't forget. And I didn't; I just pushed her out of my mind like I do all the others. No sense in hanging on to the old when I need to make room for the new.

That's a lesson I learned the hard way, from a very young age. Every woman I got attached to left me, and it doesn't take a shrink to figure out why I turned out how I did, jumping from each one-night stand to the next without a second thought. But I've enjoyed it every step of the way. Never looked back.

Until Brooklyn.

She was always hanging around in my memory, just lingering there as the first completely unforgettable piece of ass I've had in, well, ever.

I didn't do right by her. I'll admit that. I'd promised her a modeling gig three years ago, when honestly, seducing her was all I'd ever had on my mind.

I probably *could* have gotten her signed, but that would have required me to beg my brother Stefan for a favor. And to explain that that favor was for one of my conquests. I groan even thinking about the lecture on responsibility and self-respect that would have followed. After I'd come home from my MBA program and started making up for all the years of partying I'd missed while I was studying my ass off at college, my father and brother had perfected the same boring speech about "upholding the Zoric name" and loved to dictate it to me at every opportunity. I'm disgusted to think that my father was such a hypocrite all along.

So no, I wasn't really involved in the business back then, and asking a favor for Brooklyn would have opened a can of worms with my family that I didn't want to deal with. Besides, she was a one-nighter that I never intended to see again...signing her to KZM would have meant I'd have to see her often at the agency. That just wouldn't have worked for me.

I park my car, take a quick shower, and then sit at my desk, reviewing the photos of the other candidates I met today. But it only frustrates me more. Brooklyn's the only one I want.

Realizing how stressed I am, I roll my shoulders to release some tension. This damn image cleanup campaign my family tossed me into has completely messed up my lifestyle. I'm out of my element. No drinking. No one-nighters. Acting like a respectable executive and ambassador for the company. I might owe it to my family, but I don't have to like it.

Holding bogus auditions for a wife was a dick move, admittedly, but what the hell was I supposed to do? I need a decent, respectable woman to be my wife and prove that I've changed—but I don't know any respectable women. Thumbing through my list of contacts—hundreds of them—only left me empty-handed. Not one of those girls was wife material. And then Brooklyn walked in and she almost had me on my knees.

How the hell am I supposed to consider any other woman for my bride after seeing her again?

I want her for this fake marriage.

I want her. Period.

She didn't seem to remember me, though. Which is

probably for the best, considering what I did to her all those years ago. But it only took a few minutes into our interview before I texted the receptionist to clear all the other candidates from the waiting room. I'd already decided that no matter what, Brooklyn Moss was going to agree to be my wife.

I stretch again, but the tightness in my shoulders only gets worse. I'm in comfy sweatpants, leaned back in my desk chair, but I still feel wound up. Shirtless and barefoot, I carry my laptop into the den, settle onto the couch, and flip it open again. I haven't been able to get Brooklyn's image out of my mind, and the memory of our night together three years ago plays on repeat, heating my blood.

No wonder I'm so damn tense. I haven't fucked in days, and the one woman I've never forgotten is back. Those wicked dimples, those high, firm breasts. My mouth waters just remembering the taste of her sweet pussy as I spread her open on my kitchen table.

I haven't used that damn table since.

Sinking back into the couch cushions, I open my web browser and pull up a bookmark of Brooklyn's Insta account. Her perfect images pop up and I scroll through them absently, one by one. Her life in California looks amazing. The photos are aesthetically pleasing and perfectly arranged. They don't seem staged or fake like so many do, though. There's a real, visceral aspect to her photography, as if she's purposely trying to put you right there in the photo so you can be in the moment, too.

I have to admit, it burns me that she didn't remember me. Just how many men have come and gone in her life that I was so easily forgotten? My nostrils flare as I think of her parade of men. But I shut it down. I've done the same with women. It's no secret that I fuck as often as I can. I'm suddenly aggravated and edgy and I know it's from thinking of her with other men.

Like this guy that she's always with. I scroll through a few more photos. I see him again and again, in pic after pic, from social events to trips to the beach. But he's always slightly turned away, just stepping out of frame, or wearing sunglasses, so I never get a clear look at his face. I'm sure he's tagged somewhere, but I'm not going to dig. I've visited her social media pages enough in the last three years to know that whoever he is, he's important to her somehow—but if they were a couple, I'm sure she never would have talked to me about marriage.

At least, I don't think she would have.

Fuck.

I want her and it's driving me mad. I close her social media and pull up my cloud account, then the unlabeled file I have buried there. Brooklyn's image from that fashion show three years ago pops up, her lithe body wrapped in that strappy black designer dress, her heels tall and making her legs look killer. I'd nearly ripped the hem of that dress when I'd yanked it over her hips to devour her willing pussy.

My cock stirs at the memory.

I've kept these images all this time, burying them as if I could forget her and the fuck-hot sex we'd had. There'd been so much I'd wanted to do to her that night. My hand wrapped around her throat, squeezing gently while I fucked her. Her wrists, tied to my bed, her legs spread far apart, ankles bound so she had no choice but to lay there and take my cock. But once I was inside her, all my plans went out the window. All I could focus on was how good she felt, all my energy going into holding back the orgasm that threatened from the moment I slid into her.

She'd been so willing, so ready, so visibly turned on by my every touch. I know she would have done anything I'd asked.

My hand slides over my abdomen, my fingers working below the waist of my sweatpants. I'm so hard that it's mildly painful. I need to fuck—I've never gone this many days without it before. Looking at Brooklyn's photos is sending me over the edge.

Christ.

I grip my cock with urgency and give it a few long strokes. It's like something in me snaps, and I just need to come as hard and fast as I can. I need the pressure and the tension gone, and fuck, I need Brooklyn to do it. Quickly, I pull down my sweatpants. Precum lubes the head of my dick as I stroke, swirling the fluid around until my cock is slick and hot in my hand. Eyes riveted to her photo on the screen, the glistening sheen of her open mouth, I stroke my shaft and squeeze around the head. Her lips should be here, sucking me off and taking me deep in her throat.

God, yes. Her dark eyes looking up at me while she takes my entire cock in her mouth. She'd opened so wide to take me in, so hungry for me, scraping me lightly with her teeth.

I pump faster, working more slick precum where I need it the most. I'd push her over the kitchen table and pull that perfect ass back against me, spread her thighs to bury myself deep inside her. I imagine taking a handful of her hair and pulling her head back while I fuck her. Driving into her, over and over while she cries out, her pussy clenching tight around me.

Fuck. My balls get tight, my shaft swelling. I hold her image in my mind. I remember the sounds she made while I feasted on her, how her wetness burst into my mouth.

With a groan, I spill hot and wet over my hand. I give a few short jerks until every drop is out of me. I stay just as I am until my vision clears and my breathing slows, and I have to close the laptop to stop looking at her. This isn't the first time I've jerked off to her image like some helpless, horny teenager. And now that she's back in Chicago, probably right down the Magnificent Mile, I have the sense my need for her is only going to get worse.

I lean back and let out a long breath, letting the memories fade until I'm completely relaxed. The tension is gone, but I know it won't last long. I need to follow up that hard orgasm with another hot shower. Reluctantly, I get up and pull on my pants, then wander slowly through the house toward my master bath.

The doorbell rings when I've almost reached my room, which means someone is waiting in the elevator that opens directly into my home. Normally the attendant downstairs buzzes to let me know someone is on their way up. I turn on the security camera that allows me to look into the elevator when it reaches my floor.

Speak of the devil.

I immediately tap a code into the keypad next to the elevator doors. They whoosh open and Brooklyn Moss strides out like she owns the place.

She gives me a cursory glance, her eyes stopping to linger on my bare chest before she brushes past me and spins to face me, arms crossed.

"So," she says tightly. "How do you propose to pull off this sham of a marriage?"

BROOKLYN

CHAPTER 8

Now that I'm standing in Luka's penthouse, I'm not entirely sure how to play this. I'd been so sure of myself on the way over, but then he had to answer the door wearing nothing but a pair of clingy sweatpants, flashing that ridiculous six-pack and those broad shoulders I've never forgotten. It takes all my willpower to keep my eyes off the obscene bulge of his cock.

His skin is flushed and there's a light sheen of sweat at his temples, as if he'd just been working out or something. Too bad I hadn't gotten here earlier. *I* could have been his workout.

No, Brooklyn! I made a deal with myself that I wasn't going to think about sex, or kissing, or Luka naked with me under him. None of that. This is going to be a professional meeting. I know what I want from this visit, and it's not an orgasm.

I sweep my gaze over his chest, my hands twitchy with the need to trace the dips and lines there. Who am I kidding? An orgasm is exactly what I want.

He runs a hand through his hair. His eyes are lit up as if

he's happy to see me. "Hello to you, too. Does this mean you've changed your mind?"

"No." I grip the strap of my purse with both hands and clear my throat. "I just came to talk. I'm...open to discussing your proposition some more."

"In that case, have a seat while I get you a drink."

I'm about to decline the drink, but I don't. I might need something to calm my nerves.

He gestures to the end of the short hall where it opens into his living room. I swallow hard as I enter the room, remembering it from the last time I was here. I can't indicate that I know anything about this place, though. He obviously doesn't remember having me over, and I'm not about to burst that bubble.

I take a seat on the edge of the couch. "This is a beautiful place."

His right brow hitches up and I feel like he's assessing me. "Thanks."

"Professionally designed, or is interior decorating one of your talents?"

There's different artwork on the living room walls than when I was here last, large prints of antique architectural sketches, but they somehow lend a distinctly modern feel. I expect Luka to quip something about his talents resting solely in the bedroom.

"Designer. You would not want to see this place if I was left to my own devices."

He puts up a finger to indicate he'll be right back and disappears in the direction of the kitchen. I let out a deep breath and give myself a mental shake. I'm determined to stick to the script in my head. I have questions. We'll talk about it. Make a plan, and then I'll decide if an arranged marriage is something I really want to do.

Mateo's words keep playing in my head. What if this is my only hope of getting a break? I hate having so few options, and like it or not, the most promising one on the horizon is becoming Luka's wife.

He returns before I get too nervous and hands me a glass of wine. Cracking open a bottle of water for himself, he ignores the open expanse of the massive L-shaped couch and sits beside me, close enough that I get a clear whiff of his sexy male scent mixed with his high-end cologne.

"How did you know where I live?" he asks casually.

I tilt the wine glass to my lips, stalling for time. Shit. I have no idea how to answer that without giving myself away.

He shrugs as I swallow down half the glass. "You must have seen my address on my driver's license when we were comparing mug shots."

Relieved, I laugh, hoping I don't sound as nervous as I think I do. "Yes. I did."

He shifts a little and my pulse starts to race. "Okay. So let's talk."

Well, he just opened the door and there's no backing out now. *Stick to the script.* "I'd like to know what your plans are for this whole marriage thing. How would it work, exactly?"

Maybe it's my imagination because I'm nervous, but he appears way too calm. Like this is something he's really committed to, not just some whim.

"I hadn't really thought out all the details to be honest— I was going to work through it on the fly. How about this? You tell me what you'd need to make it work."

Ah, good. The door is really wide open now. I set my glass on the side table and clasp my hands together. His thigh brushes against mine. My breath hitches and I momentarily forget what I was about to say. Did he move closer to me? Why is it so hot in here?

"I want a modeling contract for the length of the marriage, with the option to renew afterward if it's mutually agreeable." The words tumble out and my confidence feeds off of them. "And I want an active role in choosing the assignments that come my way, so I can decide which are best for me. Also, I'd like to be kept in the loop about Danica Rose—you know, like if the company is bouncing back the way you're all hoping. Considering it's my future on the line, too, I feel like I should know how the general health of the business is doing."

He eyes me thoughtfully and I hope the blip of nerves I feel doesn't show. Yes, I do want to know how DRM is doing. Another scandal could put me out of a job and seriously affect my future. But also, the more info I have in my back pocket to use at my disposal, the better. Insider information could pay off for me in the long run—though I don't mention that to him.

"Anything else, Brooklyn?"

My confidence comes back as he moves along.

"I want to pick out my ring."

It's petty, I know, but if I'm doing this, I want it to be Instagram perfect. I've already started thinking about how I'd stage the ring on my hand, with a background at the Navy Pier botanical gardens, catching the flash of the diamond in just the right light.

Luka chuckles a little and spreads his hands. "Is that all?"

"I might think of something else, but those are the main requirements."

It's not my imagination; he did move closer. Our legs press firmly from knee to hip and he's looking at me as if waiting for more. Should I have asked for something else? I scramble to think of something I missed, when his hand slides over mine and my brain ceases to think.

"You don't have any conditions on when we get married, or where? No conditions on where we'll live...or where we'll *sleep*?" he asks.

Our eyes lock, and my nipples pull hard inside my thin bralette. His gaze drops there, my pulse rising as he spies the visible proof of my arousal. I can't think like this.

"Um, maybe...maybe you could put some more clothes on," I suggest.

He lets out a low, sexy laugh. I want to touch him so badly, have him flip me onto my back on the couch and cover me with every inch of that gorgeous body. I want to feel the length of his cock through his pants, grind up against him as I—

"On second thought," I say, "go get dressed so we can take this conversation to the coffee shop down the street."

"What's the problem with discussing things here?" he asks. "It's our chemistry, isn't it?"

"It's not that," I lie. "I just think professional boundaries are a good idea."

"You know, it helps that we're attracted to each other," he says. He reaches up his hand, trailing it across my cheek. I feel the sparks through my entire body. "That energy between us. That heat that makes your throat dry and your pussy wet."

Clenching my thighs together, I uselessly attempt to hold back my desire. But my core is throbbing in the way it does only for Luka.

The one man who could completely ruin me.

I can't let him sweet talk his way into my pants again.

No. Modeling contract signed and delivered, then we'll talk sex.

Luka dips his head to my ear, his hot breath washing over my skin. It's like our first meeting all over again. "It's good that you want to fuck me, Brooklyn. It'll make our relationship look real."

He takes my chin and tilts it up, and when our eyes lock, I start subconsciously leaning toward him, my lips parting almost without me realizing it.

Fuck, what am I doing?

I jump to my feet and cross my arms. "I was under the impression you needed to *clean up* your rep, not dirty it. It's obvious this arrangement isn't your main focus. Give me a call if you decide you're ready to take this seriously. Until then, I'm out."

Turning away, I grab my purse and storm out of the apartment.

As the elevator doors close me in, I slump against the wall and try to catch my breath.

I did it. I stood up for myself. Great.

But I still fucking want him.

BROOKLYN

CHAPTER 9

The little black dress I'm wearing drapes perfectly over my body, the deep V in the front showing off my cleavage. The hem falls to mid-thigh, and the sparkling silver heels I plan to wear will make my legs look killer.

Mateo is taking me out tonight, and even though I'm not really feeling it, trying on outfits is getting me in the mood. I'm going to sip a couple of cocktails and watch my bestie flirt his way into some unsuspecting man or woman's pants, and likely, I'll be taking a cab home. Alone. At least one of us will be having some fun.

I give myself a once-over in the mirror, debating how to do my makeup. My hair is still wet from the shower, and I'm not sure what to do with that, either. Up or down? Straight or curls? Rubbing some hair oil between my palms, I just start to apply it to my ends when the doorbell rings. Mateo is still in the shower, so I wipe the oil onto a towel and go to the door.

It's Luka.

I take a step back as his tall body takes up the door

frame. He's perfectly dressed in a black suit and matching dress shirt with a subtle pattern on it, a pale green tie catching the color of his eyes. His hands are in his pockets, his stance nonchalant, as if he's got all the time in the world and swinging by was a spur-of-the-moment decision.

I swallow hard and clutch the door as his cologne hits me like catnip.

"Hi," I finally manage. "What are you doing here?"

He's not looking at me. Not at my face anyway. He's feasting on my body, working his gaze by increments from my legs to my lips. His hands twitch inside his pockets, and his arms tense as if he's holding back from reaching for me. Finally, he meets my eyes.

"I may have been a little forward yesterday," he admits. "It's no excuse, but I guess I'm still learning how to deal with women in a context outside of the bedroom."

I put one hand on my hip and open the door wider. "It shows. Come in."

He wanders into the apartment and I lead him to the living room. He's on my turf this time—it gives me a sense of power. I gesture for him to sit on the sofa and he does.

"Before you say anything else," I tell him, "I've given it some thought, and you were right—I wasn't asking for enough. There are a few more things I'd need."

I sit in a chair across from him, glad to have space between us. There won't be any accidental touching, any possibility of me letting my guard down again.

"I'm happy to hear your requests," he says, sounding sincere. "And I apologize our negotiations got off on the wrong foot."

"Apology accepted," I say. "So first off, there needs to be mutual respect between us if this is going to work out. We have to act like adults and be considerate of each other's goals."

He nods. "Agreed."

Bolstered by his encouragement, I go on, "If this is going to be a marriage of convenience, it needs to be convenient for both of us."

He's watching me intently, but he hasn't opened his mouth to protest, and I decide to just lay it all out there while I'm on a roll.

"Also, if we're going to have a physical relationship at all, we have to agree that it will not get in the way of our goals." I feel my face heating at my boldness, but I push on. "I want my modeling career to have the best possible outcome. You want your image squeaky clean. Nothing can compromise those things."

I can't believe I just put the sex clause out there like that, but the truth is, I'm still into him, and there's no reason why we shouldn't be intimate with each other if we're married. Plus, I know from experience that we'd have an amazing time in bed.

Luka nods, his eyes unfocused as he seems to mull this over. I wish he didn't have such a poker face right now, though, because I'm dying to know what he thinks of my demands.

Suddenly his head snaps up and he bolts to his feet. I swivel in my chair to see Mateo wandering out of the bathroom, his ripped, muscular body glistening, a towel wrapped loosely around his hips.

"Oh. This is—" I start to say

"Who the fuck are you?" Luka barks at Mateo, completely ignoring me.

"Would you like to find out?" Mateo smiles, completely

unperturbed by the verbal aggression and lazily eyeing Luka as if he's lunch.

I've never heard that throaty tone in Luka's voice before. It's raw and dark and possessive. My middle clenches even as my panties go suddenly damp. Damn, it's hot to see him so alpha—but I can't have him going off on Mateo like this.

"Who's he?" Luka asks, turning back to me now.

Shit. I can see how this must look to him. My hair isn't dry yet and I'm not wearing any makeup—it's obvious I just had a shower, and here's a man walking around my apartment in a towel. It makes sense Luka would jump to conclusions. Still, I'm surprised he's acting like a protective alpha—if I didn't know any better, I'd think he's jealous.

It strikes me that I can take advantage of this. Especially since I need every advantage I can get with this guy.

"It's none of your business who he is," I snap, being purposefully vague. "This is exactly what I meant about respect. How dare you walk into my home and act like you have any right to decide who gets to be in my life and what I can or can't do with them. I can't be married to someone who treats me like that."

I can see Mateo hanging back in the hallway, taking in our fight with wide eyes, but I don't begrudge him for eavesdropping on the drama going down.

Luka's eyes blaze. "Well *I* can't be married to someone who's fucking other men. It'll ruin the whole 'clean image' goal, so if there's something going on between you two, it needs to end right now."

I shoot to my feet. "And I won't be married to someone who's fucking around, either! This isn't just about *your* image. It's about mine, too. I won't be the laughingstock of the modeling world just because you can't keep it in your pants."

I don't realize that we've moved closer to each other until I find him a breath away from me, both of us tense and glaring. He's either going to kiss me or walk away—I can't tell

"So, we're doing this, then?" he asks.

I cross my arms to keep from touching him. "Are you asking me to fake-marry you?"

His face breaks into a smirk. "Yes. Officially."

"Well then," I say. "I guess we are."

BROOKLYN

CHAPTER 10

I picked out my dream ring and it's almost too heavy for my finger, but I don't care. It's a four-carat radiant infinity diamond set in a diamond-studded rose gold band and I'm wearing this bitch everywhere. I've been dying to show it off on my Insta page, but we haven't made an official announcement of our engagement yet, so my e-ring hasn't made its social media debut. It's been six weeks since we decided to do this thing, and it's been a whirlwind ever since.

Luka's family seemed pleased that he'd decided to go through with it.

They also seemed neutral that he'd chosen me. I'd gotten a call from Luka's sister-in-law Tori, who was warm and personable, but she'd explained that she was going into finals week at UChicago and so I wasn't surprised that we hadn't spoken again after that. Nobody else had bothered to reach out.

While it wasn't an outright rejection by any means, it seemed obvious that the rest of Luka's family weren't exactly overjoyed about the new addition to the Zoric clan.

Meh, not that it matters. This is a temporary arrangement, and at the end of it, Luka will have his clean reputation, I'll have my modeling career, and the rest of the Zorics will have their business image healed. Everybody wins.

Luka, his brother Stefan, and their sister Mara—who everyone calls Emzee—are huddled together discussing our engagement photos. We're inside the grand hall of the Chicago Cultural Center so Emzee can photograph us against the backdrop of the historic building. Stefan thought it would help our image even more to showcase our love along with our love of the city's history, and to make a large donation to the Center in our name.

The more ostentatious philanthropy, the better. I could honestly get behind more of that.

The room has been reserved for our sole use for the next four hours and Team Zoric has been making a tour of the space, debating the best angles and how Luka and I should be posed. I'd love to tell them that the eastern wall is the best spot to catch the light coming in from the Tiffany-stained-glass dome, but the brothers are arguing now, and I don't dare interject.

Maybe I could offer my suggestion to Emzee. Luka introduced her as a photographer, so I'm sure she'd be open to discussing the best way to position us, but what I really want is for the pictures to capture the exhilaration of the moment, the brightness of the light hinting at the brightness of our future. I want these photos to have a *vibe*.

I hesitate to approach her, though. For some reason, she's done nothing this whole time but stare into space with the most impressive resting bitch face I've ever seen, and I get the feeling she wouldn't appreciate my input. She's stunning and vaguely rock 'n roll chic with her pale skin, striking black hair, and gray eyes. Stunning, and frankly, a little terrifying.

"Listen up." Stefan's stern voice echoes in the large, arched room. I snap to attention, following Luka's lead. "I want to remind you two why we're doing this and what's at stake."

"We know. We're saving Danica Rose," Luka says, sounding impatient. "Our legacy."

I'm not sure what was said between the brothers to bring this lecture on. Nor do I want to find out.

Stefan nods, but he's still tense. "We need to repair the Zoric image and turn the public's opinion back in our favor." He glances down at my left hand, where the diamond sparkles obscenely in the light, and then gazes at me. "I know it looks like a fairy tale to your social media followers—and to the rest of the world as well, thanks to our PR rep—but at the end of the day it's a business deal. One that will require your very careful attention to succeed."

"I understand," I say seriously.

"And you." He turns to Luka. "The time for fuckery is over. You need to be committed and responsible."

"Sure," Luka says.

"*Luka*," Stefan growls, his voice a deadly warning.

"Okay, yes, I get it—committed and responsible. We've been over this a million times," Luka says. "I told you, I'm in."

Stefan takes a breath, and finally seems to relax. I've already signed my modeling contract with Danica Rose, and I'm in this to fulfill my end of the agreement, but I can't help worrying that Luka may have said or done something to make Stefan think he's not going to keep up his end of the bargain. I hope I'm wrong.

Seeing Stefan up close, I suddenly realize that what

sounded like condescension a moment ago is probably just the verbalized anxiety of someone who's under an extreme amount of stress and pressure. Luka had mentioned that Stefan was the one who turned their father in to the feds, and it's obvious by the speech we just heard that the man has a lot of weight on his shoulders. Trying to repair the reputation of a company brought to its knees by such a huge scandal is no small feat.

Still, even though Stefan seems nice enough, I don't totally trust him. He's too eager to cover up his father's corruption, sweep it under the rug, and make it all go away. He doesn't seem like as much of an asshole as my future husband, but he's definitely cold. I think back to my phone call with Tori, and I shudder to think about what it's like for her to be married to Stefan.

"We're both all in," I reiterate, hoping to keep things smooth between the brothers. "Whatever it takes to turn things around for the agency, we're here to help. Just tell us what you need."

Stefan smiles, and it seems genuine. In fact, it transforms his chiseled features so completely that I almost think Luka could have some serious competition in the hottie department.

"I appreciate that," he says. "And as it happens, I've got a list of places I'd like you two to appear after your engagement is announced," he says.

"I can't wait," I say. I mean it, but I still catch Emzee rolling her eyes.

Stefan continues, "You're going to get a lot of celebrity press, which is what we want, but we need to curate that and make sure the engagement is nothing but positive if we want to shift focus from the scandal. So going forward, don't ever let yourselves be seen out in public together without huge smiles and lots of PDA."

Emzee groans sarcastically and mimes sticking her finger down her throat. Stefan gives her the side-eye, his voice hard. "Something you'd like to add, Emzee?"

"I think it's pathetic that you dragged me down here and made me cancel a gig with *Chicago Reader* to shoot engagement photos for a fake wedding. Why are we doing this again? Oh, right. Instead of pimping our models out as prostitutes, we're pimping them out as *wives*. Fantastic."

Ah. That explained the attitude. She obviously didn't approve of the fake marriage. And despite her harsh, flippant comments about the prostitution, I'd bet anything that finding out about her father's criminal behavior had been a bombshell that had probably destroyed her. No wonder she seemed so angry and aggressive.

"Ignore her," Luka murmurs to me under his breath. I just shrug, even though I'm stung.

"Mara." Stefan's voice is edged with warning.

"Leave her be," Luka interjects. "Let's just get on with this."

"Excuse me. I'm going to run to the restroom." I don't wait for their permission before I dart from the hall and find the closest ladies' room.

The tension is through the roof, not at all how I used to daydream my engagement photos would go one day. *None of this* is the way I imagined it. Yes, I'm getting hitched to a super-hot, uber-wealthy celebrity type. But what we're going to show to the world is an illusion. *Someday*, I tell myself, *I'll do it right*. Have the love, the fairy tale, the dream. All of it.

Next time will be perfect, I tell myself as I check my lipstick in the mirror. Next time.

I arrange my curled hair over my left shoulder and mentally replay the moment I signed my modeling contract, which helps me to smile like my life is about to change irrevocably and for the better—which is exactly what I want Emzee to capture.

Then my brow furrows as I realize that my new sister-in-law probably hates me. Which is extra disappointing, since I was hoping we'd get along. As an only child, I always thought it would be fun to have a sister. It could have been a nice perk to this relationship, one that didn't require the marriage to actually be real. I'd have a built-in buddy to help me navigate this crazy new world—someone to open up to, to have girls' nights with, to support and be supported by.

Clearly that's not going to happen now.

I take a deep breath and nod confidently at my reflection. Okay. I can do this. A couple of months from now, when I'm getting calls for assignments and my face starts popping up in national advertisements, I'll know that getting through this was worth it. My goals are set and all I have to do is keep moving forward to reach them.

Feeling a little more settled, I go back into the hall and find Emzee has set up her tripod and is adjusting the settings on her camera. Luka waits by one of the arches. A beautiful cream-colored velvet curtain is draped inside the arch, which makes a perfect backdrop to my lace dress and Luka's dark silver Armani suit, his hair perfectly combed to the side. His profile is masculine perfection and I swear I can see him in black and white, modeling that suit on a magazine page.

He's barely spoken to me since we got here. I'm sure he's nervous, maybe second-guessing things a little. It's natural. I mean, we're going to be tied together in a fake marriage. Of course we're nervous. His gaze moves over me as I walk toward him. The sides of his mouth twitch as if he wants to say something, or smile, but he doesn't.

"Face each other," Emzee orders.

I move to do as she asks and Luka's hands grip my hips, his fingers pressing into my hip bones and pulling me into him so our pelvises touch. His breath pulls in hard and slow as he drinks me in, and for a moment, I forget that Stefan and Emzee are even here.

"Not that close," Emzee scolds. "This is for a PG-13 audience."

I try to take a little step back, but Luka holds me tight. "No, this close. I want people to believe that I can't keep my hands off her."

"Whatever. At least you've got the 'staring deeply into each other's eyes' part right."

Emzee snaps some pictures and I panic a bit because I wasn't ready. I'm not smiling because I can't stop thinking about what Luka said, about not keeping his hands off me. The way he's holding me so tightly, his breathing notched up, his eyes shaded with that veil of desire suggests that he wants to put his hands a lot more places than my hips.

His palms move up to my waist, his fingers drumming lightly over my lower back. I bring a hand to cup the back of his neck as my breath stalls.

"Smile, Brooklyn," Emzee says. "Like you mean it this time."

"Smile like you love me," Luka whispers with a cocky grin, and then spins me so my back is against his chest. Heat pulses between my legs as his arms come around my body, his hands clasping mine across my middle. My skin feels lit up, every nerve hyperaware of him and the feel of his hard, warm body against mine.

"Time to kiss."

"What?" The word blurts from my lips.

Emzee doesn't look impressed. "You need to kiss my brother, as horrible as that probably sounds for you."

We face each other again, our eyes locking as Luka's sister explains how he's going to dip me low over his arm and kiss the hell out of me while she gets the perfect shot. *Smile like you love me.* What the hell was that for?

I don't love him. And he doesn't love me, either. He *forgot me*, for crying out loud. Doesn't even remember the amazing sex we had three years ago. I'm just another hit-it-and-quit-it conquest for him. Yet here I am anyway, playing the part of happy fiancée, while holding onto a secret motive that makes me feel guiltier every second. Putting the ring on my finger has only made it harder to remember there's another reason I'm in this fake marriage. And he's going to do the one thing that could unravel the tightly wound resolve I walked in here with.

Luka slides his arm around the dip of my lower back, his other hand clasping mine. I let him tip me back, trusting him not to drop me, my lips parting as he leans over to press his mouth to mine.

He pauses, just a breath away.

And then his lips crash onto mine, firm and hot and hungry, his taste assaulting me. It's intoxicating. I can't help letting out a soft moan as my core floods with desire and longing, the pulse so strong that I press my thighs together to stop it. But I can't. I'm at Luka's mercy, completely defenseless in this position, with his lips locked on mine.

The room starts to spin, and I want to throw my arms around his neck and pull him on top of me, inside of me, right here on the carpet. I want his touch all over me.

He chuckles, low and intimate against my lips, as if he's

reading every dirty thought going through my mind. I don't care if I'm smiling, or which way my hair is falling, or how well I'm positioned for the shot. I don't care about anything but getting through this moment. Because lord help me, I want Luka Zoric more right now than I've ever wanted anything in my life.

He's using me, I remind myself. *I'm using him.*
This is all a sham.

But is it so wrong to be attracted to the man who's going to spend the next three years acting as my pretend husband?

He pulls away finally and we move through a series of new positions at Emzee's direction. I'm a supple model, having as much professional experience as I do in that arena, and I do exactly as I'm told and play my part. I never wanted to be an actress, but I have a feeling that I'm going to have to be in order to get through this marriage.

Then, Luka flicks me a gaze that's full of heat and challenge. He wants me to act on my body's demands. The glint in his eyes feels like he's daring me to.

Maybe it's a challenge I'd accept, except that he already has an advantage over me. He can fuck me and forget about it afterward. Me? I don't have the luxury of being that callous.

I still remember every detail, and if I'm not careful to guard my heart...it could ruin me.

BROOKLYN

CHAPTER 11

Luka is really good at playing fiancé.

We're in the den of his penthouse and I can't stop the flutters in my stomach. In just a few minutes, the primetime gossip show *Celebrity Chat* will air —and millions of people will see the interview where Luka and I announce our engagement. I'm a ball of nerves.

Luka, meanwhile, is digging around in his kitchen for snacks like we're about to watch a college football game.

"Do you like olives?" he calls out to me from the other room.

"Sure," I answer, though I don't have much of an appetite.

I have to admit, it's kind of sweet that he invited me over for the airing. The interview had been a lot more fun than I'd expected. Luka was surprisingly attentive and affectionate, giving the host no reason to suspect that our relationship was all a sham. I mean, *I* almost believed our engagement was real by the time we were done. A couple of weeks have gone by since we decided to do this, and I'm finally starting to feel comfortable with my decision. We even took my parents out for lunch to break the news, and he charmed the pants off them both.

"Prosecco or water?" he asks, dropping off a couple of crystal flutes on the coffee table.

"Water's great," I say with an anxious smile. I wouldn't mind a drink to calm my nerves, honestly, but I know Luka's on a strict alcohol limit, and it feels nice to support him this way. Especially considering how supportive *he's* been.

He's gone out of his way to soothe my worries the past few weeks, exhibiting incredible patience every time I call or text him, and he readily agreed when I asked if we could color-coordinate our outfits for the *Celebrity Chat* interview. But what really blew me away was how he'd held my hand during the entire course of the filming, his grip sure and steady. Even the show host had remarked on our obvious chemistry, and the fact that Luka couldn't seem to keep his eyes off me.

I'd been enjoying it. Not going to lie. There were times it had almost seemed real.

He bustles back in and sets down an amazing spread of cheese, crackers, and other assorted gourmet accoutrements and then pours us both water with sliced lemon from a carafe.

"This is way too fancy," I say, swiping a few red grapes. "Did you really put this together yourself?"

"Oh, Brooklyn. You'll soon find out I'm a man of...many hidden talents," he says with a smirk, his gaze dropping lazily down my body and back up again.

There's a familiar tightening between my legs, and I force myself to look away. *I didn't come over here to have sex with my fake fiancé*, I remind myself.

Feeling the need to deflect the sexual tension, I tease, "You seem excited about this."

His smile gets more genuine. "Honestly, when my brother said I had to get married, I thought my life was imploding. But if I have to go through with this, I'm glad it's with you."

He puts his hand on my knee and I take a sip of water because my throat is suddenly dry. I don't want to tame his enthusiasm—it makes us look good—but I can't help feeling thrown by the fact that he's diving head-first into this whole thing while I'm still struggling with my guilt.

Being level-headed is my default, and so far, I've kept my integrity while growing my career, which isn't easy to do in the modeling industry. But in agreeing to this marriage, I made the decision to let some of that integrity slide, and now I'm struggling to remind myself that it's no big deal. People do sketchy things to reach their career goals all the time. I'll fit right in with all the uber successful. I just have to keep my head on straight and remember what this is.

A business arrangement.

I glance at my fiancé. He'll never have to know the true extent of what I've done. And in the end, it doesn't matter.

The theme music for the show suddenly comes on full blast, and my heart skips a beat.

"It's starting," Luka says, grabbing the remote. "Do you have the picture of your ring ready to go?"

"Locked and loaded," I answer, pulling out my phone.

His cologne surrounds me as he adjusts his body on the loveseat, leaning into me. Little goosebumps run down my spine as his warmth radiates against me from thigh to shoulder. I tense up a bit in anticipation of his arm going around me, but instead he reaches for a brie-smeared cracker and turns up the volume on the fifty-two-inch flat screen.

I scroll through my photos until I land on the money shot—our hands clasped over a backdrop of the Chicago skyline lit up at night, my diamond ring sparkling obscenely—already zoomed and filtered to perfection. As soon as the *Celebrity Chat* host announces our engagement, I'll be putting up the pic on my Insta account. With luck, people will care enough to keep the happy news rolling through social media until our faces are plastered everywhere.

Luka's thigh tenses against mine and my nipples perk. I'm wearing a thin bralette and an off-the-shoulder top, which I'm sure do little to hide my reaction to him, but he's so focused on the TV that he doesn't notice. I'm not sure if I'm happy or disappointed about that. I like it when he touches me, and I want more. *It's a good way to test my boundaries*, I tell myself. See how far we can take things as a fake couple. Theoretically, sex is on the table, but I'm not ready for it.

Yet.

"Here we go," Luka says.

Suddenly, I'm staring at myself on screen, cozied up to one of the hottest men alive, gushing about how in love we are. The host chats and laughs excitedly as if she just can't get enough of us. I don't remember her being so exuberant during the actual interview; I'd been too nervous to soak up much of what was actually happening.

"...such a whirlwind," I say on screen, nuzzling against Luka's shoulder.

"I'd actually taken a break from dating when we met, but you know what they say about love at first sight," Luka tells the host, managing to sound sincere, and they both laugh.

"We look great together," I say, turning to Luka to gauge his reaction.

"There was never any doubt about that," he says, absently tracing circles over my knee with his finger. A little shiver runs through me, and I drag my eyes back to the show.

It's a relief to watch myself now and realize that I got through all the host's questions without making a fool of myself on national TV. My pulse kicks up another notch as the interview reaches the moment that Luka and I have been waiting for.

"So...let's see the ring!" the host says, leaning forward, and I give her my hand with a thrilled smile while the shot jump-cuts to a close up.

"Instagram time," Luka says.

As if I needed a reminder. I hit upload, and our eyes lock as I wait for the photo to pop up on my IG account... and just like that, my beautiful diamond is out there for the whole world to see.

I flash him my phone screen. "Our engagement is officially official," I tell him.

"Here goes nothing," he says, leaning back with a relieved sigh and turning down the TV.

Within seconds, my phone starts buzzing nonstop with social media notifications. I'm almost afraid to see what's happening on IG, but Luka's looking at me expectantly. So I open up the app, and I can't believe it. I have a pretty active following, but this is *crazy*. My account is blowing up with hundreds of followers already congratulating us and sharing the pic. The comments and shares are rolling in so fast, I can't keep up.

"Whoa!" I laugh. "People are going nuts. It hasn't even been five minutes!"

He arches a brow. "No one expected me to ever settle down. I'm sure the news is worth gossiping about."

"Ah yes, your playboy ways are the true impetus to our

success." I'm teasing, even though there's a big dose of truth in that.

"This calls for a celebration," Luka announces. "Let me go rustle up some champagne."

"You sure?" I ask. "Don't want to throw off your weekend quota."

"You're worth it," he says with a smile, and I can feel my cheeks heating.

My phone vibrates with an incoming call just as he leaves the room. I glance down and let out a gasp when I realize it's Elite Image. I consider declining the call, but I don't want to risk them calling over and over again while I'm here in Luka's penthouse.

Scrambling from the sofa, I pick up and hurry to the hallway, keeping my voice low. "You can't be calling me like this," I scold in a harsh whisper.

"My apologies," says the male voice on the other line, "I should have called from another number. Just wanted to say we saw your engagement announcement. It came as a surprise to us, as you can imagine. Does this mean you aren't interested in what we discussed?"

I rub my eyes and listen for any sound of Luka returning to the living room. I've been stressing about this nonstop, but I'm still not sure what to say. Yes, I have my contract with Danica Rose now, but the company is still so vulnerable after KZM's trafficking scandal that I'd be a fool not to cast my net wide in case DRM collapses. I'm learning quickly that in this business, you can never have too many back-up plans.

"No, of course not," I gush. "I'm definitely still interested." Maybe I should have informed them about the engagement in advance, but honestly, I didn't think they'd care how I went about getting them what they want from Danica

Rose, as long as they got their results. And with everything going on, I'd tried to put Elite out of my mind as much as possible.

"Great. You'll still be able to deliver everything that we've asked for?"

"Yes," I tell him. "It won't be a problem."

"Perfect. Let's just run through the details one more time."

The sound of footfalls grabs my attention and I catch a flash of Luka coming back into the den. I cup my hand around my mouth and whisper, "Now isn't a good time. I'll call you later."

I hang up and slip my phone into my pocket. My pulse races and I hope the guilt doesn't show on my face. Thank goodness Luka hadn't been in the room when the call came in and the name "Elite Image" popped up on my cell screen. As much as I excel at vamping for the camera and playing the part of a happy, carefree model (or fiancée), I've never been a good liar when someone confronts me. It's something I'll have to get better at if I'm going to pull this off.

Putting on a smile, I return to the couch just as he hands me a flute of champagne. Then he settles in next to me with a half glass of his own.

"Who was that?" he asks off-handedly, which makes it a little easier for me to lie. If he'd acted suspicious at all, I would totally be floundering right now.

"Oh, just Mateo calling to congratulate us." I avert my eyes and quickly sip my champagne, relieved when Luka nods. "So now that we're official, I'd love to hear about what kinds of projects are coming down the pipeline. Any major campaigns on the horizon?"

Focusing on my actual goals makes me feel like less of an asshole for evading him.

He ponders the question and takes a small sip of champagne. "Actually, I'm wooing a few clients that I'd love to pitch you for. Philippa Fontaine has a new line of stilettos coming out and they asked for, and I quote, 'legs to die for.' Sounds like someone I know." He looks over suggestively. "But I want to get your face out there, too. You've heard of Shay cosmetics?"

I smile. Shay is *huge*. "I've heard they're organic and eco-friendly, and they definitely get a lot of celebrity endorsements. I'd be interested."

"You're a shoo-in," he says. "They want a fresh face, warm skin tone, someone who can pull off the innocent, girl-next-door look. If this isn't cut out for you, I don't know what is."

"Are you saying that I look innocent?"

I bat my eyes playfully as the words tumble out of my mouth. He sweeps me with a heated gaze, and I realize it's too late to take back the flirting.

"You pull it off very well," he says, his voice low. "Though I know better. In reality, you're just biding your time, waiting for your next unsuspecting victim."

I huff a short laugh and drain my flute.

"When were you ever unsuspecting?" I need to stop this game, but I can't. It's dangerous, but I don't care. I want him closer, touching me everywhere. His body on top of me.

Claiming me.

His gaze falls to my lips. "The day we took our engagement photos."

I'm almost breathless. "What do you mean?"

His fingers cup my cheek as he slides fully into my space. "You gave me a kiss I can't forget. The way your lips felt...how you taste..."

"Oh," I breathe just as his mouth closes over mine.

Our tongues tangle, hot and hungry, and my nipples harden so fast they tingle against my bra. Arching my back, I press my chest into his, needing to feel our bodies connect. I let out a soft moan and slip my hands around the back of his neck and suddenly he's pulling me onto his lap. Without even thinking about it, I straddle him, feeling him grip my ass tight.

I don't fight this. I take it. I don't care where the excitement inside me is coming from, as long as Luka soothes the ache. It's been an eternity since he's given me the release I crave.

I kiss him like I never want to stop, losing myself in the stroke and glide. His arousal is becoming obvious. A smile plays over my lips as I grind down on him, even though I know I'm playing with fire. I let him palm my breasts, moaning again when his fingers run down my sides. Then he pauses at the waist of my leggings, as if waiting for a signal to go further.

"Mm-hmm," I purr, tilting my hips to give him access. I shush the voices in my mind that tell me this is a horrible idea, and just go with it. I want him so fucking badly. The desire for Luka is like this needy little pulse that never goes away. I ignore it the best I can, but it's *always* there, tapping away at my resolve, begging for attention. Maybe giving in is exactly what I need.

My thighs open as his fingers dip past my waistband to graze over my bare pussy. He groans when he realizes I'm not wearing panties. On a subconscious level, it may have been intentional. I don't know, I'm just glad I skipped them, giving him free access.

He parts me and traces a finger up my wet slit, then swirls his fingertip around my clit. I get such a jolt I nearly jump off the couch. Deepening the kiss, he continues to glide and swirl his finger as his mouth plunders mine. I quickly lose all self-control, leaning into his touch.

"You're going to come all over my hand like a good girl, aren't you?" he growls.

The desire in his voice pushes me even closer to an orgasm. I mumble an affirmative, drowning in the way he's finger-fucking me like a pro, my pussy soaked and aching with need.

"Let's see how innocent you're definitely not," he says. Then he switches from toying languidly to plunging his fingers hard and deep inside me.

"Oh my God," I pant, frozen for a second as I try to catch my breath. It feels so good, almost as good as his cock, and soon I'm bucking helplessly against his thick, perfect fingers as they stroke me long and hard.

I grab his shoulders, bracing myself as I fuck his fingers. He increases the pace and uses his thumb to brush softly over my clit, applying pressure and then alternating back to soft brushes. I can't stop moaning into his mouth, digging my nails harder into his shoulders.

"That's it," he murmurs. "You're gonna come for me. Come for me, baby."

"Fuck," I gasp.

God, I can't believe he's doing this with his hands. I've never been with anyone who could get me off like this. My core is buzzing, hot, tingling, and I let him bring me to the brink, losing all sense of time and place...until without warning, my entire body tenses up and I peak, the orgasm slamming through me in a hot rush as I cry out against his neck.

I feel him smile as a groan comes from deep in his throat.

Desperate to feel him inside of me as I ride out the

shockwaves of pleasure, I pull his hand away and grab the waist of his pants, tugging at the button. Midway through unzipping him, something vibrates against my leg. I ignore it, but the vibration gets stronger. Irritated, I reach down and find his cellphone sticking out of the cushion near my ankle.

I grab it so I can turn it to silent, but then a text pops up from LOVES ANAL.

I'm in town. Same time and place?

My stomach lurches as Luka grabs the phone and fumbles to power it down.

"Ignore that," he says, his hands coming up to pull me back down for a kiss.

Yeah, not likely. Who the hell was that?

And even worse: why did I think I could keep my emotions out of this?

I break away from his lips and sit back against the couch cushions, my breath still coming fast and hard. Luka reaches for me, but I gently push his hand away. The moment is over.

What am I even doing? Sleeping with my playboy fake fiancé? God. He's a manwhore. Straight up. And I can't be doing this.

Sure, he said he won't mess around while we're married, but why should I trust him to keep his word? Anyone with a string of women he knows solely by nicknames like "loves anal" isn't bound to keep his stallion in the barn.

I slide off the couch and adjust my clothes, then grab my purse off the floor. I'm so disappointed. In myself. In him.

"Come back," he says, a lazy smile on his face, acting as if I might actually stay.

I shake my head and head for the door. "Thanks for the evening, Luka. Have a good night."

BROOKLYN

CHAPTER 12

Moving in together. It's momentous. A threshold I've never crossed in any of my past relationships. Not that Luka and I are *actually* in a relationship.

I step into his massive penthouse and pause in the foyer. No matter how many times I come here, the place always takes my breath away. The wall of windows framing the city's most iconic skyscrapers, the height of the ceilings, the warmth of the wide-plank wood floors, the fireplace. And now, it's my home.

But instead of welcome, all I feel is intimidated. Like I don't belong. I can't quite get my legs to move me forward, or my hand to stop clenching around the key Luka gave me. I don't even know if he's here, and honestly it would be better if he wasn't.

Was this all a huge mistake? I don't have a lot of experience with roommates, having never lived with anyone aside from my parents or Mateo. Will Luka and I just go about our separate lives, ignoring each other as we play out the next few years of this marriage? Or will it be more like what

I had with Mateo, where we'd take turns cooking each other dinner, fight over whose turn it was to take out the trash, or wander into each other's rooms for outfit checks? Actually, scratch that last one. I can't imagine Luka ever worrying about what he's wearing.

The sterile white of the walls and OCD-clean interior give me a pang as I realize what a stark comparison it is to the first place Mateo and I had together. We'd jumped up and down on the freshly assembled Ikea bed I'd picked out and then went to Etsy to order cute little throw pillows with swear words on them to spice up the plain gray sofa we'd found on Craigslist. Money was tight at the time, so we shared everything—hair and skin products, Mateo's collection of vintage rock T-shirts, food. Even our mugs of coffee, especially after staying up until the wee morning hours drinking wine and talking about our dreams for the future.

That era of my life is over now. I highly doubt my fiancé is someone I'll stay up late with, snuggling on the couch binge-watching *Sex and the City* while eating cold Chinese leftovers. Time moves on, people change. I get all that. Yet I'm not sure if I should let myself grieve over the good old days I had with my bestie, or just keep my chin up and hold it all in.

My phone rings, displaying a number with a Chicago area code. I pick it up.

"Is this Miss Moss?" a man says.

"Yep—are you calling from the moving company?"

"The van's about five minutes away," he affirms. "My instructions are to use the elevator around back."

"That's right. Security knows you're coming, and the door's propped open," I tell him.

We hang up and I take a deep breath, trying to shake myself out of this melancholy mood. Then I drop my key into the little ceramic dish on the entry table and head into the den. I've been here before, of course, but I've never really wandered around, and I don't know how many rooms or closets the penthouse has. I don't know when the housekeeper comes, either, though by the look of the place I imagine it's often. I poke around a bit and find that besides Luka's master bedroom, there's an office, a guest room, and a small home gym.

I catch a whiff of Luka's aftershave as I head back to the den. My stomach does a little flip in anticipation of seeing him. Though I paste on a smile, it wavers for a second when I see him standing there in dark jeans and a button-down that hugs his torso just right. It takes all my willpower to banish the lingering memory of his fingers stroking me until I came in his hands.

"Hey you." He nods at me, showing off perfect teeth. "Welcome to our home."

Luka runs a hand through his tousled hair and walks slowly over to meet me. He almost looks...nervous. Gone is the exuberant attitude of the other night when we announced our engagement to the entire world; all I see now is an insanely sexy but hesitant man who might actually have no idea how to handle having a woman in his house for more than a single night.

"Thanks," I say. "I was just doing a quick walk-through. I hope that's okay."

"Of course. It's your place too, now. *Mi casa es su casa.*"

He gestures at the room around us, as if I haven't seen it all before.

"I appreciate it," I say. "Look, I'm sure this must feel strange to you. I'm used to having a roommate, but you've probably lived alone for your entire adult life. I'll try not to crowd you."

Luka shrugs. "I'm honestly not home much." He pauses, reconsidering. "I mean, I didn't *used* to be home much. I'm sure we'll find a way to cohabitate here without killing each other."

I wonder if it's hard for him to be home instead of partying hard every night and waking up in random women's apartments. Or only showing up here long enough to fuck before kicking the night's flavor to the door and starting all over. Guess it's game over for him now.

I should know better than to ponder Luka's love life. It's not good for me. Tension coils along my shoulders and I rotate them to work out the knots.

"You stressed?" he asks, pulling me close and gently massaging my shoulders with his thumbs. His touch is like magic, and I find myself leaning my head into his chest, inhaling his cologne and letting out a slow exhale.

"Less stressed now," I murmur.

I'm enjoying our closeness way too much, even though I'm well aware that the power he has over my body is dangerous. It'll be a long time before I forget the way he made me feel when he fingered me...or the way that booty call text hit me like a bucket of ice water afterward.

"Anyway," I say, trying to keep my tone light as I force myself to step away from him. "I'm sure if you keep me busy enough with modeling gigs, I won't be home much myself."

"I'll do my best," he says, hesitating for a moment before adding, "so I was thinking about the bedroom situation—" His voice trails off as the elevator in the hallway dings open.

It's the guys from the moving company, and they've brought up three dollies packed with my boxes and things. Luka stands back as they wheel everything in. A man in blue coveralls holds out a clipboard to me and asks me to sign off on the items.

"Where should we put everything?"

For a moment I'm thrown. I hadn't given it much thought up until now. The boxes holding my belongings aren't that big, and the sum of them would easily fit into Luka's room without displacing anything, but I can't bring myself to invade his personal space when we barely know each other...and besides, we never talked about whether or not I would sleep in the same room. A shiver goes through me at the thought.

Before Luka can direct the men to the master suite, I point down the hallway and lead them toward the guest room, flinging open the door.

"This room is fine," I tell them. I glance behind me at Luka and see his brow lift.

"Sure," he says, shrugging. "Whatever you think is best."

It's better this way, I tell myself. Living in the same apartment as Luka is going to be challenging enough. He sidles up to me after I show the movers where to stack everything.

"There's plenty of space for you in my room," he says. "Are you sure this is what you want?"

The look in his eyes tells me it's definitely not what he wants. He probably thinks if we cozy up in bed together, sex will become a natural routine. Which it very well might.

Exactly why I'm putting my foot down.

"Yes." I keep my voice low. "There's nothing in the contract that says I have to sleep in the same room as you. And I think having some boundaries right up front is a good idea."

He cocks his head and looks as if he's about to argue. But the moving men flit around the doorway and there's no way to keep talking without them overhearing us.

"Just know my door's always open," he says, a devilish gleam in his eye.

I raise my chin. "I'll keep it in mind."

The movers finish up, and after I thank them and show them out, Luka and I stand there like neither of us knows what to do next. Though I know what my body wants to do next.

"I should unpack," I say, taking a few steps back before my animal urges can override the "boundaries" I just made such a big deal about setting.

"Sure," he says. "I have some errands to run, so I'll leave you to it."

"Right. Great. See you later."

This all feels so strange that I don't know what else to say. It's going to take a while for both of us to acclimate, I'm sure. He gives a little nod and turns, and I let myself watch his ass as he walks away from me.

My throat goes tight as I hear the door click. I'm alone in this big penthouse. It's quieter than I expected, big and lofty. And empty. For some reason, I get the sudden sting of tears. Going into my new room, I shut the door behind me, sinking down onto the plush settee. It's a good-sized room with a luxurious, impressive bathroom, a walk-in closet, and comfortable furnishings, all neutral tones and dark wood. The view isn't as pretty as the one from the living room, but it's better than the view of a parking lot filled with cars that I had back in LA.

Needing to distract myself, I grab the box of my toiletries and take it into the bathroom. I start putting things away, changing my mind, rearranging and trying again. After half an hour, I'm still working on the same row of skincare products in the huge mirrored cabinet. In between feeling overwhelmed and surprisingly lonely, I can't stop wondering what Luka is doing.

Reaching for my phone, I wipe at my eyes and dial Mateo.

Thankfully, he answers on the second ring. "This was a mistake," I wail.

He scoffs. "Don't tell me you're tired of all the banging already?"

I roll my eyes and let out a giggle. "Shut up. You know there's no banging going on. We've barely even touched."

He clucks his tongue, chastising me. "I'm sure you'll be singing a different tune tomorrow. There's no way a person can sleep next to you and not want to fool around. Trust me, I'd know."

"Very funny." I look to the ceiling, once again fighting off tears. I feel like I should say more, but I don't trust myself not to start crying. Hearing Mateo's voice is making me more and more homesick by the second.

"Ugh. I'll never understand you. So if you're not calling to tell me how many orgasms you had today, why *are* you calling me?"

I travel across the room and sit on the edge of the bed. It's big enough to hold five people. "Maybe because I miss you." I sigh. "Look, the truth is...I took the guest room. When it came right down to it, I couldn't move into Luka's room with him. It's too weird."

"Double ugh. Go get a pen and paper. I want you to write this down."

I already know what he's going to say. "Stop. I don't need to hear Mateo's Top Ten Reasons to Have Daily Sex. Not again."

"I'm going to keep telling you until it sinks in," he insists. "Sex is medicine! It reduces anxiety, lowers the risk of cancer, boosts immune function, triggers endorphins and oxytocin—"

"Stop! If it was anyone besides Luka Zoric, I might actually take your advice. But I can't, Mat. You know that nothing good will come from having sex with my fake fiancé. I'll just get attached, and it'll make things even more complicated."

He makes a sound of disagreement and I can practically hear all the words he's holding back. Mateo doesn't let his conscience get in the way of his sexual desires. Sometimes I wish I could be like that, too. Just take what I want without worrying about the consequences.

"Hey," Mateo says gently. "What's really going on?"

A tear breaks free and rolls down my cheek. I shrug and wipe at my face. "I don't know. I guess this isn't the homecoming I thought it would be. It's not warm and fuzzy and exciting like when you and I moved in together."

"Yeah, honey, I know," he says soothingly. "Hey, but I still have the 'Fuck It,' 'Hot Damn,' and 'Sexy Bitch' pillows if you want them."

That makes me laugh and silence hangs between us for a beat. Mateo sighs and I feel the weight of how much he misses me too. "You'll get used to it eventually. So will I. I promise."

Mateo is so good at getting on with life. Sex and a few mixed drinks are all it takes to pull him out of a funk. I wish that was all it took for me to put aside my emotions.

"I'm not a bad person for doing this, am I?" The question flies out of my mouth before I even realize I'd been thinking it, but it must be there subconsciously. Always hanging over me.

"God, Brooklyn, no. You're doing what you need to do

to become the person you know you are. You're not doing anything wrong."

"I'm living a lie," I murmur.

"You're taking part in a temporary and mutually beneficial arrangement," Mateo argues. "Come on, you know what people do to get ahead in this game. You're not even *close* to that level of what-the-fuck. And besides, it's all for a good cause. You're helping him, too."

I nod as if he can see me, already feeling better at his words. We talk for a few minutes more and then hang up. Suddenly worn out, I lie back on the huge bed and spread my arms out like wings. The mattress feels foreign beneath my body.

Am I ever going to feel okay about this situation? All I can do is pray that all of this will be worth it...and that I don't lose my soul in the process.

LUKA

CHAPTER 13

There's something Brooklyn doesn't know about me.

Something she's going to learn soon if this tension between us doesn't give.

As our bakery consultant bustles around Aimee Patisserie, assembling a lavish tray of wedding cake samples for us, it takes everything I have not to stare at my fiancée. Her eyes are wide, her mouth falling open as she admires the glass cases of pastel-colored desserts, flaky pastries decked with sliced fruit, tiny cakes dusted in gold flakes or studded with nonpareils. The last time I saw that much naked desire on her face, she was riding my hand to an orgasm.

It doesn't help that the bakery is closed to the public while they host our cake tasting. It'd be the easiest thing in the world to pull Brooklyn into a storage closet to have my way with her.

"Please, have a seat," our consultant says with a grin. She's an older woman in a flour-dusted apron with a maternal air, and she gestures to a cute but flimsy-looking wrought iron bistro table and chairs that I'm sure Brooklyn appreciates. "Can I get you something to drink?"

"Just water would be great," Brooklyn says, eyes flicking to me for approval. I nod. She's been incredibly considerate of my alcohol limits, which I've found oddly endearing.

It's been interesting living with her the past couple of weeks. We've had a few moments that felt like we were getting close to having something physical happen between us—Brooklyn sliding past me in her clingy bathrobe to pour herself a coffee one morning, shower fresh and clearly nude judging by the sight of her hard nipples through the silky fabric; the electricity between us as we'd sat shoulder to shoulder to review her new headshots; the way she'd opened up to me about her parents one night as we shared a single gin and tonic out on the balcony.

Yet even when we're in close proximity, sparks flying so fast and hot they're undeniable, she's kept herself closed off from me. I can't tell if it's because of something specific that I've done or if it's her way of sticking to those boundaries she loves so much.

Both, probably.

I've never been one for boundaries, though—so it's taken all my willpower not to cross hers. Especially with the chemistry between us. But ever since the night I got a text from one of my former hookups who happened to be in town, Brooklyn has had this wall up.

It's not like I haven't been trying to make it up to her. I sent flowers as a housewarming gift on her second day in the penthouse. I talked my brother into loaning out his private chef to come over and prepare us dinner, hoping Brooklyn and I could have a "moving in together" celebration of some sort. My fiancée interacted with the chef more than with me, though, drained a glass of Chardonnay in a hurry, and then went to bed before dessert was served.

Three days ago, I opened an account for her at a designer furniture gallery in River North and encouraged her to shop for whatever she liked, hoping she'd rearrange our newly shared space into something that made her feel like she had some ownership of the place. The account hasn't been used, nor has she added a single personal touch to any area of the penthouse outside of the guest room.

I'm at a loss as to what else I can do to get closer to her—to make her feel comfortable. Part of it is that the next few years are going to be a nightmare if we can't live together in peace, but I'm not going to lie: I also want her, and I'm not above doing everything I can to get her into my bed. My cock jumps to life at the smell of her shampoo in the air, the sight of her ass in workout leggings when she heads out to hit the gym, the sound of her giggling on a phone call. It's all I can do not to grab her in my arms and bend her over the couch, or the kitchen island, or anywhere else convenient and give us both release.

I just want her. And, fuck, I want her to desire me just as much. I replay how it felt to slide my hand inside her pants the night of our private *Celebrity Chat* screening party. How her smooth, bare pussy lips felt beneath the pads of my fingers. Her wetness slicking over me as I played with her clit until she soaked me. She pretends that she doesn't want me, but I've replayed that memory in my mind every night since she's moved in, using it to my advantage while I jack off alone in my room. Her body didn't lie.

She fucking wants me. I want her. With any other woman, I would have made the big moves already. But now that we live together and have this official arrangement going, I know I have to tread lightly. Be more sensitive. My usual tactics don't apply here, because unlike other women, I can't kick Brooklyn out in the morning.

Still. Something has to give before she sees a side to me that she definitely won't like. So in the interest of maintaining harmony, I've done my best to keep my distance.

Until today. It's only 10 a.m. and I'm already strung tight. I agreed to come with her to the wedding cake tasting she arranged solely to keep her happy, but now that we're sitting here, I'm over it. I've left the wedding planning entirely to Brooklyn, mostly because I can't handle being near her all the time, but also because it requires attention to details that, frankly, I don't give a shit about. I might have more patience if I wasn't horny and on edge, but I doubt it.

Venue? Who cares?

Colors? Fuck off.

Music? Nope.

I've given very little input into any of it, trusting my sister and Brooklyn and a team of professionals to work it all out. Me? I care about the honeymoon, and the wedding night we're probably not going to have. Let me plan *that*. I swear, it would be a night neither of us would forget. My body tenses at the thought of her in scant lingerie, leaning over the balcony of some five-star resort on a private island where I could fuck her anywhere, anytime.

"Sit, sit!" Our consultant is back with a round of samples, playfully scolding Brooklyn—who's still wandering around the place while I fight my urges here at the table.

Brooklyn scurries over, slips out of her denim jacket, and drapes it over the back of her chair. As she slides into her seat, I do a double take at how her breasts fill out the soft, cropped sweater she's wearing, her dark skinny jeans accentuates the curve of her hips. She'd been so intent on ignoring me this morning that I'd given her space and didn't take the time to notice how perfectly her outfit hugs her body.

Big mistake.

"Thank you so much for having us, April," Brooklyn gushes. "I've always loved this bakery. I've posted tons of your little cakes on my Instagram."

The woman—April—places a hand over her heart and smiles broadly. "I can't tell you how much I appreciate that. Word of mouth is the best advertising we can get in this industry."

She runs through the list of things we'll be sampling then, explaining ingredients and fillings in such detail I can barely keep up. We've reserved an hour and a half for the tasting, and judging by the samples laid out on the table next to us, April has really pulled out all the stops.

Brooklyn is eyeing the dishes with the same hunger I feel each time I look at her. I envy the cake. It's about to get some serious action from that pretty mouth of hers. An appreciative little moan rolls from her throat and it captures my full attention. I want to hear that sound when we're naked and my cock is deep inside her.

"Do you smell that lemon buttercream?" she asks, her eyes suddenly locking on mine.

"Uh, yeah," I say, though my mind couldn't be further from the frosting.

April smiles, delighted. "There's nothing artificial in that, dear. We use fresh Meyer lemons, local butter, and organic cream. It's so rich and decadent, it practically melts in your mouth. Would you like to try that first?"

"Yes, please!" Brooklyn says. She's so damn excited I can't help being amused.

Moving a small dish of frosting from the tray over to our table, April hands us two silver tasting spoons. "I'm going to have you try the frosting and cake samples separately, and then some of our favorite combinations together. We can combine anything you like, of course."

Brooklyn dips her spoon into the frosting, smells it, and grins before taking a small bite. She makes that sound again and closes her eyes, sucking the remainder off the spoon, taking it all into her mouth. I realize how intently I'm watching her, but I can't force myself to look away.

"Oh, my. That is *delicious*." She cocks her head at me. "Aren't you going to try some?"

I'm holding my spoon in the air, too busy watching her have a mouth orgasm to remember to get my own sample. I take a bite, barely tasting it in my eagerness to watch Brooklyn try something else. "It's fine," I say, much to the women's obvious disappointment.

A lot of descriptions get thrown around after that—espresso ganache, Swiss meringue, white chocolate whipped cream—but all I can focus on is how much I want to see my fiancée enjoy each one. I tell her they're all great, and that the choice is hers.

We finish with the toppings and move on to cake. The samples are cut into small squares and though we're given slender little forks to use, I pick up the first sample with my fingers. It's red velvet, not my favorite, but the anticipation on Brooklyn's face makes up for it. She wets her lips with the tip of her tongue and eyes me curiously. She leans in and my pulse starts to race at the thought of popping the treat between her lips, feeling her mouth brush against my fingertips.

Her gaze falls to my hand as she breaks a piece of the cake off for herself, denying me the pleasure of feeding her. Holding back my disappointment, I eat the rest myself, watching her as she starts to reach for another square—

spiced something. Quickly, I pick it up first and offer it to her, holding it near her mouth, making my intention very, very clear.

"Open up," I coax, my gaze fixing on hers.

A pulse beats between us as she slowly opens her mouth. Before I can press the cake to her lips, though, she pulls it out of my fingers and eats it. She chews slowly, making me watch her savor it, and when she's done, she licks her fingertips to get every last drop of flavor. Then she flashes me a saucy smirk.

"So good," she says, practically purring.

There's no doubt in my mind now. She's denying me but teasing me at the same time. Punishing me for something. And I'm eating it up.

I'm about to come...unglued. Everything about this is sexy as hell. I've never been one to mix food and sex, but I'm regretting that now. We finish the plain samples, and then April brings out one last silver tray with thin slices of decorated cakes, most with layers of filling inside.

"These are some of our most popular pairings," April is saying, but I tune her out.

As Brooklyn nods along, my cock twitches. She's going to kill me with this sampler. I'll either end up walking out just to control myself, or I'm going to fuck her right here on the table.

April continues her breakdown of each slice of cake, and I don't give a flying fuck, but I pretend like I do. Somehow, I hold my composure together...until Brooklyn runs the tip of her finger over a thin ribbon of strawberry champagne filling and sucks it off with a wet little smack, her eyes catching mine as she dips the tip between her lips for a final little suck.

My chest has gone tight, my cock thrumming with unreleased lust. April gets into the nitty gritty of cake toppers and decoration options and I find myself nodding along, agreeing to things I'm not fully aware I'm agreeing to. Finally, April sets down a single fat slice of traditional looking wedding cake, white on white, with a delicate rose made of frosting on top.

"This is the fun part!" She claps her hands and gestures that we should stand. I quickly adjust myself under the table before rising. Brooklyn gives me a cursory glance and then watches April with interest. I feel the weight of how my fiancée keeps her attention off me, noticing how much effort she puts into keeping her distance.

April cuts the cake in two and then pushes Brooklyn and I closer together. She has us link arms and winks as we get cozy with our arms entwined in the obligatory "feed each other cake" pose. Then she places a neat chunk of cake in each of our hands.

"Nothing like a little fun practice!" She cheers a little and stands back, watching us like an apt teacher waiting for her students to make her proud.

Brooklyn clears her throat, avoiding my gaze. I lean closer to her, smelling her scent mixed with the sweetness of the cake. A dark stirring begins like a whirlwind inside me.

"Do we get to practice the wedding night, too?" I ask quietly.

Her eyes fly to mine, lips parting in surprise. I want to see if her nipples are hard beneath that damn sweater, but I can't look away from her mouth as I slide the cake in. She takes it softly, intently, her lips pressing against my fingers with a warmth I feel all the way to my balls.

She hurriedly feeds me my cake and then breaks away to grab a napkin. April gives a pleased laugh and removes the platter. Brooklyn turns her back to me and wipes her mouth. I will her to turn around, but she doesn't. She's hiding her body's reaction to me. I felt it in the way her breath hitched and her body heat jacked a few degrees.

She wants me.

And she's fighting it.

Her cunt and her tits are all in, but her heart and head are not. Those are things I can't change through will alone, and I certainly can't rush.

I let out a breath. Wanting her won't kill me. If she wants to keep things platonic, fine. But she's going to learn real quick that being this sexually frustrated brings out the real asshole in my personality.

I guess she'll just have to learn to live with it.

BROOKLYN

CHAPTER 14

Someone needs to remind me ASAP why I can't jump my fiancé.

He looks so drop-dead sexy in his gray Armani tux that my thong just got instantly soaked. Luka adjusts his tie in the entryway mirror, his legs spread apart as he commands his space with sexy, masculine grace. I watch his hand as he works the knot in his tie, recalling those strong fingers near my mouth as he fed me cake. How I'd wanted to wrap my lips around them and suck the frosting off. How it had taken all of my self-control to act like I wasn't interested.

He turns to look at me as if he can read my thoughts, his hand falling slowly away from the base of his throat. Silently, he fully faces me, and a wicked grin transforms his face into pure, unadulterated playboy.

I enjoy the appreciation and desire on his face. I'd chosen my outfit for Danica Rose's official launch party very carefully. We'd talked briefly about matching in some way to show off how in love we are and all that, so I'm wearing a silvery gray silk halter dress with a plunging neckline, balanced by a floor-length hem and a single slit that goes up one thigh. Side by side, I'm sure we'll look like the perfect pair. We've decided to be *that* couple.

It's good not only for our image, but for DRM's as well. We're the united front of a new chapter in the Zoric empire's story. One with a brand new name and a brand new set of faces, that doesn't include Konstantin and the stain he created. Tonight is all about the company moving forward, with Luka and me at the helm of its publicity shift.

This is our first major public appearance since the engagement was announced, though, and I'm practically buzzing with nerves.

The unabashed hunger in Luka's eyes makes my stomach clench even harder. I can't hold back the grin that tugs at my lips. I'm glad he's having such a strong reaction to me. Christ, it was all I could do to hold back at the cake tasting the other day. Teasing him hadn't been entirely intentional then...but now? I'll admit I'd chosen this dress because I knew he'd love it.

I also left my hair straight tonight so it falls to my waist, begging to be touched. Perfect cat's eye liner and nude lips let the subtle sheen of my curve-hugging outfit take center stage.

"You're drooling," I scold Luka with a smile as I approach him on four-inch heels. I may want to keep a wall between us sexually, but it's still fun to be lighthearted with him.

"Can you blame me? Come here and let me get a better look at you."

I hesitate to get too close. If he touches me, I'm going to give in to what my body wants so much. I stop a few feet in front of him and do a slow turn while tossing a sultry look over my shoulder. His fingers flex as if he's holding himself back from reaching out. Breaking through his hesitation, he skims his fingers down my arms, causing tingles to race over me.

"Stunning. Look how well we match."

He gestures for me to stand before the mirror with him. I have to get right next to his body to do so, but I'm curious... I want to see *us*. Tossing back my hair, I position myself beside him and temper my urge to lean into his touch as his hand skates across my lower back and comes to rest at the curve of my waist. He pulls me closer against his side until we're touching hip to hip. I hold my breath for a fraction of a second and look at our reflection.

Luka's tall muscular body, dark tousled hair, and intense green eyes do nothing but complement my sleek stature and Mediterranean coloring. We match, but not in a sticky-sweet way—more like an elegant couple on the cover of some elite European magazine.

He catches my gaze in the glass and a pulse of sexual electricity sparks between us. He begins to turn toward me, and I watch him like he's in slow motion. I'm caught in the push and pull of desperately needing him to touch me, and just as desperately needing to prevent it.

"Luka, I—"

His phone goes off, startling us both. He works his jaw and then steps away to pick up the call with a low growl. After he says a few tight words, he hangs up.

"The limo is downstairs," he informs me.

"Better not keep it waiting," I say, relieved that we're out of time to fool around.

I rearrange my clutch in my other hand so I'm free to

take the arm he offers. My eyes work back up to his after taking another sweep of his exquisite body in that tux, and then I'm leaning against him as we head down in the elevator.

Every moment with him is charged. My heels make a determined clip across the lobby floor, the steady sound reminding me that I'm doing this for show. My fiancé looks incredible, and I know the attraction is mutual, but giving in to temptation would only muddy the waters.

He sits close in the limo and makes small talk about the event, but I'm too busy watching his lips move and daydreaming about his talented tongue to pay much attention. By the time we reach the swanky hotel venue, I'm so aroused that it takes all my will not to crawl into his lap.

Clinging to Luka, I walk into the Art Deco-style bar that's been rented out for the night and into a roomful of people I've never met. Heads turn to watch us, and the female whispers start immediately, some not bothering to temper their volume as gossip gets tossed around.

A chill goes down my spine as I realize the sheer volume of eyes on us. I'm sure our engagement has brought out a mix of jealousy and shock in more than a few people who'd hoped to gain something from Luka in the near future. For instance, the stable of attractive women he's left behind—many of them circling us like sharks in this room right now.

"Everyone's staring," I tell Luka through a clenched smile.

"That's because you're the belle of the ball," he says, his voice low and smooth. But it does nothing to calm my anxiety.

I'm the centerpiece in a room full of gorgeous, sophisticated models who have no qualms about eyeing my fiancé with lusty knowing in their expressions. For the past hour, I've been trying to remind myself why I shouldn't jump into bed with Luka, but now the reason hits me full force as we stroll through the glittering crowd.

I hear what they're whispering behind our backs. I see how they look at him. At me. Their looks are smug, or pitying, or amused.

I'm surrounded by women that have all slept with my fiancé.

It's a sickening feeling to realize there probably isn't a pussy in this room that he hasn't been inside. He glances down at me with an encouraging smile that I might find endearing if I wasn't suddenly so uncomfortable...and so angry. Everyone here thinks I'm a joke.

"Don't be nervous." He squeezes my arm encouragingly. "Our job is to tell people how glad we are to see them, smile for the cameras, and duck out as soon as possible. Sound okay?"

"Sure." I lift my chin and don't return his gaze. "Let's just get it over with."

"Ah, so you are nervous," he says, misinterpreting the edge in my voice. "Let's get you a glass of wine, then. It'll help you loosen up."

A snappy retort goes down my throat as I hold it in, hyperaware of every female here. I can't ignore the way they look at Luka like they're hungry, how they tilt their heads together to whisper and laugh. I've never been one to let gossip get to me, but this feels different. Heat tingles along my hairline and my body feels like it's slowly pressurizing.

Glancing around, I tighten my grip on Luka's arm as we head to the bar. Music thumps and vibrates through the room. I catch a glimpse of a redhead in the corner with an incredible, curvy body and a vampy, 1940s vixen vibe to match. Her bright blue eyes home in on my fiancé, her painted lips arching in a cocky smile.

"Do you...know her?" I ask Luka, inclining my head in the woman's direction.

He glances over and shrugs. "Cassandra Ronan? We signed her a few months back. Do you want me to make an introduction?"

Cassandra looks at me and then makes a show of sipping from the straw in her cocktail while dropping her gaze to Luka's crotch. Then she licks her lips before turning away.

"Um no, that's okay," I say. "I'd rather find that drink first."

I clear my throat and swallow hard, but the lump there is only growing.

Then I see a blonde dancing in a corner, her body wrapped in a black mini that shows off long, tan thighs. She's doing some sort of belly-dancing thing, swiveling her hips in smooth, suggestive motions that has a small group of male observers very, very interested. I press my lips into a hard line. Why did I think a modeling agency party would be anything other than this?

Luka makes a half turn to pass me the wine glass that seems to have materialized in his hand. "There's a good crowd here tonight—I'm sure Stefan's floored that so many people showed up to support Danica Rose. I honestly wasn't sure what the turn out would be like."

It's an innocent comment, another thread of small talk that I don't want to engage in. The hot, jealous anger inside me keeps growing. I feel suffocated. A dismissive, sarcastic sound makes its way out of me as I take a sip of the moscato.

"Are you sure this is a party to celebrate the agency, and

not just a reunion for all the women in your little black book?" I say.

"What?" Luka's eyebrows shoot up and he makes a cursory glance around. "I didn't sleep with *everyone* here." His tone says otherwise.

He takes a quick drink of water and I slide my hand out of the crook of his arm and gulp from my wine glass, ignoring the judgmental gazes all around me. I point at the redhead.

"That one over there? It's obvious you slept with her. Everyone in the room knows it." It's like I can't stop. I can't hold my tongue and I can't tamp down the bite in my voice. I nod to the belly-dancing blonde in the corner. "And what about her?"

He shrugs and thinks a moment, then looks away. I've never seen Luka truly uncomfortable, but he is right now. I'm doing this to him...but I can't seem to reel myself in.

"Right." I look pointedly at a brunette. "Her too?"

His eyes darken and narrow as he searches my face. I single out another woman and nod my head. "What about that one? She hasn't stopped looking at your dick since we walked in."

"You need to stop," Luka says, his voice low. "Let's just have a nice night out together."

I'd like to do that—but the thing is, he hasn't denied a single accusation, which only flames my white-hot jealousy.

"It's too late for that," I hiss, glaring up at him.

"Come here." Luka slips his fingers over my bicep and pulls me closer to him, dipping his head as if we're having a pleasant conversation. The tension rolling off him says otherwise. I've pushed him too far. This isn't like me at all, yet I can't find the sense to feel guilty about all the accusations I've made.

And now I'm going to pay for it.

"You want me to tell you about every woman in this room that I've fucked, Brooklyn? Huh? Does your dirty little mind want to hear every scandalous detail?"

I shake my head, but it's too late. His handsome face has gone dead serious, clouded by a dark expression I've never seen before. It scares and arouses me all at the same time.

"Don't—" I start, but he cuts me off.

"The blonde swinging her hips like that? You should see the way she moves when I have my finger in her ass. And that's nothing compared to what she's capable of when I'm pounding on her G-spot. It's sexy as fuck."

My mouth drops open, my stomach clenching and my cheeks going hot.

"That brunette over there, with the legs for days?" he goes on. "Her knees were wrapped around my head so tight I thought she'd break my neck. 'Xena,' I called her."

He pounds back another drink of water as if it's hard liquor and gives a nod of greeting to a dark-skinned woman decked out in fire-engine red as she saunters by. "That one used to be a gymnast. *So* incredibly flexible. Good thing, because the broom closet I fucked her in wouldn't have been nearly as much fun if she hadn't been able to fold up the way she did."

"Stop it," I whisper, a sick feeling roiling in my gut.

A slow, wicked grin crosses his face as he watches yet another woman with raven-black hair go by. "And her. She screamed so loud, we got kicked out of the Hilton. Twice."

I'm pulling breath in through my nose, my chest heaving to the point that I can't control it. I'm seconds away from throwing my wine in his face. These feelings inside me are shocking and I don't know what to do with them. This isn't me. I've never been the jealous type. Hell, this isn't even a real relationship. But Luka is driving me to the brink.

I feel possessive, jilted and enraged and so damn aroused, with no outlet for it. I want to pull his hair, scratch at him. Shove him and then pull him closer. I want him to tangle with me until we're sweaty and naked and my thighs are squeezing the hell out of his hot, smug face.

I set down my glass on a table, intending to head to the ladies' room where I can hide in a stall and collect myself. But I can't hold back one last jab before I go.

"Funny how you recall every tiny little detail of your whoring with these women, yet you don't have a single memory of fucking your own fiancée."

His face goes cold. I start to storm away from him, but his strong hands grip my hips and pull me back.

Luka spins me, his eyes blazing as he crushes my body up against his. "You tasted like blackberries and sin, and I'm not talking about your mouth. Which, I have to tell you, is my second favorite taste ever. And how could I forget the look on your face when you came, the feel of your soaking wet pussy rutting against my tongue while I devoured you—it's all etched in my memory so completely, it's the first thing I see every night when I close my eyes."

He's pulled me away from the bar and into a corner. We're still in the way of heavy traffic but I barely notice anyone else. I can't believe it. All this time he's known, and he's said nothing. The anger inside starts to cool. I'm simply stunned.

"So, you do remember me."

"Fuck, I never forgot you. How the hell could I ever forget *you*?"

Luka's lips crash onto mine, his tongue invading my mouth as he pulls me in and consumes me. I moan loudly, my hands wrapping around his head to hold him closer. He feasts on me and my body starts to quiver. I want that mouth all over me. Right now.

People whisper louder. I don't care.

Let them see how much I want my fiancé for all I care.

"Luka," I gasp as I grab the collar of his shirt. "Limo. Now."

BROOKLYN

CHAPTER 15

Luka slips the limo driver a few crisp bills and tells him to go get himself a drink, and then just like that, we're alone in the back seat.

The partition is up, and the windows are blacked out, but even if they weren't, I don't think I'd have a mind to care. All I can think about is ripping Luka's clothes off and climbing him like a tree. He urges me down onto the seat, on my back, his strong body hovering over me. Our eyes catch for a second before his mouth is on mine again, and that's all it takes for me to lose complete control. I rip at his tux jacket until it slides off his shoulders, then tug at the buttons on his dress shirt, not caring that his tie is in the way. I just need to feel his bare skin under my palms.

"Careful," he barks, his hands at the hem of my dress. "You're going to pop the buttons."

"Shut up," I sass him.

Finally getting his shirt open, I slip a hand over his chest and moan at the warm hardness of his naked body. Luka growls against my lips, his hands roughly bunching my skirt fabric up over my hips. I slap his hand and cock my head back.

"Don't wrinkle the silk, you beast."

"You think I give a damn about your dress? I'm just trying to get to your pussy."

I take a fistful of his hair and make him look at me. "Who says you're getting my pussy?"

His hands cup my face and hold me tight. "I do."

He kisses me, deep and hard, until I'm panting. Pulling away, I gently untie the halter behind my neck and slip the dress over my head, draping it flat on the seat across from us.

"Fuck, yes." The hunger on his face deepens as he realizes I wasn't wearing anything at all beneath the dress.

My body is spread out bare for him, and if I'm not careful, my heart will be too. I loop my hands around his neck and pull him back down to me. His lips trail down the side of my neck and work their way to my breast, and then he sucks my nipple into his mouth.

"Ahh," I moan. It's like I can feel the pressure of his tongue all the way down to my clit.

I've been so eager for this to happen, but I haven't been able to admit it to myself. And now that we've crossed the line, the floodgates are wide open, my sexual frustration finally coming to a head so intensely that I can't stop myself from giving in to all my animal instincts.

I arch my back, wanting more, and he sucks harder. One hand slides down my belly, his fingers pausing at the top of my mound.

"What the hell are you waiting for?" I growl, jerking upright to press myself into his hand, but he keeps his fingers there, just above where I need him to touch me the most. Is he teasing me?

With an impatient little whimper, I take his hand and

move it down to my pussy lips, rubbing myself against him. Luka chuckles with my nipple in his mouth and begins to stroke me. I spread my legs as far as I can on the narrow seat and shift my ass toward the edge to give him better access.

Luka puts one knee on the floor and works his mouth down...over my ribs, my belly, the arch of my hip. I moan loudly as he strokes my clit with two fingers, alternating pressure between hard and soft. The sweet tension of impending orgasm is already building. I'm not going to be able to hold back. It's been too damn long, and he's way too skilled with his mouth.

Suddenly, his tongue replaces his fingers and he's lapping me up, feasting and sucking at my clit. Glancing down at his dark head between my thighs, I wonder why I've fought this so stubbornly. The sensations are unbelievable, and I feel myself sinking down as wave after wave of hot ecstasy washes over me. It's the best drunk I've ever been—my head and body heavy and light at the same time. Every nerve standing on end just waiting to feel his touch.

"God, you're good at that," I groan, grinding against his tongue. "Don't stop."

Luka shifts to slide his fingers into my soaked hole as he sucks harder on my clit, moaning so my whole pussy feels the vibrations of his mouth, and when he starts to pump his hand in a pounding rhythm, I can't stop myself from coming fast and hard.

I cry out, my voice loud and jagged, not caring if anyone outside can hear. My body has taken over, thighs tight around Luka's head, milking every last second of pleasure. When he finally rises from between my legs, his gaze triumphant but tender, something pulls at my heart.

It's the same sensation that pushed my jealous anger

earlier. Of all the women in that room tonight, he chose *me*. He could have had any of them—again—but here he is, in the back of this limo, with his hands all over his fiancée. Keeping his promise not to sleep around during our arranged relationship. Is it possible he really cares about me? Or is this all part of the deal?

Before I can think about it more, Luka moves closer and I reach for the zipper on his pants, pulling it down and releasing his thick, glorious cock. It springs free, hard and ready, the head glistening with pre-cum. I grab his ass in both hands and urge him toward me.

With a wicked grin, he climbs further along the seat. I sit up just enough to meet him as his cock lines up with my mouth, the tip just brushing my wet lips. I open up and pull him in, stroking long and hard with my tongue and sucking deep until he hits the back of my throat. He groans a couple of curses, his pleasure driving me to suck him harder, longer, pulling him in and pushing him out. He swells in my mouth and I grip his bare ass tighter to keep him inside of me.

Luka starts to thrust his hips, working his cock in and out of my mouth as he looks down to watch. He's bracing himself with one hand on the back of the seat while the other holds up the hem of his shirt so he can watch me suck him off.

"Yeah," he groans. "Take all of it. Every fucking inch. You like that?"

"Mm-hmm," I moan around his length.

His taste is heady in my mouth and I love it. Pressing my thighs together as my lust starts to grow, I realize that Mateo was right: I've been missing out by denying both of us this pleasure. It's fucking amazing. Luka suddenly pulls out of my mouth and shifts so he can bend down to kiss me.

I close my eyes as I dig my fingers into his hair, lost in the tangle of our tongues.

I'm into this, I realize. Like, really into this. Making out with Luka feels good, sucking him off feels good, and it's obvious he enjoys putting his mouth on me. Maybe this could be more than just a transactional arrangement, or a shared opportunity for solidifying our futures. Maybe, if we're open to it...this could actually turn out to be something real.

Luka moves between my thighs and adjusts my legs so they wrap around him. Then he lines up the tip of his cock at my entrance and pushes in just enough that he fills my opening. Then he stops.

"Ooh," I gasp, digging my nails into his back. He's so big, I'm practically throbbing around him.

Spreading my pussy lips, he stays where he is and slides a finger down to circle my sensitive clit. The sensations are too much and not enough, his cock unmoving but stretching me wide, his fingers working their magic all the while. He strokes me until I'm nearly vibrating off the seat, his hard length still buried inside me, making me ache for him to pound fully into me. The tension is almost painful, and I hear myself whimpering, "Fuck me, please, Luka, fuck me."

"Yes," he groans, thrusting his cock all the way inside, filling me completely.

My breath catches in my throat and for a moment we just cling to each other, both of us gasping for air. Then he starts to move, slowly and then faster, working steady and deep inside my pussy. His name flies from my lips and I toss my head back against the seat. It's all I can do to hang onto him as he fucks me while working my clit.

"You feel so good," he pants, picking up the pace. "So...fucking...good."

Another orgasm is building, and I squeeze my legs tighter around Luka's waist and bury my face in his neck. I don't ever want him to stop. I think I'm actually seeing stars.

"I'm coming," I murmur, kissing his jaw, his mouth, his cheeks.

Suddenly, I shatter with the most intense climax of my life. It pulses from deep within my core, moving outward in radiating waves of bliss. My fingers and toes and scalp tingle as pleasure rolls over me and I hear myself crying out, but I can't tell how loud. It's just his name, over and over until he pulls out and finishes in a hot spray over my belly.

Wide-eyed and dazed, I watch him stroke off the last of his release, his face clenched in pleasure, lips parted. With a final exhale, he comes down off his high and opens his eyes. I smile lazily. All the anger I'd had earlier is gone. My body is light and sated and for the first time in a while, things just seem right.

He averts his gaze when I try to catch it, grabs a few tissues from the box across the seat, and gently cleans me up. I sit and stretch my arms above my head.

"How bad is my lipstick right now?" I joke. Maybe from now on we can be more lighthearted with each other, less formal and walled-off.

He looks quickly at me, then focuses on pulling on his shirt and getting his pants back on. I wait for him to answer me, but he doesn't. Instead, he dresses with practiced quickness, and before I have a chance to reach for my dress, he's completely put back together.

I hitch a brow, a sinking feeling suddenly spreading in my gut.

He pulls at his cuffs and straightens his cufflinks. "Since my brother has banned me from fucking our models, I've had to leave every one of these events with blue balls like you wouldn't believe. Having you around is very convenient. Thanks for the help."

And just like that, I remember exactly who he is.

Nausea rises in my throat. He reaches for the door handle. Quickly, I grab my dress and cover myself just as he opens the door and slips out, slamming the door behind him.

I stare after him as if he's going to pop back in with a big smile and a "just kidding." But, of course, that won't happen.

Luka used me.

Just like he used every woman at the party.

I'm too shocked and gutted to drum up tears. Sitting there, clutching my dress, I stare into space until my skin grows cold and pebbles with gooseflesh. I can't believe I allowed that to happen. I had sex with my fake fiancé, the one rule I was so adamant about not breaking.

And in return, he threw it in my face and broke the thread of faith I was starting to have in him. I have to go back inside to the party, but I'm not sure how I'm going to keep it together.

The only thing I do know with one-hundred-percent certainty is that Luka just showed me who he really is—who *I* am—and it's the last time I'll let myself forget it.

This will never, ever happen again.

BROOKLYN

CHAPTER 16

After all these years, all those pounded pavements, the endless revolving door of hopeful auditions and crushing rejections and the small-time gigs I hustled for that kept me going but just couldn't launch my career...perfume is taking me national.

I don't care for most perfumes, personally, but if this is what's going to put my face in the pages of every popular beauty magazine and on a billboard in Times Square, I'll take a bath in it.

I was so nervous this morning that I ended up arriving a few minutes early, and now I'm standing here in the studio glancing around at all the chaos with sweet, but tense, anticipation. Admittedly, I'm a tad overwhelmed. I've done plenty of shoots before, but this is a really big deal. It's my first campaign as a Danica Rose model, and it's a doozy. I'm going to be the face of a brand new celebrity perfume called "Soirée" and there's a lot riding on my success.

"The photographer is all set up and ready to go," Luka says, coming up to me. "How are you feeling?"

"I'm great," I lie. I've been so wrapped up in everything

that I almost forgot Luka accompanied me. He wanted to oversee the shoot—not as my fiancé, of course, but as a DRM exec who needs to shake hands and ensure all goes well with the company's newest signed face.

Luka checks his watch. "Almost time for the walk-through. The photographer will show you the set with the stylist and you'll get some notes on what's expected of you. After that you'll sit for hair and makeup and then go to wardrobe."

"In case you forgot, I *have* done this before," I say, forcing a smile through gritted teeth.

"Just trying to help," he says, walking away from me.

Things have been a little tense between us—okay, a lot tense—ever since we had hot, angry sex in the limo and Luka thanked me for "helping" with his blue balls. Even still, I was initially kind of excited when he offered to come to this shoot with me. I thought this could be an opportunity for him to finally see what I'm capable of. To prove that not only is he not wasting Danica Rose's time by signing me to an exclusive contract, but that he made a *serious* misstep three years ago when he let me slip away.

But now here he is being a dick to me. Treating me like an amateur and mansplaining things that I know the photographer is going to tell me all about in a few minutes anyway.

Why did I expect anything different? After forcing myself to get through the remainder of the disastrous Danica Rose party, I've stayed in my corner and Luka has stayed in his. Not that I haven't been aware of his presence 24/7. The penthouse is big and lofty, but I can still smell his damn cologne everywhere. Still hear his footsteps padding into the kitchen every morning when I know he's walking around post-shower with only a towel around his hips. He also likes to take his phone calls on the upper deck outside, the deep tones of his voice rippling back to me inside. Basically, there's no place that I can go when I'm at home to be completely free of him.

He's always around in one way or another to remind me that I made a huge mistake in that limo. A mistake that my heart and pride still haven't recovered from. He's done nothing to reassure me about that night, either, which only serves to remind me what an ass he can be.

"Brooklyn? I'm Ady, the stylist."

I turn to find a gorgeous woman with box braids and glowing dark skin holding out a hand to me. "Hi! It's great to meet you," I gush, glad someone has finally said hello.

"Just wanted to let you know there's coffee and breakfast over there," she says, pointing. "Feel free to feast. You've still got a few minutes to scarf."

With a wink, she's gone, and I wander over to grab half a bagel and make myself a cup of hot green tea—more to give myself something to do than because I'm actually thirsty.

Luka wanders back over to stand beside me with his hands in his pockets.

"You sure you want to be eating right before they start snapping photos?" he asks.

I shoot him a death glare. "What's wrong, Luka? Worried I'll get a cramp?"

With that, I stuff a huge bite of bagel into my mouth. The fact is, the reason I work so hard at the gym is so that I don't *have to* worry what might happen if I eat a bagel before a photo shoot. And I'm not going to let Luka make me any more anxious about this than I already am.

He's ignoring me now, looking around and assessing the set. I've already studied it myself. There's an exposed brick wall for the backdrop and a black fainting couch with velvet throw pillows on it. Two antique-looking lamps arch over the couch. A white Persian cat is milling around inside a huge animal carrier, waving its plume of a tail. Spread out on the prop table is a slip of lacy fabric that must be some sort of lingerie, and a fur stole. There are three of the same bottle of perfume carefully lined up on mirrored trays.

The whole thing has a vintage feel to it, and I wonder how they'll do my hair and makeup. I'm thinking bold, early-Hollywood movie star style with a red lip and soft waves, or maybe they'll pin my hair up to make it look shorter. Either way, I love the vibe.

The photographer, Hans, bald and black-turtlenecked with huge horn-rimmed glasses, waves me over onto the set. I go eagerly, pointedly ignoring Luka.

"I'm going to have you do a few quick poses for me first, so I can get a sense of how your face and body play against the backdrop and the lighting. Then we can make adjustments while you're getting ready."

I nod and wait for his instructions. Luka is a few feet behind the photographer now, his expression intent as if he's going to watch and critique my every move. He steps onto the set and waves a hand.

"The lighting in here is all wrong," he says, brow furrowing. "Brooklyn's hair is so dark that you need to put a separate back light on it. Otherwise your key light is going to wash out her skin tone and blow the whole exposure. That thing shouldn't be over 3,000K."

The photog and his assistant whip Luka wide-eyed looks. A tingle goes down the back of my neck. What the hell is he doing? When no one responds, he slowly wanders the space and continues his perusal of the set. Hans ignores his suggestions and positions me a few different ways, then looks through the camera lens. He motions for me to sit on the couch, but before I can get there, Luka moves behind me and pushes the couch to the side, angling it differently.

"The fill light needs to move now, too," my fiancé says, grabbing the stand that holds the umbrella behind the light.

"What the hell is this?" I hiss. I'm mortified, but I have to keep my professional face on.

Luke frowns. "I won't have the Danica Rose name on something that looks this unprofessional. None of this is staged correctly."

Hans clears his throat and juts out a hip. "The lights may look unorthodox to you, Mr. Zoric, but I was going for a more experimental play of shadow and light—"

"I know what I'm doing," Luka cuts him off.

Hans waves his hand, starts pacing, and simply waits Luka out. A few minutes later, the set is completely rearranged. Luka studies his handiwork and then nonchalantly steps off the set and crosses his arms.

"If you're all through now, Mr. Zoric...?" Hans says drily.

"Go ahead," Luka says with a nod.

Hans motions me back into place and nods to himself before stepping back from the camera again. "It'll do," he tells his assistant. "What we're losing in saturation, we're making up for in contrast. Which is basically what I was going for."

"Cool," the assistant says, looking relieved that she won't have to break up a fight.

As much as I hate to admit it, I'm not surprised that Luka was right. I've done my share of shoots, and the suggestions he made about the lighting *did* make sense. He's grown up in this business. Of course he's developed an instinctive eye for details.

Satisfied, Luka finally fades into the background and lets Hans and me do our thing. After a few more minutes, Hans nods and waves me away.

"Very good. Go see Ady, Brooklyn. And thank you."

"Thank you," I say back, starting to relax.

I find Ady by a wardrobe rack, scrolling through her phone in a director's chair.

"There you are," she greets me. "Let's talk styling."

She holds up the scant bit of lacy fabric as if she's imagining what it might look like on me. The situation is professional, totally par for the course, and in no way creepy. Yet all of a sudden Luka is standing here once again, getting in between us as if Ady was about to undress me herself, and plucks the lingerie from the stylist's fingers.

He tosses it from hand to hand and holds it up again, before balling it up and throwing it on a table. "No, that won't work. It's too sheer."

"Excuse me?" Ady scoffs.

"Luka," I say tightly. "It's fine. I've worn less. You don't need to defend my honor."

"This isn't about you being my fiancée, it's about our reputation," Luka insists.

"Ah." Ady looks between us, her expression going from annoyed to understanding.

She sighs but exhibits more patience than I would expect in this situation, explaining the concept to him. "*Soirée* is French for 'party,' as I'm sure you know, and the story the client wants to tell with these photos is that Brooklyn is a mysterious, sexy woman who's getting ready for a night out," Ady is saying. "Hence the risqué, Prohibition-era themed vibe."

He nods as he listens, but I can tell by the way he's tapping his foot that he doesn't like it.

Maybe Luka is always like this with his models at photo shoots. The thought gives me pause. Just how many of them did he accompany to stuff like this? Rationally, I know that he's a one-and-done kind of guy—not the kind to hover, normally. He's only here today because he's worried about the agency's reputation and trying to make sure this campaign upholds the new Danica Rose brand. Still, he might have to concede to things he's not comfortable with.

"Why can't she be getting ready in a robe?" Luka asks.

Cocking my head pointedly, I widen my eyes to signal him to knock it off.

Ady smiles. "Believe me, Mr. Zoric, I'm on your side. But I'm not the client."

Hans hustles over, exasperated. "What's the problem?" he asks.

Before I can say anything to smooth this over, Luka says, "I just don't see the necessity for this...lingerie."

For a moment, Hans just stands there nodding. Finally, he says, "That's a great point, now that I think about it. And the client wasn't explicit regarding the model's wardrobe."

I'm stunned that he seems to be agreeing with Luka. Ady also looks taken aback.

Hans goes on, "The face of Soirée is a sexy risk-taker, the type of woman who draws every eye whenever she enters a room and loves to shun the rules." He smiles at me, gesturing to the discarded lingerie. "How do you feel about nudity in lieu of wearing the bodysuit?"

Luka tenses beside me. "That's not what I had in mind—"

"I'm perfectly fine with it," I say, interrupting him. I've done nude shoots before. It's never bothered me to take off my clothes for the right photo shoot. "It definitely fits the vibe."

"Excellent," Hans says, tilting his head as he looks me up and down again with an artist's eye. "I'm thinking we go black and white, then, with you stretched out on the sofa, relaxed. I can't think of a better way for a woman to break all the rules than to be naked—"

"Hell no." Luka finally breaks in, straightening to his full height. His arms are crossed so his biceps bulge beneath the sleeves of his white dress shirt, and he's radiating aggression.

"Luka," I warn.

He ignores me. "I said no."

I can't believe him. What the hell is he doing?

"If you'll excuse us for a moment," I tell Hans and Ady.

Taking Luka by the wrist, I lead him away to a darkened corner of the studio. He won't look at me, so I get right in his face, making it clear that he's really pissing me off.

"What are you doing? This is my *career* and you're acting like a controlling, possessive asshole. Are you trying to screw this up for me?"

He doesn't flinch. "I'm looking out for DRM's image. If a shoot featuring one of my models doesn't feel right, I have the authority to negotiate for change."

I spread my hands wide. "You're not negotiating. You're just being a dick about everything."

"Your job is to do what you're told. Do you understand that?"

His words cut right through me, leaving me momentarily speechless. How could I have ever considered that there might be something real between us when he can stand here and be so condescending about my livelihood? He's not taking my career—or my own feelings about this—into consideration at all.

"My 'job' is to be an extension of the photographer and

the client's artistic construction," I tell him, my voice raising involuntarily. "I am their prop and it's my *job* to do what they need me to do in order to fulfill my contract for this campaign. I'm trying my best to be professional about this and to do what they tell me, but you're interfering, and you don't seem to give a shit that my career is on the line!"

He steps into me until we're inches apart. I glare up at him, trying like hell to keep my temper under control. I don't want my face to flush and get splotchy, or even worse —for tears to build up. Taking a cleansing breath, I let it out slowly through my nose. I'll be mad at Luka later, when it doesn't matter if it's etched all over my features or not. His jaw works to the side.

"I won't shut up. And I won't back down. Did you forget about the contract you signed? The family and the agency always come *first*. My wife isn't going to look like a slut."

And there it is. The truth, revealed.

I smirk. The irony isn't lost on me, but it probably is on him. Luka's worried about me appearing too slutty when he's the biggest manwhore in Chicago. I'm about to tell him that, but I bite my tongue. Nothing good will come from having an all-out pissing match right now.

"You know what, Zoric? Fine. You might own the rights to my body in print and behind the camera. But in real life? You'll never own me, Luka. Never."

I storm back to Hans, ready to get to work. I've spoken my mind a lot in my life, but I've never meant the words more than I did just then.

BROOKLYN

CHAPTER 17

After the almost-disaster that was my first huge modeling gig, I'm ready for a good bitch session with my bestie.

No, scratch that. I'm dying for one.

I went straight from high school to professional modeling, and with all the fierce competition and backstabbing that goes on in this business, I've never had a ton of friends —though believe me, I've tried to make them. But just look at the models at the Danica Rose party the other night. Those women were ready to eat me alive. In contrast, Mateo and I connected from the get-go because he was always so real with me. Nothing about him is two-faced or shady or judgmental. And he's the one person I can be completely myself with.

He's been my lifeline for years: confidant, personal assistant, therapist, teddy bear... A teddy bear with off-color jokes and a therapist who occasionally tries to flirt his way into my bed every now and again, sure, but intense friendships like ours are always a little complicated. Point being, no one else would understand what I'm dealing with. Or at

THE SHAM

least listen, hug me, and feed me drinks to help me cope with it. I need to vent about what went down with Luka at the Soirée shoot, and Mateo's the only person I want to talk to. He's the only one I trust.

It's what everyone wants in a partner. Lord knows I'll never have anything even close to this level of emotional intimacy with Luka.

I brush off the sting that the thought gives me and pull out my cellphone to text Mateo.

This is a 9-1-1. A really bad 9-1-1-1-1-1-1-1.

Uh-oh. What happened, boo? he quickly texts back. *Everything go okay at the shoot?*

I type back, *It wasn't the shoot. It was Luka.*

He sends back a sad face emoji, and I'm already anticipating an evening in with him curled up on the couch, watching horrible movies and eating a pile of cheat food, with some cheap wine to wash it down. He'll listen when I bitch about Luka and the hate sex we had in the limo, and how he ruined my very first national photo shoot. He'll crack jokes and talk smack with me while feeding me chocolate. It'll be perfect, just like old times.

So here's the plan... he texts me back.

Pacing the guest room, I wait for him to fill me in. It's getting late in the day. Luka is out doing who-knows-what, and I'm feeling more and more cooped up in this penthouse by the minute. At this point I'm more than ready to bolt over to the Wicker Park apartment.

I have to be at the opening of this new club downtown—Geo Blu. I'm committed, so I can't bail last minute, but meet me there and we can leave early, k? You need to be vetted to get in, but I'll handle it.

I tap a finger against my bottom lip. Ugh. This wasn't the BFF night in I was hoping for. Mateo has been making friends in the industry and always seems to be off to some gallery show or restaurant opening or something. Normally he fills me in on all of his invites, but I don't recall him mentioning Geo Blu. I'm actually a little hurt that he didn't ask me to go with him before.

Sure, I've been tied up with wedding planning and getting used to my new life with Luka...but am I losing Mateo in the process? I pause as I stare at the phone. Maybe I've been letting my new life get in the way of our friendship. Now that I think about it, that's exactly what's been happening. I lift my chin and text back as I march over to the walk-in closet.

Be there in an hour.

You won't regret it, he texts back. *Promise. Hit me up when you get here.*

I smile as I run my fingers along a row of dresses, playing a little game of eenie-meenie-miney-mo with my most revealing selection of clubbing outfits. There's the bodysuit with the sexy shredded fabric along the sides, the micro mini with an oval cutout over the chest. I have an all lace bodycon dress that shows, well, everything. Bandage dresses, little black dresses...

None of it feels exactly right.

Going into the bathroom, I plug in my curling iron and twist the ends of my hair into big, fluffy curls. I work a little product through them until I'm satisfied, and then turn to my makeup. I go dark and heavy with the palette. My eyes are all smoky shimmer, with big, black fake lashes. Next I stain my cheeks pink and create bold lips with a slick of deep burgundy gloss. The finishing touch is a spray of body glitter, just for fun, and then I go back to the closet.

My gaze falls to a matte, metallic silver dress hanging in the back. Plucking it from its place, I turn it over and over, remembering what drove me to purchase it in the first place. It's a little "Vegas" for me, not something I'd normally wear. Mateo talked me into it back in LA, I think to wear to an audition, but I haven't worn it since.

Slipping out of my clothes, I stand there naked for a moment, trying to decide, and then slip into the dress. It's got a vintage feel, with ruching at the waist, thin halter straps, and a cowl neckline, but the way it hugs my body and flashes my cleavage screams all modern. There's a slit up the back nearly to my ass. I slip into black heels and do a turn in front of the mirror.

I decide that I kind of love it. It's sexy, different, and totally glam. And the perfect party outfit for a club opening with my bestie.

Luka still isn't home by the time my Uber arrives. It crosses my mind to let him know that I'm leaving for the evening, but he never extends me that courtesy, so fuck it. I give myself one last look in the entryway mirror—the same Luka and I had stood before not long ago—and smile. I look positively slutty. Raising my middle finger, I pretend it's him I'm giving it to.

Take that.

Mateo meets me with a hug at the door of the club.

"Look at you, little miss Studio 54!" he teases.

"Is this okay?" I ask, suddenly self-conscious. "I look like a disco ball."

"Okay? You look fucking *amazing*," he says, and ushers me in like he's got VIP access—which it turns out he does.

"How'd you get in on opening night?" I ask, looking over my shoulder at the mile-long line of hot young things still waiting behind the velvet rope. "Is this a paid appearance, or…?"

"Sleeping with both the club manager and CEO at the

same time has it benefits," he laughs, nudging me with a swish of his hip as he pulls me inside.

Music thumps straight through me, strobe lights bursting into shards of color all over the darkened room. I head for the bar, but Mateo shakes his head no and pulls me out onto the dance floor. We're immediately swallowed by swaying, gyrating bodies as the music shifts to an even louder song with more bass. The crowd cheers and I forget about alcohol long enough to dive into the music with Mat. We used to go dancing often in LA and then head home to crash on the couch and eat tacos we picked up from a parking lot food truck at 3 a.m.

What I wouldn't give for those good old days.

The crowd suddenly parts and the flash of a camera takes me by surprise. I spin to find two photographers working the room, snapping pics as they mill through the crowd.

"Hey, is that the model who's marrying the younger Zoric?" someone yells.

"Uh-oh," Mateo drawls. "You've been recognized." He throws an arm around my shoulders and pulls me in.

"Brooklyn, can we get a picture?" someone else is shouting now. "Brooklyn, over here!"

I initially freeze because I'm not sure what to do. Mateo nudges me. "Do you want the pictures to look terrible? You're a professional, girl. Smile!"

Suddenly on autopilot, I manage to paste on a huge grin just as the photog snaps a few rapid-fire pictures. Mateo spins me around and pulls me back into his arms. We bump chests and I laugh. He kisses me on the cheek, clearly loving the media attention more than me. He's a pro. I'm used to being in front of the camera, but not out in public. Luckily, the photographers snap a few more pictures of

Mateo and me and then work their way back through the crowd.

I sigh in relief when they leave. "Okay. I really need a drink now."

We head to the bar, order, and find a spot at the end to sip our drinks in peace while watching the crowd.

"I really needed this tonight," I say over the noise. Mateo moves closer to hear what I'm saying.

"Continued trouble in paradise?" he asks around a drink, lifting his brows.

"You could say that."

The club gets more packed by the minute, and soon bodies are pressed in all around us. Disappointed at the lack of privacy, I move away, thinking Mateo will follow. But he's watching the crowd, moving his body to the beat of the music, totally oblivious to my exit.

He probably wants to dance and mingle and find his hookup for the night. My need to vent about my personal life is obviously holding him back. I hug a wall and sip the rest of my drink, and he finally makes his way over to me after getting another drink and double fisting it.

"So tell me what the hot asshole is up to now," he says.

"Luka?" Silly of me to ask. Who else would he be talking about? "Well, what do you want to hear about first? How he humiliated me at the Danica Rose launch party, or ruined my first ever national shoot by being a raging dick to the photographer and the stylist?"

"Ooh, raging dick. My favorite. That one first."

I tell him how he acted in front of Hans and Ady and the assistant. "He refused to let me wear the vintage lingerie. And then he flipped out when the photographer suggested I go nude."

His eyes flash. "Nude, huh? Sounds like he's a bit

jealous at the thought of you stripping in front of someone else."

I roll my eyes. "There were three people there, and they were all professionals."

Mateo shivers. "Sounds like my kind of fun. So, what did you end up wearing?"

Setting my empty glass on a table, I say, "After my hair and makeup was done, Luka wrapped me in a silk robe, like one of those old-fashioned Oriental ones, and set me on the couch. He opened it just enough to bare *one* of my shoulders. How scandalous, right?

"And then?"

"Nothing. That's it. I got to bare one shoulder."

"What about later? Did you bare anything else when you got home? The caveman thing can be a pretty big turn-on..." He takes a long suck on his straw, eyeing me with hope.

I laugh. "You're terrible. No, Mateo, nothing when we got home. I was too pissed to even think about it. I wanted to punch him in the face."

I want to tell him about angry limo sex, but I don't. His eyes are glassy, and he's got that excited edge he gets when he's on the prowl. Just like with Luka, sex is Mateo's main motivator.

"I bet he likes it when you're mad." Mat winks at me. His eyes narrow as if he's reading my mind about angry limo sex. "I also bet Luka is a beast when he's pissed. Probably just throws you down and fucks you silly until he gets all that hot rage out."

Okay. That's the end of my night. When Mat gets like this, I turn him loose to go have some fun before his balls explode, or else all that sexual energy of his gets directed at me. Disappointment fills me. This was fun, and I'm glad I got to blow off a little steam on the dance floor, but it wasn't quite the one-on-one time I needed.

"I'm gonna ago," I tell Mateo, gesturing toward the exit.

"Hey," he says, grabbing my shoulder. "Let me just throw this out there. I am *all in* to be the filling in an angry Luka-and-Brooklyn sandwich. I'll do the filling; I'll take the filling. Whatever, I don't care. Just let me know if you ever want to open things up for a third party."

"*Seriously*, Mateo? God!" I spin on my heel and take out my cell, opening the Uber app. "Call me when you're sober."

"Brooklyn—"

I whirl back on him, still angry. "I'd rather be holed up in my room alone than have to listen to this. I came out tonight because I needed my friend, and instead I get...this. Thanks for nothing." I give a last, halfhearted wave and weave my way through the crowd.

"I'm sorry!" I hear him holler as I make my way to the door.

I sink into the seat in my Uber, picking at the hem of my silly shiny dress. I can't wait to take it off and bury myself in a pile of bubbles in a bubble bath. I check my cell for anything from Luka. Unsurprisingly, there's nothing. It's really late, and I wonder if he's finally home.

The penthouse is quiet when I walk in and put my clutch on the entry table. Turning on a light in the living room, I'm startled to find Luka standing at the living room windows. He turns and holds out his cellphone to display a photo of Mateo kissing me on the cheek, both of us grinning like maniacs.

Luka's eyes are steely and cold.

"Well, well. If it isn't my soon-to-be wife, sneaking back in after a night out with another man."

LUKA

CHAPTER 18

"Just what the fuck did you think you were doing?" I growl, using every ounce of my self-control to keep my hands at my sides.

I'm so angry—no, enraged—that I can barely think straight. Imagine my surprise when my phone started blowing up with social media notifications about my fiancée whoring it up on the dance floor of some club with another man's lips all over her.

I know it's her friend Mateo. But the rest of the world doesn't.

Besides, no man's mouth should be anywhere on her body.

Only mine.

Mine.

"You don't own my body," she says, copping an attitude and throwing a hand on her hip.

She thinks I don't own her? She's about to learn otherwise. I storm toward her. She lifts her chin and holds her ground, watching me approach. How can she be so calm in the face of the storm I'm creating? I want to punch some-

THE SHAM

thing. To take her in my arms and show her just how much I own every inch of her skin. I stop before I touch her, keeping enough space between us that I don't do something stupid, like tear that damn silver dress off her perfect body.

"Your *image* is owned by me, in case you've forgotten, and I have the contract to prove it," I tell her. "It doesn't matter whether you're out at a club or on a set—the same rules apply."

Brooklyn's jaw clenches. "Mateo asked me to go to an opening with him, so I went. It wasn't an official public appearance."

"Oh really? Because it looks pretty official to me."

I flip through the images of her on the dance floor, holding them at an angle so she can see. They're still popping up all over social media, one after the other. She's not looking at the photos, though. She's looking at me, as if waiting for my next move.

I thrust the phone closer so she has to look. "I didn't give you permission for this." A picture of Brooklyn laughing, drink in her hand, half of her perfect breast exposed, has me especially angry. "And what about this, huh? Did I approve this?"

She glares at me. "Did you approve *what*? I don't need your permission to go out with a friend, Luka."

"You put yourself in a public space without any of my input into your creative choices, or the setting."

She scoffs at me. "Creative choices? You're being ridiculous."

I take a step back and gesture to her dress. She looks down at herself, then back at me with confusion. I know that I'm being a dick, but I don't care.

"Image is everything right now," I insist. "Your image tonight was all wrong." I lean in toward her, but she shifts back, diverting the touch she thought was coming. Her aversion only flames my anger.

"The club choice was a mistake," I go on. "Did you even think to research the place before you made a public appearance? I'm guessing not, or you would have known that the owner recently got out of prison for running cocaine in the pockets of underage girls. How's that for DRM's stellar new image?"

Her face pales a little.

"And what about this outfit?" I say, gesturing at the dress. "Do you really think this was the best choice? Don't get me wrong, Brooklyn, you'd look stunning in a paper bag, but silver isn't your best color." I tap a finger to the base of her throat. She eyes me but doesn't move. Her cheeks color with anger. Good. Let her get pissed.

"I would have put you in gold, to show off your burnished skin. Play up your golden glow." I look at the photos again and shrug. "The background was fine, your co-star? Less so. Mateo might be hot shit right now, but nobody's going to remember his name in five years. He's second-rate at best and does nothing for your image."

Her eyes flash knives at me and I smirk, knowing that I got under her skin. Professionally speaking, Mateo is a very attractive man—he didn't skyrocket to fame for no reason. I'm straight as you can get, but it's part of my job to know good looks.

The truth is, I'm lying. Brooklyn's best friend looks great beside her. Almost as good as I do when she's on my arm. They're happy in these photos, their body language demonstrating how much they're enjoying each other, how comfortable they are together.

It burns me to see her so damn happy in another man's arms. They clearly have an effortless, undeniable chemistry between them—hell, the huge smiles on their faces as they dance together would be very appealing if this photo was a shampoo advertisement, but that's beneath Brooklyn's talent.

Besides, I can think of much better ways to have her posed. With me. I should have been on the dance floor with her, behind her while she grinded that round, tight ass against my cock. In front of her, holding her tight enough that I could feel her nipples through our clothes. I should be on top of her right now, commanding and dominating her body.

Heat ripples through me, making my cock twitch. Her eyelids flutter, the flush on her face fading from angry red to soft, aroused pink. I know that color…I know that expression and the set to her lips. She cocks her head and takes another step back. The wall is directly behind her and she leans her ass against it, placing one hand palm down on the wall next to her. Her other hand slides up the center of her body before going up and over her head.

"Maybe I'm not the model you're looking for, then," she taunts. Her breasts thrust out as she moves her arm higher and pretends to relax with the wall supporting her. "Maybe I'm not the right image."

She knows exactly what she's doing by redirecting me from my anger with her body. My temper starts to wane as I wander toward her. "Oh, you're definitely the right model." I pull my cellphone out again and open the camera, snapping a few pictures as she gazes into the lens. "You just look better here. In this light. In front of my eyes."

"Oh really?" she asks, her voice throaty and turned on.

I don't take time to overthink it. "Put both hands palms down against the wall by your hips and lean forward. One shoulder higher, and look up."

She blinks twice and slowly moves her hands along the wall to do as I ask. With a little push, she leans slightly forward and tosses her hair over one shoulder, then flicks those smoky eyes up toward the ceiling. I keep the camera clicking the whole time, moving closer so I can get a better shot of her cleavage. God, her tits are fucking perfect. I want them free so I can see her hard pink nipples on my screen.

"Untie the straps of your dress and let the top fall down."

She lifts her chin, eyeing me with a combination of defiance and lust. A long beat of hesitation passes before she pushes away from the wall and slowly reaches behind her neck. She unties the knot and the silvery fabric slips down loose over her breasts. She catches it with one arm across her chest, waiting for me to take another photo, and then she lets it fall.

"Perfect," I breathe, ignoring the tightness in my pants. "Now lean back."

She does, her bare breasts bouncing as her back hits the wall. "Like this?"

I nod, snapping a few more pictures.

"Bend your right knee and put your foot on the wall," I go on, directing her. "Arms above your head."

She complies, the blush on her face deepening. I know that if I thrust my hand between her legs right now, I'd find her soaked and swollen for me. I'm strung so tight that I can barely work the camera as I take a few more photos.

"Now look at me," I say. "Like you want to fuck me."

She looks directly at me and I reposition the camera to catch what I'm seeing, her big, dark eyes so telling of her desire. Then she moves her head a touch, lining up better with the angle, and then flashes me a look so hungry it makes my breath catch.

"Take the dress all the way off now, and hold your tits in your hands." My voice is ragged with lust, but she never breaks eye contact as she complies.

Suddenly, gorgeously naked, Brooklyn spreads her legs apart and squeezes both breasts into one hand, exposing her entire body to me as I capture her image.

I walk toward her, taking a few more until I can't go any further. Taking her chin in my hand, I direct her gaze to the last picture that I took.

Her cheeks are perfectly pink, her eyes heavy with desire.

"Did Mateo make you look this good? Did he make your cheeks glow like that?"

She lets out a breath as I run my hand down her body and cup her between her legs. She jumps with a little moan. It's exactly what I expected. She's perfectly soaked. I lean into her until I'm whispering in her ear. "Did he make your pussy this swollen?"

She moans again and I pull her away from the wall and gently push her to her knees. "Remember when you said I don't own your body? Your pussy just admitted otherwise."

I unfasten my button and pull down the zipper so my jeans hang open. A small grin tugs at the corners of her mouth as she looks up at me, but it fades fast as if she didn't intend for me to see it. Too late. She loves this game as much as I do.

"You're going to suck me off," I tell her, angling the camera just so. "And I'm going to show you how good you look doing it."

Her throat moves as she swallows, and then she turns her attention to taking my cock out of my pants. The phone is unsteady in my hand as she wets her lips and takes me between her lips, wrapping her tongue around me.

Clenching my eyes with the first roll of pleasure, I enjoy the hot suction of her mouth for a few minutes before I focus the camera again. She pulls back, the tip of my cock on her tongue, the shaft glistening as she looks up at me. I take the picture, then another. And another. Until she's working fast and hard, with long, wet pulls that have my balls tightening faster than ever and I forget all about taking pictures.

"Fuck yeah," I groan, gripping her hair in my free hand and pumping my hips, thrusting back and forth in her mouth. The light scrape of her teeth against my shaft is a fine line between pleasure and pain. She sucks hard, bobbing her head as I push in deeper and hit the back of her throat. I glance down and see she's taken me all the way to the balls, moaning softly. Fuck.

"That's good," I encourage her. "So good."

When she looks up at me again, my cock still fucking her mouth, I snap a pic at the same time I lose all control, shooting my release down her throat. She closes her eyes and works to swallow every drop, prolonging my pleasure with each contraction.

I can barely breathe, my head spinning from the force of the orgasm. Brooklyn palms my body as she gets to her feet and slides a look over me. She wipes her mouth with the back of her hand, then wordlessly picks up her dress and tosses it over one shoulder, her perfect ass swaying as she walks away to her room.

I run a hand through my hair as a thought suddenly goes through my mind.

Who owns whom?

BROOKLYN

CHAPTER 19

I've always loved the movie *Pretty Woman*.

Who wouldn't want to be Julia Roberts in that role? All the luxury and wealth and the company of a handsome Richard Gere in exchange for pleasure. Seems like a no-brainer. Yet she was never quite comfortable, too afraid that the higher-class social circle would sense that she didn't belong, would see her for what she really was.

That's how I feel sitting in the back of the private car taking me downtown. Like this isn't my world at all, and everyone can tell just by looking at me. I didn't even realize I had access to my own car and driver until it showed up this morning to take me to my lunch reservation with my future sisters-in-law, Tori and Emzee. The driver introduced himself and gave me his cell number so I can call him when I need a ride, any time of the day or night.

No more cabs or Ubers for me now.

When I showed him the address that Tori had texted me, he'd looked impressed, seeming to know exactly what the place was. I didn't have a clue, nor did I ask. I'm still a bit shell-shocked by my new life and all the privileges that come with it. The penthouse is starting to become more comfortable, but I still don't really think of it as mine. It's just a place where I keep my things and go to bed at night. Although I've been venturing out to the other rooms a bit more, watching TV on the sofa, making small meals in the kitchen instead of ordering out.

I even learned the housekeeper's name—Denise, a different woman than the one who'd kicked me out the morning after my disastrous one-night stand with Luka all those years ago, thank God—and left her a thank-you card and a small plate of chocolate chip cookies that I made. Acclimating to my new life is taking effort, but I'm trying.

Taking a compact out of my bag, I do a last quick check of my hair, which I've left down in loose waves, the light touch of makeup I put on, and my teeth. Check, check, double check. But I still can't shake my nerves no matter how much I try to tell myself I'm not an imposter.

My outfit is a sleek jumpsuit in dark navy and a few pieces of gold jewelry. I hope it's appropriate. Luka gave me a heavy black credit card with no limit and set up several store accounts for places he thought I'd enjoy shopping, but I haven't taken advantage. I don't want to feel like I'm in his debt any more than I already am, and on top of that, I don't love the idea of running around town blowing money on shopping sprees just because I can. That's not me.

I grew up in a modest home on the outskirts of Chicago, born to a middle-class family. Peanut butter and jelly was my school lunch standby, my recreation was school-sponsored activities, and I took the bus. No fancy dinners. No drivers. No private schools. I look at the back of my driver's gray head now, feeling a twinge of guilt and hoping he gets paid well enough that taking care of his own family isn't a struggle.

Rationally, I know that paying people to take care of your needs is part of the package deal. This is what it's like when you move up in the world, and I should lean into it. But I'd always imagined I'd get myself here, one step at a time, by way of hard work and modeling gigs.

Not by signing a marriage contract.

The car slows in traffic and my stomach twists in knots. I don't know Tori and Emzee very well. Tori has reached out a couple of times, wanting to get to know me better since we're going to be family. We've had a few short conversations that were nice, but nothing too personal—Tori's always studying or working on a school project or rushing off to one of her linguistics classes at UChicago. Emzee, on the other hand, made it clear she wasn't interested in any sort of relationship with me at Luka's and my engagement photo shoot, and I haven't spoken to her since. I understand. She's probably worried about my intentions with her brother.

Maybe they see me as a gold digger, or some kind of modeling mercenary. Which I guess I am. I mean, furthering my career is the whole reason I agreed to this marriage, isn't it?

My throat goes tight as my mind begins to race. Tori's husband Stefan pushed for Luka to get married, of course, but I'm not sure my soon-to-be sisters know the details of our contract, or if they even care. As long as our union helps Danica Rose's reputation, they're probably happy to stay out of it. They have no idea how hard Luka had to push to get me to agree.

The car pulls up to a nondescript modern building with one side all gray brick and the other side all windows. A bifold sign on the sidewalk is the only indicator of where we are, but I know the name as soon as I see it. Alinea is an exclusive restaurant, accessible by (impossible-to-get) reservation only. I've heard about this place, of course, but I've never been here. It's always being mentioned in the papers and Chicago society and culture magazines, but I never imagined I'd dine here. By the looks of it, it's not even open for business this time of day.

"Are you sure this is it?" I ask as the driver opens my door.

"Yes, ma'am. If you'll follow me."

I glance down at my jumpsuit and nude sandals and wonder if I should have dressed up more. But the driver opens the front door of the place and gestures for me to go up the staircase to the right. I step inside and hear the door close behind me, leaving me alone to climb the stairs.

Hearing laughter, I follow the sound up and find the intimate dining area basically empty, with the exception of Emzee and a gorgeous blonde who must be Tori. They're nestled side by side in a plush velvet booth, laughing about something, and a pang hits me. I'm an outsider about to intrude on their fun. Tori's eyes light up when she spots me, and I feel a little relieved.

"There you are! Come, sit!"

Emzee's smile fades but her calculated expression isn't totally unfriendly as she watches me cross the room toward them. Something about Emzee unnerves me. Probably because she's Luka's sister and I want her acceptance, even if I won't admit that to anyone. It matters to me that the important people in his life like me. Luka and I will be spending a lot of time together, after all, and we both need their support in order to make this whole marriage thing work. I lay my beaded clutch (a vintage Melrose Avenue find) on the table and sit, unsure what to do next.

"Isn't it nice they opened early just so we could have a private lunch?" Tori goes on.

And there's the difference between rich and *rich*-rich. Alinea opens early just for you.

"I've always wanted to come here," I say, nodding.

"Nice bag," Emzee says, eyeing my purse. I can't tell if she's being sarcastic, especially given her edgy style—a too-cool black leather jacket and silk blouse—but I thank her anyway.

A server comes by and pours wine for us, then sets down heavy glass bowls filled with a scant amount of something purple and gelatinous with little orange beads glistening on the side, a few slices of parsnip sticking straight up from the pile, and a garnish of some kind of flower. He quickly gives a description and then he's gone.

The bowl is pretty, but the food doesn't look like anything I want near my mouth. I take a sip of perfectly chilled white wine. It has a delicate sweetness that hits every corner of my palate. I take another sip just as my stomach growls and kick myself for not having breakfast.

"This, um...looks interesting," I say, trying to keep my tone light.

"Oh, come on, Brooklyn," Emzee teases. "Don't tell me you've never had trout roe with grape paste before?"

I'm fairly certain roe is another name for fish eggs. "I'll try anything once," I say, hoping I come off as adventurous and fun rather than inexperienced and ignorant. It earns me a giggle from Tori, but Emzee cocks a brow, seeming unimpressed.

"Well, it's two-hundred a course," she says, "so for the love of God, eat up."

It's obvious there's no room for argument. Emzee may

be younger than me, but she definitely makes her dominance known.

I pick up a small spoon and hover it over the dish. "How many courses are there?"

This draws another laugh from Tori. "We're only doing five. You'll live."

Emzee adds, "Normally there's like sixteen."

Tori takes a small sample of the roe, her expression delighted. "We're mixing art and food today, ladies. I asked the chef to surprise us with the menu, so make sure you save room to try it all."

Truth be told, I would have no qualms whatsoever with trading whatever this is for a Big Mac right now, but that wouldn't go over well. I need to fit into my new world, not sidestep it. Forcing a smile, I take a small bit of the roe, mirroring Tori, who tried the paste separately. I do so too, chewing quickly, not sure I want to taste it. To my surprise, the roe bursts cleanly in my mouth, leaving a briny but not unpleasant flavor behind. I don't love it, but it's okay.

I go in for a second taste, mirroring the other women so I don't make a fool of myself. Before I know it, my bowl is empty save for the flower. Emzee eats hers but I let mine be.

Our dishes are taken away and I catch Tori nudging Emzee, tilting her head in my direction. Emzee sighs, clears her throat, and says, "So Brooklyn...I want to apologize for getting off on the wrong foot with you. I know I was a brat at the engagement photo shoot."

"What do you mean?" I ask. When it comes to good manners, sometimes it's more polite to play dumb.

"You know what I mean," Emzee says, narrowing her dark-lined eyes at me. "Nobody told me about the deal with Luka, and I thought you were just another greedy model trying to land my brother and take advantage. Stefan told me later that he organized the whole thing."

Tori tosses her hair, looking a little peeved, and leans forward to add, "I think what Emzee means is that she's super protective of her brothers and she tends to be a little quick to jump to conclusions when it comes to people who try to get too close, too fast."

"I really get it," I tell Emzee, meaning it. "It's obvious you love them like crazy, and I can't be upset that you're looking out. In fact, I'm kinda jealous. I always wished I had siblings."

"Aww," Emzee and Tori chime in unison.

"Well, now you have us!" Tori says.

I smile. She's sweet, and I wish it really were that easy, but I still feel a million miles away from the women sitting across from me.

All of a sudden, the server comes over to our table to set down a bundle of branches—*actual* tree branches—with feathery greenery coming off them. On top is a piece of burlap covered by an arrangement of what appear to be sandwich cookies topped with toasted pine nuts, herbs, and little dabs of honey.

"Wow," I blurt. "I've never eaten anything off a branch before."

Emzee and Tori start cracking up, and for a moment I think they're laughing at my expense, my cheeks going hot, until Emzee reaches across the table and squeezes my hand.

"This *is* pretty...extravagant," she says, dabbing a tear from the corner of her eye. "But whatever it is, it smells amazing. Is that cedar?"

The server, who has been waiting patiently this whole time, gestures at the dish and gives us another rundown, spooning sauce along the branches as he talks. I have no idea how we're supposed to utilize this to our advantage. Apparently, it's some exotic bean and sassafras pâté sandwiched between celery root, chervil, and sumac crackers served over fresh juniper. When the server walks away, we all exchange perplexed glances.

"Screw it, I'm using my hands," Tori finally says, reaching for one of the cracker sandwiches. She takes a bite and grins as she chews, clearly enjoying whatever it is.

Emzee and I join in, and soon enough we've devoured the course in all its bizarre deliciousness. As out of my element as I am, this whole concept is kind of fun.

Next, we're served huge round plates with intricate Moroccan-style designs around a painting of a cow's head. At the tip of the cow's nose is a tall, round pastry holding a soft filling. Some herbs poke out of the top, and two smears of paste on the plate resemble yellow petals.

I poke at the food without thinking. "Who's down to hit up the nearest Taco Bell on our way out of here?" I cut through my pastry and take a bite. They both laugh.

Emzee takes a long drink of her wine and then shakes her head slowly at me. "You're actually really funny. And fun. I feel like I was completely wrong about you."

"In what way?" I ask, keeping my tone light, not sure I'll like what she has to say.

Crossing her arms at the edge of the table as she chews, Emzee regards me and my apprehension grows. "I guess, when I first met you," she says, "I assumed you were like all the rest of my brother's harem."

Tori puts down her fork and looks between us, her mouth puckering as if she's concerned about what her sister-in-law might say.

"Every woman he's with ends up using him," Emzee says. "Money, photo shoots, contracts, that kind of thing.

And probably sex, but I don't even want to think about that." She grimaces in disgust.

"*Emzee*," Tori chirps, overly cheerful. "Why don't we tell Brooklyn about that cool avant-garde florist shop you found on Insta—"

But Emzee's already picked up where she left off. "You're different, though. He actually seems—and this is insane to me, only because it's Luka—but he actually seems invested in this marriage. In you. I didn't think he'd last a week before breaking off this engagement, but..."

Our server is back with a helper this time, and they start clearing our plates. Then they set down what looks like a chunk cut from a log. The top is smooth and glossy, the center hollowed out and holding a single, hot coal. Three pieces of meat on skewers sit on top of the coal. Other finger-food type items are arranged around the outside. Emzee wastes no time digging in.

"The thing about Luka is," she says between bites, "he never had any stable female relationships growing up. Our mom was gone. We had plenty of nannies, but they were all temporary, and our dad sure didn't keep any women around long enough to get attached to.

"Point is, I know Luka can be a real dick, and I'm not trying to excuse him, but he never had a solid relationship in his life to look at and learn from. I don't expect you to understand and I'm not going to explain it any more than I have. But I can see that you're different in a way that counts to my brother...so it counts with me, too. Even if this whole thing was arranged by Stefan and has, oh, a ninety-percent chance of being a disaster." She laughs.

I'm reeling from Emzee's words, my chest gone tight. I don't know how to respond.

Tori circles her fork in Emzee's direction. "Need I

remind you that my *own* arranged marriage started out as my dad trying to land me a Zoric?"

"You guys had an arranged marriage, too?" I ask, totally floored by this revelation.

"Yup," Tori says. "And it's turned out fine."

"Has it?" Emzee teases. As she grins at me, I realize she's accepted me into the fold, as much as she can, I suspect. Warmth floods through me, pushing out the doubts I had earlier.

"Yes, it has!" Tori says. "I didn't expect to fall for Stefan. We went into our marriage with our own goals in mind, and they had nothing to do with love." She takes a bite of food and savors it before continuing. "Just goes to show, you never know when love will find you."

"Right now, I'm just worried about Luka keeping his nose out of my photo shoots," I say.

Falling in love with Luka? I can't imagine our relationship will ever develop to that point. We have attraction, sure. Okay, fine, it's lust. But love is a whole other part of the brain, and the heart. Changing the subject is the only way I know to not think about that right now.

"Oh, do tell," Tori says. "How have the jobs been going, by the way?"

Our conversation turns to my latest modeling gigs and Luka's domineering alpha mentality in making sure everything goes his way during each shoot. By the time our dessert course of freeze-dried fruit, chocolate mousse, and various edible flowers arranged on a slab of rock arrives, I feel light and warm and completely included.

Tori and Emzee like me. They believe in me and in my ability to help DRM's image. I'm on the right track, I'm a player in this game, and I'm *this close* to having the career of my dreams.

And maybe things will progress with Luka in a way I never thought possible.

My driver arrives and I give Tori and Emzee hugs, feeling more optimistic and energized than I have in weeks. Slipping into the back seat, I realize that I really might have it all.

Now, if I can only keep Luka in check at my next photo shoot, things will be perfect.

BROOKLYN

CHAPTER 20

"You're not wearing that."

Luka gestures at the thong I'm wearing. I start to protest but then stop myself and take a deep breath. We're in the lobby of The Platform, a brand new, sixteen-story luxury office complex with exposed steel beams and floor-to-ceiling windows. The lighting is perfect right now, and Jane Otembe, the famous fashion photographer I've been dying to work with, is more than ready to get started.

Unfortunately, I'm having some trouble managing my fiancé's douchebaggery.

I look down at myself and put my hands on my hips. The set assistant took my robe, leaving me in a demi bra and dental floss-style thong. My hair sports huge, elegant curls that flow down my back and around my shoulders, and my makeup is shimmery and gorgeous. I feel sexy and confident, not easy emotions to drum up considering the whispers going around the room about my fiancé. There are two other models here beside me, but I'm the headliner, so makeup and wardrobe have been fussing over me for most of the morning. The attention hasn't won me any favors with the other models, who have made it perfectly clear they're jealous, despite my efforts at chatting casually with them and learning their names (Heather and Sasha).

I don't let it bother me. I'm still feeling amazingly better after lunch with my almost sisters-in-law yesterday. For the first time, I feel as if I have this whole situation under control. If I could only figure out how to get Luka out of my modeling life, everything would be great.

He glances around, spots the wardrobe assistant, and snaps his fingers at her. "Get her a full bottom panty. She's not wearing this."

The young girl gives him a deer-in-the-headlights look. "I'll have to check with—"

"I don't care if you have to ask the Pope. Just make it happen. Now."

Okay. I've had it. It would be bad enough if it were only the styling crew staring at us, but it's literally everybody in the entire room.

"Luka!" I grab my robe and slip it back on as I approach him.

Over by the windows, I see Jane throw her hands up and storm away with her phone in her hand, mumbling something that I'm glad I can't hear.

"You're not doing this to me again," I hiss. "No one is going to want to work with me if you keep this up."

He folds his arms, clearly not budging an inch. "Keep what up? Demanding perfection? Wanting what's best for you?"

Irritation washes over me in a flood. "What's 'best for me' is for you to let the other professionals in the room do their jobs."

He smiles but it's icy. "I've been in the game for years,

Brooklyn. I know what I'm talking about. And I'm not going to let a DRM model get a reputation as a slut."

I scoff. "Well, you're very likely going to end up with a reputation as an asshole."

Before I can say another word, he's walking away. He goes straight to the set, ponders for a moment, and then starts rearranging the furniture. Jane darts back over, waving her hands. I tap my foot, listening to the steady clip, clip, clip of my three-inch heel as I take deep yoga breaths, attempting to gather my frustration into a little ball and toss it away.

The other models chatter behind me, sighing and laughing in animated whispers. I hear one of them say something about Luka's ass—or maybe that he's being an ass—but I don't eavesdrop. I'm not going to be pulled into their gossip.

Striding over to the set, I stand there making my presence known as Luka plays with a light meter to gauge the temperature of the bulb. I try to give an apologetic look to the photographer, but she won't hold my gaze.

I can only imagine how hard it's going to be to please her after this. None of the shots will meet her expectations, or else I won't pose right. Hell, I might not be able to get inside my own head enough to play my part effectively. Suddenly, the set designer comes running over, yelling at Luka in what sounds like Portuguese. They get into a shouting match over the position of the bar stools, and I look to the ceiling.

I'm going to get totally blackballed because of him.

I can't stand here and let this happen. My heels click loudly on the tile floor as I stalk over to Luka. He and the set designer pause to look at me, and I place both hands on my fiancé's chest before he can say another word, pushing him back. His eyes flash daggers at me but he doesn't resist.

"I don't know how many times I have to tell you this. You're fucking this up for me big time. I need you to stop, I'm saying please, and I won't say it again. I know that you're worried about my image, but you're overdoing it."

"I won't have you walking around with your ass on display. It's gratuitous."

"Are you kidding? I've worn a similar outfit clubbing before, Luka." That gets his full attention. "And I've worn a string bikini on the beach, okay? This thong isn't scandalous. It's just an undergarment. All models wear them."

His hands go to my hips. "Well, you won't be. You're going to wear something with full coverage."

Kicking Luka in the shin right now wouldn't do anything but make me look like a toddler throwing a tantrum, but I'm seriously tempted. "Why are you so worried about my virtue? I'm a model. I'm paid to wear what the client wants. And this is what the client wants!"

His fingers press into me through the thin robe. "The only person who gets to see you running around looking like a little slut is me. That sexy-ass bombshell who sucked my cock while I took pictures? *She's mine.*"

My breath hitches at his crudeness. Yes, he's being an asshole, but it's hot to hear him talk about me that way. He's displayed possessiveness before, but he's never actually claimed ownership over me until now. His eyes drop to my lips and I watch him with anticipation. There might not be love between us, but lately there's been something new, something neither of us can deny—a flirtatious awareness of each other, a spark. His behavior on these shoots might be annoying, but I have a sneaking suspicion that it's his passive-aggressive way of displaying his emotions. It's obvious that he cares enough to not want my body on display for everyone to see.

He pulls back, looking over his shoulder for someone. "I said brown-red, not pink-red lips," he's yelling out into the room. "Where's the makeup artist?"

He breaks away from me and storms off, leaving me almost panting and staring after him.

I roll my eyes and shake my head. It feels good. It would feel better to give him the middle finger, but I don't. Instead, I hug my middle and head to the refreshments table where I pour a glass of cucumber water and take a nice long chug. This might take a while. In fact, if Luka has his way, I'm sure all my makeup will need to be redone.

"That's quite the show the two of you put on."

Heather, one of the other models, pours herself a glass of water across the table from me. She's gone sans robe and has been strutting around in her lingerie like a peacock despite the slight chill. I've spent the past few hours trying to be pleasant to her and Sasha, but I'd have to be blind not to see how her gaze lands on my fiancé now and follows him around.

"He's got a vision," I concede, not wanting to say too much about Luka, or my relationship with him.

"Really?" she says. "Because to me, it looks more like his compulsive need to dominate is the problem." She lifts a brow at me over the rim of her glass. "Though he's always had a bit of a temper. Especially when he doesn't get his way."

Ah. Another one of Luka's conquests. She's opened the proverbial door, but I don't want to walk through it. I move to leave, but she sets her glass down hard, drawing my attention. With a catty grin, she refills it while staring at me.

"I told him once that I wasn't going to have a threesome

with him and my best friend. Crossing lines and all that. But you know how persuasive he can be and, well, I gave in. Turns out it was the best sex I've ever had. He's...quite talented in that department."

I stand to my full height and find myself smiling. It feels surprisingly good to put my shoulders back, straighten my spine, and look down at her. In these heels, I'm a solid two inches taller than she is. Her sneer fades quickly. She probably doesn't want to crease her makeup, but if she keeps talking, I'll be happy to mess it up for her.

"You know what the craziest thing of all is?" I say. "I'm not even bothered by what you just said. Because you're right. He is talented. In that department."

I smile again, and realize my words are genuine. A couple weeks ago, her admission would have wrecked me and twisted me up inside, killing my confidence. But not today.

She crosses her arms, narrowing her eyes. Clearly this battle isn't over for her. "How does it feel to know he's been inside every woman in this room?" She glances over her shoulder pointedly. "The makeup artist, the hairstylist? And the other model, Sasha? He fucked her twice, once in front of an audience at an underground club. Members only, of course."

I can't help it. I actually laugh.

"I hope he had fun with that," I say. "Especially considering that his bachelor days are over now."

"Mmm, you're right." Heather pulls her hair over one shoulder, still catty as hell. "Though I also recall that he's a real asshole when he doesn't get laid enough. Considering how pissy he is today, I have to wonder if you're not doing a good enough job in bed to keep his temper under control."

My fists clench. I've never resorted to actual violence in

moments of anger, but I'm getting pretty close to going in for my first right hook. Luka and I have been dancing around each other ever since the day he took those pictures of me sucking him off. Every time I get near him, it's a struggle not to just give in and beg him to let me ride his cock, but I'm still too afraid of getting my heart involved.

For now, I can handle pissy Luka. And I'm not going to let this woman get the upper hand. If I don't make any new friends in this industry, oh well. I've got Mateo, my family, and maybe even my new sisters. Time to lay it all out for this bitch.

"You know, Heather," I say sweetly as I set down my glass and start around the table to her side. "I honestly don't care if every woman in the state of Illinois has fucked Luka. Because that's all in the past. And now? I have something they don't."

She stiffens when I stop before her and slap my left hand on the table beside her. She looks down, her nostrils flaring a little as my ridiculous glitter bomb of a diamond ring flashes in the light. I smile big and warm, though I'm sure she can see the murderous glint in my eyes. Lord knows I'm feeling it.

"And for the record, no one gets to talk shit about my hot-as-fuck fiancé but *me*." I take one more step toward her and she backs up. With an indignant huff, she turns and clomps off.

I don't bother lowering my voice as I wave and call out toward her retreating back, "He's in my bed now, sweetheart. Be sure to tell all your friends. Bye bye now."

I glare after her with one thought flashing in my mind.

I may not love Luka...but that man is mine.

BROOKLYN

CHAPTER 21

I stay near the table sipping my glass of water for a few more minutes after Heather storms off. My heart is pounding, but not from stress. Instead it's pure adrenaline and a heady feeling of self-assurance. I stood up to her. It was empowering, and not something I would normally do. I've never been a complete pushover, but I'm not confrontational, either. Being diplomatic is the way to go in most situations. But you need a strong backbone to make it to the top, and though I've been working on it, standing up to that bitch was a big step for me.

I can't have women with agendas like Heather constantly trying to plow me over with their jealousy and gossip. And I just proved to myself that I have the strength to prevent them from getting to me. Guess I'm a little bit of a badass, after all.

With a barely suppressed smile, I glance to where Heather has rejoined the other model, Sasha. Their heads are bent together, but I don't even care what they're talking about. I'm already over it. Just then, I catch the sight of Luka's long, muscular body leaning against the wall in the shadows off to my left. He's pretty relaxed, as if he's been there for a while. Was he eavesdropping this whole time? That controlling ass.

An arrogant grin tugs at his gorgeous lips as he saunters over to me with his hands in his pockets, which is more than enough answer to my question. I set my jaw, annoyed that he would lurk, and equally irritated that he did nothing to step in and back me up.

"How long were you standing there?" I cock my head, challenging him to lie to me.

"Long enough to appreciate the fact that you can fight your own battles."

Pride washes over me, and suddenly I'm glad he didn't try to intervene. "That's something you should know by now," I say, matching his cockiness with a bit of my own.

He reaches for a glass and pours some water, takes a small sip, and eyes me over the rim of the glass. "You know, the way you talked to Heather about me—got all feisty and possessive? That was pretty hot."

I give a nonchalant shrug. "If I'm going to be fully invested in our agreement, I have to act the part. Do you really think I wouldn't defend our 'relationship' in public?"

Luka's smile widens and he puts his arm around me, drawing me close.

"Is that all it was?" he asks, looking down into my eyes. "An act?"

Tingles race down my spine. "Of course. What else would it be?"

Our lips are inches apart, body heat flaring between us, and Luka's gazing at me with an intensity that makes my pussy ache. I almost wish someone would bring me the damn full-ass panty that he was barking orders about so I'd have more of a barrier than this tiny thong between us.

Female voices get closer and I glance over to see the other models walking our way. Heather gives Luka a wink and makes a show of sneering at me as they sashay toward us.

His eyes narrow with a spark of his asshole side—I know he's about to do something. But I'm still not prepared as he takes my chin to tip my face up, and suddenly he's kissing me, his arm tightening around my waist as he pulls me tighter against him.

"Luka," I half moan, finally drawing away a little to catch my breath.

Instead of letting up, he steals another searing kiss, cupping my face and tilting my head back so my neck is bared and my breasts push forward. He grins against my lips as if he's enjoying the little display he's putting on for the benefit of the other models.

"You're mine," he growls, but it's only loud enough for me to hear. The timbre of his voice jacks my need and it takes all my willpower not to wrap my leg around his and pull his hips closer to mine. Luka nibbles at my neck and works his way up, and I gasp at the contact.

Regardless of the fact that this is all for show, the chemistry between us is real.

My chest hitches at the warm luxury of his mouth brushing across mine gently before he takes my lips again fully, demanding that I part them with a push of his tongue. I do, and his tongue slicks along mine until I'm completely breathless, practically panting in his arms. He cradles the back of my head with the palm of his hand as he pulls away. His eyes are clouded with desire and also something I haven't seen in him before.

Pride.

"What was that for?" I step back and smooth my robe with my palms, realizing that Heather and Sasha are gone. They must have gotten the message after seeing Luka all over me. "And why are you looking at me like that?"

Glancing around, I see that the photographer and everyone else on the crew has left, too. The set area is empty save for me and Luka, the space completely quiet. They all must have left to take a meal break.

"Just pleased to see my fiancée turn into such a lioness," he says.

"No thanks to you," I huff. "You could have stepped in. Backed *me* up some."

The dark lust in his eyes deepens and all at once I'm glad everyone is gone...because I'm two seconds away from getting on the table and fucking him right here.

"You want me to back you up, Brooklyn?" he says. "How about I back you up against the wall and wrap your legs around my waist so I can fuck you hard and deep? Or maybe I'll back you up against the couch over there and bend you over it so I can take you from behind."

"Jesus." My face flushes hot and I'm so needy and wanting that I can hardly stand still.

He takes my hand. "I prefer when you call me 'Oh, God.'"

"Is that so?" I say, my voice a challenge, my pulse racing.

Our eyes catch for a hot second and then we're hurrying from the room and down a hallway. He makes quick work of checking door handles until he finds a room that's open. We tumble inside, into semi-darkness. He shuts the door quietly, and suddenly my back is pressed against it and his hand is on my hip. He flicks on a light and we both go completely still.

My eyes dart around the room and I laugh. I can't help it. Of all the places to fuck in this luxury building, we found a storage closet. The corners of his eyes crinkle. "We're the adventurous kind, aren't we?"

"You could say that," I agree.

He laughs, and this banter feels good. It's light and easy, and sexy because we're sharing this odd moment in an even odder place. Just then, the overhead light shuts off. He laughs again, and then the soft glow of his cellphone flashlight illuminates the room.

"Oooh, ambiance," I croon.

"Now you don't have to worry about stepping in a mop bucket while I make you come."

His hands and lips are suddenly everywhere, and I surrender to his ministrations. He opens the tie to my robe. It flutters open, bringing cool air over my desire-heated skin. I shiver and Luka responds by running hot kisses over my collarbone, between my breasts, and down my torso. Clutching his head between my hands, I run my fingers through his hair and let my head fall back against the door.

Trails of electric pleasure follow the path of his lips across my skin. His kisses are eager and urgent, but soothing. I moan softly at the delicate pleasure, panting when Luka traces a finger along the front of my thong. The fabric is fragile, and he could easily rip it off me. Instead he brushes it carefully to the side, taking care to let the pads of his fingers trail along my sensitive, needy skin. Then he drops to his knees and pulls my left leg over his shoulder, his finger tracing the seam of my bare pussy.

With a gasp, I push into his touch, needing more.

He looks up at me. He's so wickedly handsome on his knees for me that I swear I might orgasm just from the sight of him. The light gives him an angelic glow, and I want to crack a joke, but the intensity of his expression robs me of clear thought.

"I like it when you're possessive, Brooklyn."

"You do?" I'm so breathless, I can barely get the words out.

He parts my lips and his tongue slicks across my clit. I cry out and have to brace one hand against the door to steady myself. Luka storms a crazy assault on my clit, his tongue lapping and swirling and flicking until I can barely control the volume of my cries. Clenching my jaw to keep from screaming, I sink into the sensations he's causing and ride them as they flood my body, grinding my pussy against his hot, hungry mouth, until we find a rhythm.

The edge of my release wraps around me and I tense, ready to welcome it.

"I'm gonna come," I moan.

Luka pulls away. I'm barely aware of anything except the sudden loss. I'm about to protest when I hear the sound of his zipper, and my heart rate doubles as I realize he's about to fuck me. *Yes.* He grips my waist and hitches me up, urging my thighs around his waist. The fat tip of his cock nudges at my wet opening, and all the heady sensations come flooding back.

I want to come so badly, yet I crave the overpowering feel of his thick cock inside me.

"I want you to always be possessive of me," he breathes against my lips. "Show everyone who gets to take this cock every day."

"Yes," I murmur against his mouth, in between kisses. "Yes, yes, yes. Give it to me."

He thrusts up inside me, hard and deep, filling me completely in one strong move. I can't hold back my jagged moan as I dig my nails into the fabric of his shirt to clutch his shoulders. Slipping a hand between us, he finds my clit and begins slow circles around it as he thrusts. His movements are careful, as if he's gauging the level of my pleasure so he can build on it. And it's working. He's so good, he knows exactly how to jack me up, higher and higher, until the pressure inside me is so strong I need to scream or come, or both, to relieve it.

"Oh, God," I moan. It's definitely working.

His lips find the side of my neck, an intimate touch that he drags along the sensitive flesh as his cock and fingers drive me toward the edge again.

"Fuck me, Luka," I pant. "Fuck me, fuck me."

"You're mine," he growls, picking up the pace. "Your body is mine. This pussy is mine."

"Yes. Yes."

The tension between my legs is painful. *I need...I need...*

"Tell me I'm yours, Brooklyn. Like you're screaming it so every woman in this building knows it."

I loop my hands around his neck. "You're mine...you're fucking mine, Luka Zoric." My voice is aggressive, feral. I've never heard myself sound like this before.

"And you're mine," he says. "All mine."

Our mouths find each other in the dim light, hot and desperate and almost violent. I feel myself start to break apart and I can't hold back. "Oh, God," I murmur.

My release crashes over me, pulsing in deep shockwaves, leaving me shuddering. Luka groans softly into my neck, his body going tight as he pumps his final release into me.

We're holding each other tight, our breaths mingling, our moans echoing each other's. Emotions flood me, unbidden. I don't recognize them as anything except...they're something new. Something...different. My chest goes tight with whatever it is as Luka gently lowers me to my feet. My arms are still around his neck and I lean into him, closing my eyes as I listen to his heart pounding in his chest. He doesn't speak, just lets me hold him, stroking my lower back.

Finally, I pull away. I have no idea what that was. I'm not sure I want to.

He finds some tissues and carefully tidies me up, even pulling my robe around me and tying it again. He's gone from possessive, domineering asshole to tender lover so fast that I'm not sure what to think. But it's done something to my emotional center, and I'm shaken. It hits me then: Luka Zoric isn't actually the standoffish ice king that he wants me to believe he is. There are real emotions hiding inside him and they keep coming out and getting in the way.

"Let's turn the light on and make sure you're all in one piece," he says.

He reaches beside me to turn on the light, but I stop him. I rather like the soft glow of his cellphone and the intimate haze hanging over us. The way he'd kissed my body and touched me with care was different from whatever sparked between us in the past, and I'm sure we both felt it. Once he turns the overhead light on, it'll all go away.

"No, leave it. I don't mind looking like I've been freshly fucked."

He flashes me a wicked grin. "Really?"

"What better way to stake my claim, right?"

A low groan comes from deep in his throat. He kisses me lightly before moving me away from the door and opening it. Then he slips an arm around me as we head back down the hall, toward the shoot. I steal a glance at him as we walk. He looks almost happy. Almost content. He catches me looking, and smiles.

"You really impressed me back there," he says.

"In the closet?" I tease. "Or back at the shoot?"

He laughs. "Both."

My instincts were right today, I realize. The way I dealt with Heather was ultimately for the best. Everyone—including myself—will respect me more for owning my piece of this relationship. Even if it is a sham. And as long as I continue to stand up for myself, I don't have to lose who I am. I can still be my own person. I can own myself.

Maybe Mateo was right. Luka's domineering, possessive ways are kind of hot. Yet I can also see that he's been an asshole during these photoshoots because at the end of the day, he wants what's *best* for me, for both of us. He's looking out for our professional reputations. And today, I'd been looking out too. Though I have to admit, I kind of enjoyed the shocked look on Heather's face when I'd given her a verbal middle finger.

As I stroll back onto the set with Luka at my side, my body still tingles with the aftereffects of hot sex. Yes, I'd liked being that possessive woman. But Luka liked it way more.

And if it's going to make both of us feel this good, I have no intention of loosening my claim on Luka Zoric any time soon.

BROOKLYN

CHAPTER 22

Our penthouse looks like the set of a television show.

Lights and cameras are in position around the sofa, crew members with headsets and blaring walkie-talkies stroll back and forth with various types of equipment, and a team of sound people gather in a corner trying to troubleshoot a problem with the boom mic.

I force myself to take a deep breath and a long drink of water. It'll all be over soon.

Stefan set up a last-minute interview for Luka and me with a reporter named Kyla Chung, a former supermodel who has kept a big name for herself by transitioning to entertainment news. She happened to be in town filming at another event and called Stefan to ask if Luka and I had time to do an interview before she left Chicago. Of course, Stefan couldn't refuse.

He thought having the camera crew come to our home would give the interview an "intimate" feel, and also be a great way to show the public how wholesome Luka and I are. Emzee had even sent over a few framed pics from the engagement shoot so that we could decorate the place with some of our "happy couple" photos. Seeing them on the bookcase and the walls, I had to admit they looked pretty good.

Luka's older brother had whipped everything together in an impressive amount of time, including an intensive session over dinner last night to coach Luka and me on how to respond to questions about Konstantin and the prostitution scandal. Up until that point, neither of us had realized it would be *that* kind of interview—we'd expected more of the usual fluff. But Stefan insisted it was time to step back from the engagement, work harder to clear the Zoric name and rebuild the family's reputation as founders of the newly minted Danica Rose Modeling agency. While I understand that and agree, this interview is making me more nervous than I expected. Probably because the pressure is on me and Luka to be the bright new face of the agency.

I glance around the penthouse again and feel my chest go tight with anxiety. I've never had to speak about my future father-in-law really, or about the things he's done. I'd rather keep it that way. The truth is, he deserves to be rotting in jail—but I can't say that on TV.

Over and over during dinner last night, Stefan had grilled us. *How much did you know about the trafficking, Luka? Were there rumors in the industry, Brooklyn? How has this affected the business going forward? What about the effects on the Zoric family?* It had felt a lot like a police interrogation, but by the end I finally felt confident I had my answers down perfectly.

After all that practice, there's no way I should be feeling so off my game, but as a production assistant leads me to the sofa to sit next to Luka, and I catch a glimpse of Stefan pacing in the kitchen with a glass of whiskey in his hand, my jitters only get worse.

My fiancé looks dashing as always in dark pants, Italian leather shoes, and a deep green pullover with buttons open at the neck. It brings out the color of his eyes and the olive undertone of his dark skin. He looks like an exotic treat, his black hair glossy and perfectly styled. A hint of a five o'clock shadow covers his jaw—a change from his normal baby-smooth face, but I like it.

I'm wearing wide-leg gray pants and a silk blouse with embroidered sleeves and a scoop neck. The thin wire of the microphone that's clipped to my shirt suddenly feels uncomfortable against my back and I resist the urge to fiddle with it as Kyla takes a seat across from us.

"Last checks!" someone yells, and the hair and makeup crew dash over to pat down Kyla's hair and dab her nose with a powder puff. A young guy leans over and tucks my hair behind my ear, and I almost jump at the contact.

"Try to relax, Brooklyn," Kyla tells me kindly, in a low murmur. "It's just TV."

"Thanks," I say, but I'm nowhere near calm as the director calls "Action."

Kyla starts her intro, her words flawlessly rehearsed, but I have a hard time concentrating until I feel Luka's hand on my knee, warm and reassuring. I smile, feeling a little more centered.

"Brooklyn, it's safe to say your engagement to Luka took the modeling world by storm. Not only is he Chicago's most notorious bachelor, but notably, the engagement comes on the heels of the KZ Modeling sex-trafficking scandal." Kyla's brows knit together in concern.

I nod and mirror her expression, anxious for her to ask the first question.

She goes on, "So I'm wondering, as a model on the outside, did you know about Konstantin's actions? Was there a lot of talk in your inner circles about what he'd done?"

My face feels tight as I offer a small smile. "It was impossible not to be aware of the rumors, but I didn't know anything for sure. No one did. The truth came out much later."

Kyla tilts her head. "And yet, you chose to sign with the agency anyway...and become engaged to Luka, effectively binding yourself to the Zoric family and their questionable legacy."

The hours of coaching kick in. "As you know, Kyla, KZ Modeling has effectively closed its doors for good. I signed with Danica Rose Management, the Zorics' new agency, and the company is fully committed to upholding standards of transparency and integrity in this industry.

"Beyond that, Luka isn't his father, and he and his brother have gone on record stating the majority of KZM staff had no knowledge of or involvement in the company's illegal activities. With Danica Rose, Luka and Stefan are publicly moving forward to forge a legacy all their own. I'm proud to be a part of that. Professionally and also on a personal level."

Though I know I'm performing my lines well, I feel like I'm on the witness stand, giving rehearsed testimony instead of a casual interview full of wit and cute banter. What if I'm coming across as robotic to the viewers? My face heats as I imagine how I look on camera. There's another squeeze on my knee and I try to relax.

Kyla gives a nod, her eyebrows going up. "Before you signed on the dotted line, did you worry about long-term repercussions of the trafficking scandal, and how that might affect Danica Rose's chances—your chances—of success?"

"I—" I look to Luka, then wonder if people might think I'm looking at him to coach me in some way. I mentally shake myself. *Transparency, integrity, legacy.* Stefan's script echoes in my mind but I can't form a sentence.

"That's a fair question," Luka cuts in. He lifts my hand in his own and kisses my knuckles. "To be honest, the shadow of KZM's past was certainly a concern of mine with respect to Brooklyn's career. A model of her talent has a world of possibilities open to her, and we did discuss how Danica Rose was just one option. But in the end, she chose us, and the agency is honored to have her. Brooklyn's work speaks for itself, though, and she's been in extremely high demand since signing with us. It's clear the industry is embracing her."

"That's wonderful," Kyla says. She sounds like she means it.

"I think the industry and the public are ready to move forward," I tell her confidently. "We can't hold the entire Zoric family accountable for what one man did."

"So you'd go on the record saying you have full trust in Danica Rose Management?"

Trust? My stomach falls as I think about the huge lie I'm keeping. "Of course," I say with a smile. "I absolutely trust DRM. And I trust my fiancé and the rest of his family."

I'm careful to keep my smile schooled, though the butterflies inside me keep growing. I think back to the other day at the photo shoot when Luka and I hooked up in the supply closet. He'd been so gentle with me afterward, and the good vibe between us had followed us the rest of the day. In fact, he's been extra attentive ever since then, including an impromptu dinner at my parents' house where he seemed totally in his element. It's like we're finally connecting in a way we haven't before. And...I like it.

I enjoy the side of Luka that asks how my day went, or what I want for dinner, or if I'm warm enough. I like it when he opens the door for me or holds my purse while I get into the car. Over the past few days, we've been acting like any real couple would.

"Luka, did you really have no idea what your father was up to? Was there no indication that something illegal was going on?"

The question makes my smile fall. Which isn't a bad thing given the question, so I don't plaster a new one on.

Luka shakes his head, his face grim. "If I'd known, I would have turned him in. No one in the family knew about it. You hear people talk about criminals leading double lives, and I guess my father was a textbook example of that. It was a shock for all of us."

Luka may have practiced his interview questions, but the emotion in his voice is real. Suddenly, I realize I've never asked him how the scandal affected the rest of the family or their relationships with each other. They've certainly presented a unified front to clean up their image, but the news that their father was a predator must have shredded them.

"I can't imagine what you've all been through," Kyla says gently, showing some real humanity. "How would you say the scandal has affected the new modeling agency?"

Stefan is standing off to the side near one of the large windows now, observing the filming from a closer standpoint, and I catch the barest glimpse of him stiffening at the question.

But Luka remains cool and steady. "Even with the

rebranding and the new company name, the bad press created a ripple effect. There's no denying it. But the majority of our clients and models were willing to talk things through with the new management—Stefan, mainly—and give us a chance to prove that we have their best interests in mind. We're thriving now."

I try not to stare at my fiancé. He's on fire. He answers so calmly and smoothly, as if giving interviews about hard topics is just something he does. From the corner of my eye, I spy Stefan nodding along approvingly. I wonder if he's proud of how his younger brother is doing right now. The Luka in front of this camera is certainly different from the playboy, party-all-night version of himself that the media is used to seeing.

Kyla shifts in her chair, her face lighting with an animated smile. "On to something more fun. Tell me about the two of you. Where did you and Brooklyn meet, Luka?"

I snap to attention at the question. Where did we meet? Oh boy. My mouth goes dry as our eyes catch. Luka gives an adoring smile and by God, it looks genuine. As if he's truly remembering the sweet moment he knew that I was the one and not making something up.

"We met at a runway show a few years ago," he answers. "I knew the moment I laid eyes on Brooklyn Moss that she was special. Other models were storming down the catwalk, glaring and posing, but then Brooklyn walks toward me with this Mona Lisa smirk, like she had a secret that nobody else knew. I was a total goner." He pauses, and Kyla smiles dreamily at him. "Then we ran into each other at the after-party and spent the whole night together. We just...clicked."

"People talk about love at first sight for a reason," Kyla says with a wink.

Luka smiles and pulls me close. "We lost touch soon

after that, but when we finally reconnected, I knew I couldn't let her go again. I proposed almost immediately."

"And I said yes," I say with a giggle, playing my role.

Part of me is wistful, though. If only Luka meant it. If only that was the way it had *really* been. We'd spent the whole night together, all right. After he'd promised me that modeling contract just to get me in bed. And I'd eaten up his every word. God, I'd been so stupid then.

"Brooklyn, what's it like to live with a former hardcore bachelor?"

I hear the question, but I don't know how to answer. All I can do is hope that I'm not still that stupid girl, making stupid mistakes. Luka laughs and takes my hand in his own, making a show of our fingers twined together.

"It's so good, she's speechless." Everyone laughs, including me. Luka continues and I'm grateful he's taking the attention away from me. "Look, relationships are tricky no matter what, and living together is definitely an adventure. But this place has never felt like more of a home than it has since Brooklyn's come into my life." He gestures around the room and Kyla nods.

"Brooklyn, how about you? What do you love most about living with Luka?"

"His avocado toast," I blurt. Kyla throws her head back and laughs, as if I was joking.

"I make her breakfast every morning," Luka interjects. "I like taking care of her."

Kyla smiles. "It's very apparent how much the two of you care for each other. Which brings me to the one thing everyone wants to know. Are you planning on having kids?"

I hesitate, and Luka squeezes my hand. We look at each other and once again, I silently thank him for taking the lead. I'm supposed to be the one who's good at putting on a presentation for the world, but today it's Luka who's excelling.

"We're just enjoying the wedding planning right now, and our time with each other. We'll all just have to wait and see what the future brings us." He grins.

"Time will tell," I agree.

The interview winds down, Kyla leading out with a few chitchat questions. Luka and I take turns answering, but I'm in a daze. Everything about this interview seemed so real.

I can't get my heart out of it.

His hand is on my knee again, absently running a thumb over my kneecap as if he's subconsciously trying to comfort me. Did he mean it, about seeing what the future brings us?

What's happening here? It's all for show, yes. I know that. Yet I can't help but fantasize that his words had actual meaning. That he wasn't just placating the press with sugar-coated lies.

He aced the interview so hard that I find myself envisioning what our life could be like. If we had a house with a yard. Kids. Family dinners, holidays with the rest of the Zorics, vacations. The future we've painted could be real, not just words.

This doesn't have to be a sham.

BROOKLYN

CHAPTER 23

An image of Julia Roberts tossing her bouquet into a packed church pew as she bolts from her wedding in *Runaway Bride* ripples through my head.

My wedding is two weeks away and I'm daydreaming about calling everything off, walking away, and forgetting all about Luka Zoric. Ditching this arrangement once and for good.

I'm sitting at O'Hare Airport, waiting to board my flight to LA. It's raining outside and I can't help thinking it's a sign that I need to get the hell out of Chicago and never come back. The past few days with Luka have me completely confused and twisted up in knots—ever since our interview with Kyla, I haven't been able to keep my head straight. I *know* the image we've created isn't real, but the more time I spend with Luka, the more it *feels* real. But I can't let myself be seduced by the lie. It'll only cause heartache later.

Still, I've seen so many instances of what could be for us. This dream doesn't have to be just a dream. What if everything we're faking could be real? I don't know what I want anymore.

I haven't slept in days as my mind cycles through all the what-ifs and analyzes every word Luka has said to me to try to determine if there's hidden meaning behind what I've been taking at face value. The interview really threw me. I was still reeling from how gently Luka held me in the supply closet at the photo shoot and how much my possessiveness had turned him on, and then he had to go on national television and talk about how he'd fallen for me at first sight. Was that total BS? Or was there some real truth to it?

Do I risk my pride and face him and confess the feelings that are creeping in, or do I wait it out and see if anything blossoms on its own...or if things resume to what they've always been? Putting myself out there doesn't seem like the best option right now. Not with the wedding so close. All I need is his emotional rejection to stain a day that's already tainted with lies.

And if what I'm feeling are real feelings, and he has them, too? Then what?

We can't possibly have a real life together. Not when this whole thing started out as a sham...and especially not with the secret I'm keeping from him.

The stress is accumulating, and I need to temper it before I explode or do something stupid like run away from my wedding—and my picture-perfect future.

I flip my cellphone over in my hand and glance to see if I have a text from Mateo. He doesn't know that I'm coming. Nobody does, aside from the people I have an appointment with tomorrow afternoon. Another blip of guilt courses through me. Mateo is staying at his condo in LA for a job this week, which works out perfectly for me. I need an alibi, so to speak, to cover for what I'm doing tomorrow, and I need time with my bestie so I can unwind and relax from all this emotional pressure. I'd texted him earlier to call me, but I haven't heard back yet.

After I'd gotten the call this morning about the top-secret appointment, I'd packed a light bag and headed to the airport without even notifying Luka. His schedule is packed today and by the time he gets home, I'll be curled up on Mateo's sofa drinking wine.

I grip the phone tightly and glance at the ceiling, feeling suddenly terrible that I didn't give Luka a heads-up. I'd thought about it, but I wasn't sure what to say that wouldn't raise his suspicion. We have an unspoken thing where we come and go as we please. Lately, neither of us has gone very far, and never overnight. He comes home every night and so do I. But maybe I'll luck out and he won't notice I'm missing until my plane is already in the air.

My phone chimes, and joy pumps through me when I see that it's Mateo.

"Hey!" I'm so excited to speak to him. It feels like forever since we've caught up.

"Sorry it took me so long to get back to you. What's going on? You sound stressed."

Of course he knows how I'm feeling even though I've only said a single word. He knows me better than anyone... even Luka.

Aware of the people seated all around me, I lower my voice and turn toward the window for a measure of privacy. Below, I can see planes taxiing on the runway. "It's the wedding. Well, not just that. I guess it's everything." I tell him about the photo shoot and the interview and how sneaky feelings are weaseling into my common sense.

He's quiet, as if he knows I'm not quite done. "A part of

me wants to call off the wedding," I finally say. Dread floods me as I say the words out loud. "I don't know what the right thing to do is."

"Oh, Brookie, you're never lacking on the drama lately, are you?"

"I never used to have any drama!" I exclaim.

"I know. You were so boring. And look at you now."

I huff a little laugh. "Thanks...I think."

Mateo sighs. "Look, I can't tell you what to do. Emotions are just products of hormones. They come and go, you know? He's being sweet and loving because it's part of the game. Or maybe he's really starting to fall for you. But you know what? It doesn't matter. Because in a few years, it will all be over and you're going to walk away with everything you ever wanted. Maybe you need to focus on that, on the reasons you agreed to this marriage in the first place."

I take a deep breath through my nose as his words sink in. He's sassy and full of himself, but Mateo is a surprising voice of reason. He's right. No matter what I think I feel, no matter what lies ahead for me and Luka, I have to keep my eyes on the ultimate prize.

"Thanks, Mateo. I knew you could talk me down from the ledge."

"Yeah, yeah. That's what I'm here for."

"You free tonight? I'll be landing at LAX in about four hours."

I laugh at his excited holler. In a rush of profanity and rambling sentences he hangs up, only to call me back a few minutes later, right before I board the plane. I can hardly keep up as he excitedly chats about the impromptu bachelorette party he just tossed together with some friends of ours who are in town, too. By the time I get to my seat, I'm genuinely excited to get to LA, despite the growing guilt that I didn't mention it to Luka.

I try to rest during the flight and figure out what I'm going to tell him. He can't know the real reason I'm going to California. No one can. Several possible scenarios play through my mind, but why make it complicated? All I have to say is that I wanted to get away and see my bestie. Even better, friends wanted to throw a very impetuous West Coast party for me since they couldn't make it out to Chicago for the bachelorette party that Tori and Emzee had hosted, and how could I refuse? I'll call him as soon as I land to explain. That should erase the guilt...I hope.

Mateo is waiting for me when I get out to the curb to stand in the taxi line, surprising me by being there. He whisks me off for a late lunch and then to his condo, and before I know it, we've been talking and laughing so much that Luka slips my mind and I never make the call.

Until my phone suddenly rings and all the excitement drains from my body. Mateo goes quiet and makes an exaggerated anxious face when he realizes who's calling. Excusing myself, I go to the bathroom, shut the door, and answer the call.

"Hey," I say cheerfully.

There's a beat of silence that makes my chest hurt. Damn, I can't believe I didn't ward this off by calling him first. "Where are you, Brooklyn? It's almost 10 p.m."

I clear my throat and compose myself. "About that. So, Mateo decided to throw me a *very* impromptu bachelorette party with some friends out in LA, so I got on a plane and—"

"You're in *Los Angeles*." His voice is hard, the tone rising just enough that I can feel his anger through the phone.

"I—yes, I am in Los Angeles."

More silence and I imagine he's clenching his jaw the way he does when he's getting sudden emotions under control. Right now, I wish I was one of those people who didn't feel guilty or anxious over anything. Both are tearing through me right now.

"With *Mateo*." It's not a question.

My cheeks go hot. "Yes."

"I see." His tone is even harder, with an edge I've never heard from him before. "Be honest with me, Brooklyn. Do you have something going on with him?"

Luka shocked me the other day when he expressed pride over the way I stood up to Heather. He's done it again right now with the pure jealousy in his voice. He's always been a little standoffish about my relationship with Mateo and I've never lied to him about our friendship being just that, friendship. I thought he'd come to accept it, but now, I'm not so sure.

He's jealous. And I kind of like it.

A small grin pulls at my lips. Maybe Luka does care about me.

"You know things between Mateo and me are strictly platonic," I remind him. "It's never been otherwise, and it never will be."

"Regardless," Luka says gruffly, "don't you know how shitty it looks for my image if the paparazzi get more pics of you partying it up with another man, weeks before our wedding? Did you forget what happened the last time you two went out to a club? We nearly had a fallout thanks to the pictures that got circulated."

His words are like a bucket of ice water over me. Of course. His *image*. His reaction had nothing to do with us. It was about all the ways I could potentially screw up his PR.

"Don't worry," I say quietly. "We're just going to dinner and our friends will be there."

"When can I expect you back home?" he asks.

"I'm just here for the weekend," I tell him. "I'll be back Monday."

"Fine. See you then."

He hangs up, and I stare down at my phone feeling like my chest is caving in.

I can't believe I thought there was something more blooming between us. I've really let my own emotions override common sense lately. Of course Luka doesn't actually care for me. This is still, and always has been, just a business deal. One we made to elevate Danica Rose's image, which by proxy means Luka's, too. That's all I am to him—a means to an end.

∼

THE NEXT MORNING, I slide into a black leather chair across from the head of Elite Image, Austin Spears, who greets me with a smile. I'm feeling zero anxiety about being here at their swanky Hollywood office. There's a pit in my stomach over this meeting and what I've agreed to do for Elite, but for once, it's not filled to the brim with guilt.

If anything, I'm even more motivated to see this through.

"Glad you could make it." Austin slides a piece of paper across the mahogany desk. "Here's our official offer. I'm sure you'll be more than pleased with the terms."

My heart begins to pound, my palms growing damp as I read the contract. They're offering to make me the premier face of Maxilene cosmetics. International contracts. More dollar signs than I've seen in my life. I'm trembling by the time I'm done reading all of the perks Elite is offering in exchange for the terms we privately discussed before.

I pull my bottom lip between my teeth and read it again. At least, I try to, but the words begin to jumble. This offer is a much bigger deal than what Danica Rose is currently giving me. So much more. And yet, I'm not sure how easily I can walk away from what I'm already locked into. On an emotional level, the guilt wants to come back and remind me that I already have a deal, even if it's not the absolute dream that's outlined before me on paper.

Austin steeples his fingers, a knowing grin on his lips. "Anything DRM is currently giving you will be null and void once you sign with us. This contract overrides anything you currently have in place. You can walk away from them, free and clear."

"I know," I tell him.

He pulls a pen from the inside breast pocket of his suit coat and hands it to me. His smile is meant to be reassuring, but it does nothing to make me feel that way. I slowly take the pen as he watches me intently, probably gauging what my next move will be. Joke's on him, though, because even I don't know what I'm going to do.

Positioning the contract in front of me, I lower the pen until the tip rests on the signature line. But the pen begins to feel heavy in my grip, and I set it down.

"Are you worried you won't be able to deliver?" he asks, concern knitting his brow.

"I can deliver. It's not that."

It's true; I can give Elite exactly what they've asked for. Luka's already unknowingly given me everything that I need to make Austin and his bosses very, very happy. A flash of my fiancé's face plays in my mind and guilt begins to trickle into that pit in my middle. I'm so tired of feeling this way. *Why* should I feel guilty? Luka has no trouble making everything we do about business. His end game is all about looking out for himself and the agency.

So why shouldn't I look out for myself, too? It's business.

I slide the contract back toward Austin. The flicker of disappointment in his expression is visible. "I need to think it over a bit longer," I say, lifting my chin. "I'll get back to you soon."

He drums his fingers on the desk, eyes narrowed as if he's trying to think of some way to persuade me to sign right now. But then he sits up straighter, pulls the contract over, and scribbles his signature on one of the bottom lines.

"Take it with you and mail it back when you're ready." He slides it my way again and gives a resolved tap of his hand on the desk. "You're a smart girl, Brooklyn. Smart enough to know where the opportunity lies. I'm confident you'll come around."

I thank him and tuck the contract into my bag on my way out the door. I still have no idea what the right move is.

Because no matter what I decide, somebody's going to get hurt.

LUKA

CHAPTER 24

The floral musk of Brooklyn's perfume greets me as I step into the penthouse Monday evening, telling me she's back.

I barely slept the last few nights, knowing she was so far away, doing whatever she was up to with Mateo under the guise of a bachelorette party. It was the first time I've been alone in the penthouse since she moved in and I swear I could feel her absence like a tangible thing. It created a sort of tension that could only be broken by one thing.

Her coming home.

Her keys are lying in the little ceramic bowl on the side table; her purse sitting on the edge as if she'd simply tossed it there instead of putting it away like she normally does. I walk quietly down the entry hall to the living room, listening for her. The gentle beat of the shower trickles through the open space and my cock immediately comes to life. She's home and she's naked in the shower. Two of my favorite things. I'd love to barge in and join her. I think to her haphazard purse on the table. Why was she in such a hurry to get home and jump in the shower?

What kind of lies is she washing off?

Setting my jaw, I resist the urge to barge into her ensuite bathroom and demand to know what she was really doing in LA. My sister and sister-in-law already threw her a lavish party here last month, along with a few of her model friends. Granted, Mateo hadn't been able to attend, but still. I don't believe the bachelorette party cover-up for one second. Her departure was so last minute. So impromptu. Brooklyn has to be up to something.

Either she's fucking Mateo, or—

Fuck! My whole body goes tense and hot at the mental image of her underneath that guy—any guy, I don't care who. I can't shake my anger at her for running off. Especially given that the past few weeks have been different between us. More real. I'd been slow to realize it because I didn't want to face it, but there's no doubt in my mind that things've changed. Yesterday morning it came to me clear as crystal while I was sweating out my shitty mood at the gym.

I like taking care of Brooklyn, doing little things for her. I fucking loved it when she got all possessive over me at the photo shoot. What the other model had said about me was true. I had fucked every female in that room at one time. It's an uncomfortable, even caustic, situation for a fiancée to find herself in—but instead of cowering, or taking the socially acceptable high road, Brooklyn had stood up for herself, and for our relationship. And I swear it meant something—that *I* meant something more than just the agreement we've made.

Loosening my tie, I remove my cufflinks and roll up my shirt sleeves. My clothes feel too tight all of a sudden. Needing to calm down, I go to the large windows and look out over the city. Dusk is beginning to fall, and lights dot the buildings in different hues of silver and gold. Streaks of purple and orange fade into the encroaching night. Brooklyn should be here right now, her naked body pressed against the glass. I swear I'll make her forget every man she's ever fucked.

"Luka? Hi."

I turn to find Brooklyn rubbing her hair with a towel. A pink robe clings to her curves as if she put it on while her skin was still damp, her nipples perking beneath the silky fabric.

"I texted you earlier to let you know I was home. Did you get it?"

Ah, so now she's trying to play nice. She couldn't be bothered to tell me she was leaving town on her very sudden, very secretive little trip, so why have a change of heart now?

"I did." I just chose not to respond. Two can play at this game.

"Oh. Okay." She drapes the towel over her forearm. "How was work?"

The mundane small talk sets off my frustration. Turning to fully face her, I run a hand over my mouth. "Why did you go to LA, Brooklyn?"

Her eyes widen. "I told you. For a really last-minute bachelorette party."

"My family just threw you one a few weeks ago."

She looks away, and I can't tell if it's guilt or lies she's trying to hide from me. "I know, and it was lovely. But my LA friends had to miss it, and Mateo was already out there for work, so he thought we should have a second party so I could celebrate again."

I'm not buying it. "What LA friends? You never mentioned them before."

Brooklyn shrugs and pauses, probably scrambling to

come up with more lies. "Just, you know. Anjali, who models part-time and runs a non-profit magazine, her boyfriend Jacob. He's a dental student or something at USC. Pera Lutz, you've heard of her. She modeled for that luxury car company last year—she played the secret agent in all the commercials. And then Bowie and Harper from YouTube, they run a makeup channel."

The names are familiar...so maybe she's not completely lying. I take a couple steps toward her, my pulse racing. Part of me is glad she's back. The other part is still too suspicious, too jealous, whatever, to fully embrace how nice it is having her in my—our—home again.

"Where did you have the party?"

Her smooth brow crinkles. "Why the hundred questions?"

I move closer. "What aren't you telling me? Why can't you just answer them?"

"I *am*."

"Okay, then tell me what you did last night. Tell me all of it." I'm so close to her now that I could touch her. I want to, but I might not be gentle, so I don't. As if she senses how tense I am, her eyes track up to mine as she crosses her arms over her chest.

"We had a couple drinks at Mateo's. Then we went to Shin Ho's on Sunset for pad Thai until about eleven. And then to meet Anjali at some whiskey bar downtown that I've never heard of, and then home. Happy?"

"Your home is here." The words drop from my mouth like rocks.

Her entire expression changes to one of disbelief. "Are you saying I'm not allowed to ever leave here? You know what I meant."

There has to be another reason she took off. "And this morning, before your flight?"

She backs away with an irritated sound. "You know what, Luka, the whole possessive thing was kind of fun when I thought it meant something, but now you're just being a dick."

I put my arms on either side of her, caging her against the wall. "I'm just curious what my fiancée has been up to."

She looks up at me, glaring, her breath coming faster. "I might be your fiancée, but I'm still my own person and I'm allowed to have my own life. I've already told you everything you need to know. There's nothing wrong with me keeping some things to myself!"

"Fine." Stepping closer, I press my hips into hers. "As long as you remember that your body belongs to me."

A desperate whimper comes from her throat, her mouth parting willingly as I dip my head to kiss her hard. Her soft taste floods me and I'm overcome with how much I want her. Remembering my earlier wish, I walk her back across the room, feasting on her mouth like a starving man as we go. She gasps as her back presses against the cool glass of the window, her thin robe doing nothing to protect her from the slight chill.

I'm angry and aroused and I don't want to control myself. I want to strip her bare and fuck her against the backdrop of the night sky and the lights, where anyone with a good view could look up and see her luscious body pressed to the glass.

Stripping the robe off her, I can't get enough of the sight of her body. My cock is so hard for her it's almost painful. Her chest heaves, her heavy breasts thrusting out for me, those pebbled nipples just begging to be sucked. Taking her face between my hands, I press into her and claim her mouth, kissing her until we're both breathless. She squirms and twists with a little pant, face flushed with anger. Our eyes lock and I feel the force of her raging emotions like a blow to the chest. It's pissing her off that she wants me so much.

She grips the front of my shirt. "You're an asshole."

"Get used to it."

"Fuck you."

"Oh, Brooklyn, I plan to fuck the memory of every man you've ever had right out of you. Starting now."

I reach between her legs. She's soaked, her juices coating my fingers as I pump them into her. She bucks against me with a moan and palms the window to steady herself. I wrap my mouth around her nipples, sucking hard, one after the other, and then trail a line of kisses up her throat until I reach her lips again. All the while, I fuck her with my hand until she's panting my name, completely helpless. She's so slick, it's running down my wrist.

"I thought about this last night," I growl against her lips. "Thought about your sweet pussy so much I had to jack off just to get to sleep."

"Luka," she moans, head tilted back, eyes closed.

Her cunt swells around my fingers and a flame of satisfaction lights inside me. I use my thumb to stroke her clit while I thrust, her hips rocking against my hand as I work her, feeling her getting closer and closer to the edge. She's taking me with her, but it's not purely sexual. I'm tiptoeing around the rim of something I don't understand—a longing, a need to have this every night. To be the only one who makes her feel like this.

Fuck.

"Listen to me, Brooklyn." I flick my thumb over her swollen clit. She cries out, one arm locking around my neck in a death grip. "I'm gonna make sure you never think about another man when I'm fucking you."

"Your ego would love that, wouldn't it?" Her eyes flash.

Instead of answering, I lower the zipper on my pants and let my cock spring free.

"Tell me you don't want this," I challenge, pressing against her wet cunt.

She licks her lower lip with her tongue, and I lose any sense of self-control. Grabbing her hips, I spin her so she's facing the window and then pull her smooth, firm ass back to me. I grab one perfect globe in my hand and then slap it hard enough that it will leave a mark. She gasps with pleasure but doesn't resist—just pushes back against me, wanting more.

I smack her ass one more time, grab a handful of her silky hair, and nudge her legs farther apart before driving into her in one perfect, hard thrust. We both cry out and I swear I could explode already. She drives me insane, pushes me further than any woman ever has. The craving never goes away and I can't get enough of her.

"No man has ever fucked you this good." I pull her hair until her head snaps back. A hard tremble courses through her body, her pussy clamping hard around me as I jackhammer into her. "Whatever you were doing out in LA, *whoever* you were doing, I'm gonna make sure you can't think about him while I'm inside you. I'm gonna fuck anyone else right out of you."

She makes a desperate sound as she drives her hips back to meet my thrusts. I ram into her harder, harder, the burn of jealousy surprising me. All the tension and anger and worry of thinking about her being with Mateo or another man floods out of me as I ride her until we're both strung tight.

"Luka, please." Her soft, desperate plea drives me to finally push her over the edge. I reach around and stroke her clit as I increase my pace. It only takes seconds and she's crying out with the force of her orgasm, her whole body tensing up as the climax slams through her. I lose control and come with her, pressing her into the glass with both hands until we finally go still.

Breathing hard. Sweaty. Lost in our own thoughts.

I want to stay pissed at her, but I want to carry her to my bed and feel the warmth of her body next to me all night even more. Running a hand through my hair, I pull away and slip an arm around her waist to steady her as she turns to face me.

Brooklyn searches my eyes as if she's waiting for me to say something…or maybe she has something to say herself, but in the end she doesn't. Goosebumps rise on her body and I quickly retrieve her robe and wrap it around her shoulders. The moment is over, the possessive jealousy fucked right out of me. But I still want her.

Even as she walks quietly away to her room, I wish she would turn around and run into my arms.

But she doesn't. And I don't do anything to stop her.

BROOKLYN

CHAPTER 25

The wedding is tomorrow.
We're at the rehearsal dinner and I'm on my second glass of champagne to help steady my nerves, but it's not working.

It feels as if there are a million people here—Luka extended invitations to the majority of the wedding guests, not just the wedding party—most of whom I don't even know. Luka's family. Family friends. Friends of friends. Godparents, cousins twice removed, random children. I try to keep my sights set on my parents and Mateo and those who have become closest to me in the short time Luka and I have been engaged. His sister, brother, sister-in-law. They're my tribe.

I take another sip as a sudden realization sinks in. Luka's family *accepts* me. They are fully on board with this sham wedding, and even his ice queen sister Emzee has come around to actually liking me. In fact, she texts me silly pictures of her dog Munchkin almost every day now, and in return I send pics from my modeling gigs—anything visually interesting that would appeal to her photographer's eye. But in the end, I'm still keeping secrets from all of them, and the guilt I've been struggling with has only gotten worse since this damn dinner started.

"Excuse me," an imperious female voice says.

I glance up to find the scrutinizing face of an older woman with perfectly styled gray hair, a sleek pinstripe pantsuit, and heavy gold earrings. She offers the tips of her fingers in one of those dead fish-type handshakes. I make it fast and plaster on a smile. Before she can say more, Luka gives her a warm hug with a genuine smile.

"Brooklyn, my aunt Vivian. She flew all the way from Morocco to be here and was hoping to get to know you before the wedding."

"So you're Brooklyn Moss," she says, smiling tightly and giving a cocky tilt of her head as she side-eyes me. I feel judged, as if she knows what I'm up to. Then again, Luka comes from money. Lots of money. She'd probably scrutinize anyone he chose to marry.

"Yes. It's wonderful to meet you," I say pleasantly.

"Mmm-hmm. Well, they do say the heart wants what it wants." She sniffs at me and then turns a bright gaze on Luka, patting his cheek affectionately, and my heart sinks. He doesn't speak about his family much. I know he lost his mother at a young age and was raised by a series of nannies and babysitters, but never had a steady maternal influence in his life. Whatever relationship he has with his aunt, though, makes his eyes light up.

Once again, my guilt nearly suffocates me.

I'm a horrible person.

I start to rise to go get some fresh air, but then my bridesmaids come over to swarm me with hugs and hand me a shot of something dark and creamy. I toss it back, wishing we had more time together, but they have to rush to take their seats since the meal is about to be served. I don't know if I'll be able to eat a single bite. I'm so ready to get this over with.

Another relative of Luka's comes over to meet me, and then another, and finally I'm standing because there are two more waiting in line to say hello and my arm begins to ache from lifting it while sitting to shake hands. My head is swimming, and it's not from the alcohol.

Something warm touches between my shoulder blades and I look up to see Luka's smiling face. His brow crinkles. "You look pale. Do you need to step out for a minute? I can cover for you."

I smile and wave him off. "I'm fine. Just hungry, I guess."

He looks like he doesn't believe me. "I know this is probably overwhelming for you, but so much of my extended family flew in for the wedding that there wasn't going to be time to visit with all of them tomorrow, so it seemed best to just invite everyone—"

"We talked about it already, and I really get it," I reassure him. "Besides, it's your wedding, too. Enjoy your family time."

He rubs my back in a little circle—a gesture of appreciation. He's being sincere, once again showing me the side of him that might really care about me. But I truly can't tell if he's into me, or just going through the motions because of the wedding, or trying to make up for the angry sex we had after he got so jealous over my trip to LA. No matter his reasons, though, I can't shake the feeling that something amazing could really blossom between us if we let it. And I have to admit, I want that. We both deserve it, but I don't know how to get from here to there.

Especially considering the contract that's folded up in

my purse right now. It's a reminder that I haven't fully committed to Luka the way I should if I want to be his real wife. Real wives don't purposely deceive their husbands or play dirty to get what they want.

No. I could have Luka *and* a healthy relationship. My name is already getting around in all the right circles thanks to my connection to him and my contract with Danica Rose Management. I've had job after job lined up ever since I signed, and though most of them have been smaller campaigns, I know that in time I'll be a household name, and everyone will know my face. I'll be making a ton of my own money, if I just stay the course.

Or...or I could sign the Elite Image contract and become a household name right now. No waiting required. The Maxilene contract will propel me to international fame and recognition in the blink of an eye. But if I do sign, I lose Luka.

Forever.

"And then he said, 'Spirulina is nothing more than fancy algae. Why don't you just scoop some out of the fountain on campus and put that in your smoothie?'" Everyone behind us starts laughing at Tori as she tries to impersonate her husband's commanding, overly serious voice.

"I do not sound like that," Stefan protests, sounding commanding and overly serious.

"You do too!" she insists. "And for the record, you've already been drinking fancy algae in your smoothie every morning. That's why you're so handsome."

"Ah. So I have *you* to thank for that," he says, finally cracking a smile and pulling her in for a kiss.

Everyone *ooohs*. Everyone but me. I'm too torn up over the line I'm walking with Luka.

The teasing continues, much to everyone's delight.

"You're lucky you have me to take care of you," Tori says. "You know who else is lucky?" She puts her hands on Luka's shoulders and gives him a kiss on the cheek. "I'm sure Brooklyn will be forcing you to drink your greens soon, too."

Luka gives a look of mock horror. "In that case, I better double down on tempura and cheesecake while I still can."

They're all looking at me while they jest and have fun. I force a smile, but my soul hurts too much to really join in. They hope that I'm going to take care of Luka, that things will work out splendidly for us the way Stefan and Tori's arranged marriage did. But the difference is, they love each other for real. They take care of each other for real. They're happy just being together.

The meal turns into a pleasantly chaotic mess, everyone standing or walking around the room, taking a bite of this or that and then finding someone else to talk to. It's nice seeing all the people in Luka's life having such a genuinely good time. I just wish I felt their lightheartedness.

I push the food around on my plate, the burning in my throat preventing me from enjoying any of it. Water isn't helping, nor is the champagne.

"Brooklyn!" a voice hisses.

When I look over my shoulder, I see Emzee triumphantly marching over with a stack of magazines under her arm.

"What are those?"

She grins. "Travel magazines, *National Geographic*, a Lonely Planet guide, and a few random others. These all have articles on romantic destinations, so you can start getting ideas for sightseeing on your honeymoon! I've been pulling this stash together as part of your wedding present, but I thought you might want to get started now."

My mouth falls open. "Oh, wow. Thank you, Em. That was so thoughtful."

"I'm going to put these with Luka's coat so you can take them on your way out. You guys are going to have the *best time*," she gushes, before heading back to her table.

I take a deep breath. I can't keep holding my secret inside. Tomorrow is my wedding day and for all it's worth, I want my marriage to start out right and not on a foundation of lies. We might not be able to change the reasons we became engaged, but I can do my part to make it better from here on out. Just not with the contract mocking me from the depths of my purse.

Luka takes his seat next to me and I study his profile as he laughs with the woman next to him. Slowly, I run my hand over his thigh beneath the table, a tingle going up my arm at his firm warmth. I know what I want to do. It's time to come clean.

He turns to me, the smile fading from his lips when he sees my face. "What's wrong?"

"I, um, I need to tell you some—"

"Brooklyn, you haven't eaten a thing!" Stefan interrupts. "I know you probably have pre-wedding jitters and all that, but you're missing out." He leans over my shoulder and spears a piece of tempura shrimp with my fork, then brings it to my lips with an expectancy I can't deny. I eat it to appease him and he starts talking to Luka. Before I know it, he's feeding me another.

"Why am I feeding your bride instead of you?" Stefan teases his brother with an amused laugh. They banter back and forth for a while, and my future brother-in-law goes back to his spot to retrieve his drink before mingling with someone else.

I wipe my mouth with a napkin. "Wow. Stefan seems to be in a good mood. He usually seems more...serious."

"True." Luka leans closer toward me. "To be honest, I can't remember the last time I saw my family this laid back, especially not about something as big as a wedding. They're actually *relaxed*. Stefan's been downright easygoing. I guess we've really been nailing the PR stuff."

My stomach clenches and I clear my throat. "Yeah, that must be it. I'm glad."

Luka glances at my full plate. "Are you nervous? Is that why you're not eating?"

I'm not going to lie to him. It is nerves, and so much more. "Yes."

His warm hand wraps over mine and he kisses me on the cheek so gently that I shiver. I quickly eat a prosciutto-wrapped scallop before I blurt everything out right here and now.

"What did you want to tell me?" he prods.

"Hmm?"

His brows knit together in concern. "Earlier, you said there was something you wanted to talk to me about."

I look around to see if we can possibly leave for a few minutes without anyone stopping us. For the moment, all the guests are seated and talking, their attention anywhere but on Luka and me. It's the perfect time to escape for a little bit. Which is necessary, because he may not take this well.

In fact, it might go over like a fucking bomb.

"Can we have a few minutes alone?" I ask, my heart in my throat.

"Hey-o!" a voice interrupts. "I haven't had a chance to meet your smokin' hot bride yet!"

Luka rises to greet the man rushing up behind us. I

THE SHAM

recognize him as one of Luka's groomsmen, someone he went through his MBA program with, but we haven't been formally introduced. Luka makes the introductions and small talk ensues. Before I know it, the dinner plates are being cleared and dessert is brought around. Everyone resumes their seats and the din of conversation hums loudly in my ears.

People I barely know stand to raise toasts to Luka and me, but it's Mateo's speech that has my eyes stinging. It's brief but heartfelt, and when he says he wishes me and Luka an amazing journey together, I can't help wishing the same. I should burn that contract from Elite Image.

Or should I just sign it and guarantee my success?

Fuck, why is this so hard? I know where my heart is... and it isn't with Elite. But what if I'm making a huge mistake, letting my feelings for Luka get the better of me? My brain says this arrangement with him isn't a sure thing. But betraying him feels wrong in every way.

By the time a selection of cakes and pastries are passed along with brandy and carafes of coffee, the noise has dimmed, and the guests are winding down. True to his word earlier, Luka eats two huge pieces of cheesecake, then leans back in his chair and stretches his arms over his head. He looks satisfied and...happy.

"Brooklyn, look at me," he says quietly. I glance at him and he's holding a bite of dessert on his fork for me. "Consider it practice for tomorrow when I feed you cake."

"When you smear her face in it, you mean?" someone across the table hollers.

I hold Luka's gaze as I take the offered treat, and everyone cheers. We're not going to get a moment alone. I don't have any choice but to ride the rest of this evening out and put my conscience behind me.

"You better not even think of smearing it on my face." I try to join in on the fun, but I'm two seconds away from losing my composure. The papers in my purse whisper to me, reminding me that I can't have true happiness unless I clear the air. I want to. I'm trying! I need to get him alone for a couple of minutes and explain everything.

"Brooklyn, when you have a minute, can I show you something?"

It's the wedding planner. Glad for the escape, I excuse myself and meet her in the lobby to go over a couple of last-minute details. There's been a small change to the color of the ribbon on the flowers. The seating arrangement for the reception was altered slightly. Did I want the ring bearer to carry the ring in his little tux pocket or on the silk pillow?

By the time I go back inside, the guests are leaving. Luka rushes over and kisses my forehead. Emzee and Tori come up behind me and loop their arms through mine.

"She's ours now. Bye-bye, loser." Emzee waves him off.

"See you tomorrow," Luka calls to me. He looks back as if expecting me to reply. I don't, because I can't get anything out.

"Oh no, she already has stage fright!" Tori pats my hand. "Come on. The hotel room we booked has a fully stocked bar. We'll get you through this."

My future sisters-in-law whisk me off to the luxury hotel we're staying in tonight and I know they're going to take good care of me. They'll have to, because I'm in no shape to do anything except drown in the guilt over not coming clean to Luka before I become his wife.

BROOKLYN

CHAPTER 26

I'm getting married.
I am getting *married*.
Today. Soon. In a few minutes.

I let out a slow breath as Tori adjusts the lacy folds of my voluminous, hand-beaded veil. We're standing before a tall oval mirror and I'm having a hard time believing the princess in the glass is me. The ivory Vera Wang dress fits like an absolute glove, the strapless bodice cupping my breasts and giving me killer cleavage. The skirt conforms to my hips and bursts into a pile of gorgeous, fluffy ruffles about mid-thigh to the floor, accentuating my statuesque figure. It's simple and expensively elegant. Stefan, my brother-in-law to-be, surprised me with an antique teardrop pearl necklace on a rose-gold chain ("Something old, as the saying goes," he'd told me with a wink. "Tori helped pick it out."), and it's the perfect adornment to my dream dress.

My hair cascades down my back in big, glossy curls. I instructed the makeup artist to go with a light touch, except for a bold lip to match the unexpected pop of the bright red heels that peek beneath my hem when I lift my skirts.

Diamond studs borrowed from Tori sparkle in my ears, setting off the glitter of my engagement ring. As I give myself a final once-over, I have to admit I look perfect. All of it feels simply perfect.

Forget the princess. I look like a queen.

"I know you're a model and all, but seriously, you are absolute perfection." Tori spins me around so she can fiddle with my veil from the front. She and Emzee are in fabulous dresses of nude and dusty rose; my only requirement for the bridesmaids was that they wear warm neutrals.

"Thank you," I say, feeling unexpectedly emotional.

My inner well is full. Despite everything, there's joy in there, and it's surreal that I have Tori and Emzee here to fuss over me, just like real sisters would. I've been complacent and quiet, letting them primp and fix and fluff to their hearts' content. They're genuinely happy to see Luka getting married—something I can't quite wrap my head around, considering this is all a sham. Maybe they're hoping this will really turn into something and Luka will finally have a little family of his own to love. Maybe...he'll finally have that intimate connection with someone in the way he never did when he was growing up. I know that I want those things for him.

But can I really be that person?

"We're just so lucky to have you!" Emzee grins and gives me a tentative hug, careful not to muss my dress. I squeeze her back. She was the one who had my garter custom-made with a tiny blue bow stitched to it, to make sure I'd have my "something blue" for the wedding.

"Remember, you guys promised not to say anything that would make me cry," I say. "Five-hundred-dollar makeup over here." I point to my face, trying to keep things lighthearted.

My mom just left the room a few minutes ago to take her seat. Meanwhile my dad is waiting outside to walk me down the aisle, and I've been reminding myself over and over not to cry the moment I see him. This wedding isn't real. It's *not*. I have to remember that, or I'll never get through it dry-eyed.

"I wonder if Luka's as nervous as I am," I say.

"I'm sure he is," Tori says. "But you shouldn't be. It's going to go by so fast you won't have time to feel nervous. Trust me. My wedding was a total blur."

Despite Tori's kind words, I doubt my fake fiancé is feeling much of anything. There's no way he's as caught up in the excitement of the day as I am.

My impending nuptials aren't the only reason I'm anxious, though. When Emzee and Tori whisked me away from the rehearsal dinner last night, I didn't get a chance to tell Luka what was on my mind—the Elite contract. To avoid the lingering guilt, I turn my thoughts to imagining him standing there waiting at the other end of the aisle. He's already breathtaking, and I'm eagerly anticipating the sight of him decked to the nines in all his wedding glory.

"I bet he looks amazing," I say with a sigh. "Have either of you seen him in his tux?"

"Sure," Emzee says with one of her signature eye-rolls. "And he looks just as plain and unattractive as ever."

I can't help laughing, even as Tori tsks her sister-in-law.

They both comes close to stand next to me, and the three of us look into the mirror. "He looks great," Tori says. "And I've honestly never seen him so excited."

Excited?

Luka's family has taken this sham wedding in stride and elevated their acceptance of it by actually embracing it as if it's real. Planning everything has definitely had its perks and moments of excitement for me, even though I've kept the end game forefront in my mind. Luka hadn't seemed excited over any of it. He'd simply gone through the motions, letting me handle the decisions. But he'd been different at the rehearsal dinner last night, enjoying himself like a true groom might.

"Are you sure?" I ask. "Maybe he's just trying to talk himself out of backing out."

"He's not going to back out!" Emzee gives my bare shoulder a little squeeze and I cover her hand with mine. We share a smile in the mirror and then she slips out of the room for a moment, then comes back to crack the door and wave at me.

Beside me, Tori's shoulders bunch around her ears with excitement. "It's time! Ready?"

She hands me my bouquet, a custom creation I chose made of huge blush-colored peonies, exotic succulents, and fragrant hydrangeas. I can only nod.

Suddenly, I'm whisked out of the dressing room and into the hall of the nineteenth century mansion we rented for the ceremony and the reception. My one ask in regard to the venue was that we be married someplace that had "history," and our wedding planner hadn't disappointed. The Esmoor Estate rarely allows weddings as large as ours, but they had been happy to make an exception for the Zorics, of course, and the wedding planner spared no expense or detail in creating the ultimate fairy tale out of the place.

Above my head, sparkling chandeliers hang between drapes of sheer fabric. The polished marble of the hallway floor is dusted with pale pink rose petals. The hem of my dress swishes against them as I take my father's arm.

"My little girl's all grown up," he chokes out. He lowers

my veil and wipes his eyes and I have to look away so I don't start to cry, too.

Then he leads me to the yawning ballroom where the ceiling above us is hung with arrangements of rose branches, lush ferns, and creamy wisteria in abundant groupings intermixed with garlands of crystal drops hanging delicately between the blooms. An ivory runner lines the walk between rows of chairs. The soft prelude music flutters to silence as everyone rises.

I grip my father's arm tightly as we pause at the end of the aisle. Tori and Emzee are standing beside the pastor, lined up beside Mateo, my "maid of honor," in his dashing pale pink Dolce & Gabbana suit. I'd told him that beige was fine, but he'd wanted to go all out.

And then I spy Luka on the other side, just as I imagined, waiting for me beneath the elegant arch covered in greenery and tiny fairy lights. My chest hitches, my mind suddenly whirling. I force myself to focus on the music. The wedding march will start any second—

Suddenly, there's a musical beat, then another...then another, and I immediately recognize the song. My dad looks at me with surprise that probably mirrors my own, and I can't hold back a shocked gasp. Billy Joel's *She's Got A Way* begins to softly play in all its musical glory.

I can't believe Luka remembered!

I look at him and wish he was closer so I could fully see his expression. I'd once mentioned to him that this song had been a favorite of mine and my dad's, kind of "our song" since we danced to it at my middle school winter festival dance. Luka had seemed a bit shocked when I told him but wouldn't explain why, until I finally got it out of him that the song was special to him, too. A housekeeper had taught him to slow dance to it so he could impress a girl in fifth grade. It was something we shared that unified us with the people who'd helped us grow.

And now we would be helping each other, and the song would connect us in our own special way. A collective sound of delight comes from our guests as the song softly plays, and with a gentle squeeze to my hand, my dad walks me down the aisle.

A shiver goes down the back of my neck as Luka comes into focus. His tux is bespoke, the lapels glossy black satin. A crisp white shirt makes the dusky hue of his skin pop. Diamond cufflinks sparkle, reminiscent of my engagement ring. His lips part as he watches me approach, eyes wide with an emotion I can't read.

"Awestruck," my dad whispers with a smile. "That look is called completely awestruck."

He kisses my cheek and places my hand on Luka's arm, and I realize that I haven't stopped staring at the gorgeous face of my almost-husband. We must stare at each other too long, because we're softly directed to turn inside the arch and face the pastor. Luka's hand slides over mine with a warmth I can feel flowing through every inch of me.

"Dearly beloved..."

The ceremony starts and it really is like a dream. Words I've heard in romantic movies a million times are now applied to me. Words that are intended to have real meaning and conviction when they're repeated. My heart is racing.

We turn to face each other, and Luka takes my other hand in his. The weight of my dress becomes palpable, but not because I'm scared or second-guessing—instead, my body feels weak from the intensity in Luka's eyes as he begins to state his vows.

His tone is clear and steady and confident, and so full of conviction that I believe what he's saying. He's sincere.

Our fingers twine together as if we intend to never let go, and now it's my turn to make him believe I mean each and every word.

I repeat the vows, saying them as clearly and confidently as Luka did for me. As each word comes out of my mouth, the intention with which I repeat it grows. This may have started out as a sham, but it doesn't feel like it now... and I want nothing more than to make my life with Luka work. He cups my face in his hands at the exact moment I decide what I want for our future, his grin stealing my breath right before he kisses me softly, tenderly. Lovingly.

Everyone claps and cheers and I barely have time to pull my emotions back in before we're ushered down the aisle as man and wife, flower petals raining down on us.

I'm Mrs. Luka Zoric in name, and if things continue like this, I will be in heart, too.

I don't let myself overthink anything as we follow our guests up the curving, split staircase that leads to the reception upstairs. The intricate gilded iron railing is decorated in pink and cream flowers with plumes of natural greenery, and tea lights glow softly at the edges of each step. I laugh a little as I take it all in. Even the stairs are perfect.

"Take a deep breath, Brooklyn," Luka whispers in my ear. "The hard part is over."

I smile up at him and enjoy the depth of emotion rippling through me. Finally, we enter the second-floor ballroom, hand in hand, to loud cheers and a few whistles.

Above us, billows of organza drape from the ceiling. Perfectly arranged tables are set with lightly patterned china and cut crystal glasses rimmed in gold. Four-foot tall crystal flutes hold floral topiaries, and live cherry blossom trees stand at each end of the long table for the wedding party. The pale pink fabric napkins I picked out have our initials monogrammed on them and look amazing beneath the golden glow of the flatware.

As much as Luka left the wedding decisions to me and the planner, I also encouraged him to incorporate some personal elements of his own. I spy the first of our little personal touches as a server comes around with his favorite gold label Veuve Clicquot champagne. Another has a tray with hors d'oeuvres of my favorite Great Lakes whitefish with rosemary and cucumber on rye toast, and Luka's requested crème fraîche and caviar tartlets. We're handed champagne and we clink our glasses together before taking a sip.

With a quick pull of his hand on my wrist, I'm up against my husband and he's kissing me with the sweetness of champagne on his lips. Tilting my head, I take his mouth deeper, pressing into the warmth of his body.

Luka presses a hand to my back, his fingers splaying against my bare skin. His breathing picks up, his grip on me tightening...

"Groomsmen! Gather around Luka!"

My head is swimming as Luka is peeled away by a man with a camera on a tripod. Luka insisted we hire an outside professional to take pictures so that Emzee could just enjoy herself, but as the resident photographer in the family, she couldn't help bringing her own camera to the wedding. I've already spotted her snapping photos, and I'm glad. I know they'll be way more fun, intimate, and candid than any of the posed pictures that our hired photographer will get.

Tori loops her arm through mine and spins me out of the way just in time for me to see Luka and the groomsmen pull up the legs of their pants to reveal knee-high Minnesota

Wild socks, resplendent in the hockey team's garish red and bright green team colors. Even our littlest groomsman, Tori's adorable eight-year-old half-brother Max, is in on the tacky sock flashing.

Luka winks. I laugh. He warned me that he might add a few crazy elements to the wedding, and considering the huge smile on his face right now, I'm glad that he did. The evening flows on like a dream. Every time I see Luka across the room, each time he takes my hand, or kisses me at request of the guests, or gives me a heated, lusty glance, I melt a little more. Watching him joke with Mateo, the rift between them mended now, is the icing on the cake.

When there's a lull, Mateo comes over to me with a glass of champagne and a smirk on his face. "Girl, you are glowing," he tells me.

"I'm happy," I can't help gushing.

"Of course you are," he says. "Have I ever steered you wrong?"

"Never," I say, pulling him in for a tight hug. "Thank you for...just everything."

Finally I find myself in Luka's arms for our first dance as husband and wife.

"Well, hello, Mrs. Zoric," he croons as he pulls me against him.

"That has a very nice ring to it, Mr. Zoric."

He tilts his head and gives me a questioning look. "Do you really think so? You won't mind having my name?"

It feels so right. I've made the right choice, and the content look on his face says he feels the same. For the first time, we're completely connected. I want it to stay that way.

Resting my head on his shoulder, I nuzzle against his neck. "I'm proud to have your name, Luka."

A warm kiss presses against my temple right before he tugs me upright and gives me a spin. The crowd cheers.

My heart cheers.

Everything feels exactly right, like my life with Luka is finally coming together perfectly. And as I look into his eyes, I know—I won't let anything stand in the way of our future.

BROOKLYN

CHAPTER 27

I've changed into a classy white pantsuit that looks amazing with my red heels, but all I can think of is how eager I am to have my new husband strip me naked.

The well wishes and cheers of our family and friends fade into the distance as we drive away in our limo. I indulged during dinner and ate two pieces of our gorgeous triple-layer strawberry champagne cake from Aimee's and had more than a couple glasses of the thousand-dollar-per-bottle champagne. But while my soul is content, there's one thing I *haven't* gotten my fill of. I want my husband inside me, repeatedly, until we're both too spent to move.

With a happy sigh, I settle into my seat and slip a hand onto Luka's knee with a gentle squeeze. His arm slips around my shoulders and he pulls me in tight against his side. He also changed into something more comfortable for our long night of traveling ahead. I've wanted to wrap myself around him since the moment we locked eyes as I walked down the aisle. It's an ache that hasn't lessened a bit this entire time.

He kisses the top of my head. "You should get some rest. It's going to be a long night."

Playfully, I walk my fingers up his leg to the inside of his thigh. "Since when does Luka Zoric want to rest when he has the opportunity to do something more fun?" I press the button that closes the partition between us and the driver and give him a saucy wink. A dimple forms in his right cheek with the wicked smile he gives me.

"Darling, we're going to Paris. I want nothing more than to fuck my wife for the first time with a view of the Eiffel Tower right outside my window."

He stiffens as I brush my fingers along his crotch. "You want to wait that long?" I tease. "It's a long flight." Nuzzling into him, I take a draw of his masculine scent. "We could be on round three by the time we land."

Luka takes my hand. "I love how eager you are. But I just want everything to be perfect."

"Really?"

"Really," he says.

I cup his jaw with my palm and lose myself in his eyes for a moment. I *am* eager. Now that I've decided what path I'm going to take and how I'm going to handle this marriage, I'm content. More than content. I'm happy. "The wedding was...unbelievable. Thank you."

He nods and kisses my knuckles, drawing a shiver over my skin. "I didn't have a lot of say in the planning, so the credit is all yours. You put on an amazing wedding, Brooklyn."

"Thank you. Now it's time for you to put on an amazing wedding night."

He moves to run his fingers into the back of my hair where the curls hang down. I look up at him hungrily as he leans down to kiss me, but his lips are soft and gentle.

Sparks of pleasure burst through my body as I enjoy the feel of his mouth, and the way his tongue dances slowly with mine. He takes his time, drawing out every zing of pleasure. I moan. My nipples tingle and I shift my hips to get closer to him, but it's not enough. I want the length of my body pressed against his, our nakedness mingling with waves of heat and pleasure until we can't take it anymore. My desire ratchets, promising to surpass any need I've had for him before.

This already feels different. Maybe because I've never had sex with Luka when I've been at peace with my intentions. I can't wait to experience it now that I'm whole and confident. Sex with him is already amazing. This time? I shiver at the thought of how intense it could be.

His palm presses to mine as he pulls away, our fingers intertwining. I feel how much he wants me through that simple touch, how pleased he is with how today turned out.

"We're almost to the airport." Luka rights himself in the seat but doesn't let go of my hand. I've never seen him this contentedly quiet before. A less confident version of myself might wonder if he's having second thoughts or regrets, but I can feel how relaxed he is, and it makes my soul soar. We're on the same page. It's amazing.

The car exits the highway and soon, we're parking at a runway where our private jet is waiting to take us to Paris. Luka helps me from the car, never letting go of my hand as we embark onto the plane. Ducking my head to enter, I pause to take it all in. This can't be real!

"*Wow*." I glance back at Luka, then do a double take as I fully enter the plane.

The interior is sleek, with cream-colored leather seats, a mahogany table, and gold trim around the oval windows. An arched doorway stands open, revealing a bedroom with a queen-sized bed and en-suite, fully functional bathroom. The front offers a mini-kitchen and wet bar. A flight attendant greets us as she appears from the kitchen area and immediately takes our bags.

"Welcome, Mr. and Mrs. Zoric. My name is Miranda and I'm here to serve your every need. We'll take off as soon as you're comfortably seated. Congratulations on your nuptials."

The luxury is a bit overwhelming and I'm not sure where I'm supposed to sit. Luka gestures me to a plush double recliner against the back wall. There's a mini fridge at the base of my seat. It's filled with tiny bottles of alcohol and a variety of snacks. There's also a heated blanket on the armrest, waiting to warm me up if I catch a chill.

"Watch this," Luka says with childish delight. He presses a button and a huge flat screen television slowly descends from the ceiling a few feet in front of us.

"Impressive," I admit.

"You could live on this thing for a month and never feel deprived," Luka says. "Though I'm glad we're only on board for a few hours. Let's get you comfortable."

He positions the television back into place, then shows me how to operate the buttons on the reclining chair. It gently falls into a chaise position and I'm in heaven.

We settle in and the flight attendant brings out feather pillows and lap blankets. Luka settles in next to me as we take off, and once we've reached altitude, Miranda brings out a round of drinks. I'm not sure if I should drink more after the multiple flutes of champagne I had at the reception. Seemingly to sense my hesitation, Luka takes both tumblers and hands one to me.

"We won't get to Paris until the wee hours of the morning. You'll sleep it off by then."

I want to make a quip about preferring to work it off, but Miranda is still standing there. The huge bed in the other room calls to me. I'm not scared of flying, but I've never been on a flight this long, and never this late in the day. As the adrenaline of the wedding begins to recede, fatigue creeps in more and more. My body feels heavy and light at the same time, my mind tired yet buzzing, and I don't make it halfway through my whiskey sour before I lean into Luka.

"I think I'm about to have a post-wedding crash. I'd better lie down."

He starts to get up. "Of course. It's been a long day."

"I want you with me," I tell him.

His eyebrows go up playfully. God, I love his face. He taps the tip of my nose before taking my hand and helping me to my feet. "Are you going to behave yourself?"

We move to the doorway and go through, Luka softly shutting the door behind us. I spin into his arms and loop my hands around his neck. He's never turned me away before, but I'm getting the clear impression that wedding night sex is not on his radar.

I kiss him softly. "Is it bad if I don't want to behave?"

He groans deep against my mouth before kissing me slow and easy. "I want our wedding night to be special."

"Luka—" The protest dies on my lips as his expression grows serious.

"Can I be honest with you?"

"Of course."

He fiddles with a strand of my hair, raising tingles all over my scalp. Leaning into his touch, I close my eyes at the pleasant sensation.

"This isn't my usual MO. You know that. I take what I want and don't think twice about it. But the truth is...it's different for me this time. I want our wedding night to be amazing."

My legs go weak at the sincerity in his voice. He actually cares about this, about me, and is doing the one thing he knows will elevate our union beyond the sham it's founded on. He's showing me the most vulnerable part of himself, and I'm not sure how to react.

"I have to say...I love that idea," I murmur.

I smile at him and he kisses me again and leads me to the bed. We lie down on top of the covers, facing each other, and the last thing I remember is how lazy and relaxed I feel.

"Brooklyn. It's time to wake up."

I blink to the sound of Luka calling my name. He's looking down at me, his hair disheveled, eyes heavy with sleep. Realization seeps in and my pulse ticks up excitedly.

"We're here? In Paris?" I push myself up to a sitting position.

"Just about to land."

Slipping out of the bed, I pat at my hair, finding that my curls have gone limp in my sleep. Luka chuckles and makes quick work of helping me remove the bobby pins so I can pull it back into a loose ponytail. Then he leans back and looks me up and down with a slow smile.

"Beautiful."

"Thank you."

We take a few more minutes to get ready. Butterflies swirl in my middle. I've never been to Paris, and I've never felt as close to a man as I do to Luka right now.

But I still haven't told him about Elite...

"Come out here and sit with me." Luka opens the bedroom door and waves me through. We sit and buckle in just as the plane begins to descend. Soon after, we're taxiing on the runway at CDG through the early morning darkness.

THE SHAM

A car is waiting to take us to the Shangri-La Paris, and I can barely contain my excitement as we drive toward the city center just before sunrise.

There is so much to take in: gorgeous old stone buildings with sloping mansard roofs, the postcard-perfect, pre-dawn view from the bridge over the Seine, a few people out walking their dogs or setting up woven chairs outside of tiny sidewalk cafés. Luka leans over my shoulder to point out the window at the domed roof of the Sacré-Coeur and a few other famous sights in the distance, clearly familiar with the city and the arrondissement where we're staying.

We pull into the hotel's circular drive lined with lamp posts, and a valet opens my door.

"*Bienvenue à Pah-ree*," he says warmly.

"*Merci!*" I respond, glad I can at least say "thank you" properly in French.

Luka and I step into a sprawling, luxurious building with white marble floors, softly glowing crystal sconces along the walls, a domed ceiling with a mural painted on it, and a wide staircase to our right with ornate black and gold wrought iron railings. A gentleman rushes to us, speaking rapid-fire French—which, of course, Luka seems to understand—and just like that, we're immediately shown to our room.

My husband opens a wide set of cream-colored double doors, then cocks a brow playfully before picking me up in his arms and carrying me through.

"Does a hotel room threshold count?" he asks.

"It's a threshold in *Paris*. Of course it counts!"

He doesn't give me time to look around, closing the door with his foot and hurrying to the bedroom to set me gently onto a massive bed with a golden brocade quilt.

"Watch this."

He moves to the French doors a few feet from the foot of our bed and opens them. A small balcony is lined with flowers and topiary trees and just off to the left, the Eiffel Tower is still alive with lights against the backdrop of a pink- and orange-streaked sky.

Leaving the doors open, he makes his way toward me from the foot of the bed until he's straddling me. His fingers dance across my chest as he unbuttons my shirt and leans low to nibble at my ear. My desire sparks immediately back to life. I've been holding it back for hours and it's a physical relief that I don't have to anymore.

"Did you ever think you'd get fucked on your wedding night with a perfect view of the Eiffel Tower outside your window?"

"Never," I answer honestly.

I swallow hard as he pushes my top off my shoulders and down to my waist. Then I shimmy out of the rest of my travel-wrinkled suit. Catching his eyes, I arch my back as he unhooks my bra and pulls it off me. I want to say something sweet about never thinking I'd have any of this, including a man like him. But it's not the right time. I want him too much to talk.

Neither of us says anything else. My brain sinks into the moment, losing all sense of time and our surroundings. It's just me and Luka and the sinfully delicious things he's doing to my body. His mouth is everywhere—sucking at my nipples until I can't lie still from the pleasure, working down my belly to my pussy where he feasts like he's never tasted me there before. He's tireless, letting me guide the rhythm, and he doesn't stop until I'm coming all over his face, moaning his name. Then he leans in again, licking and sucking until a second orgasm follows.

I'm breathless and overcome with the reality that this

man is mine. He's fully and completely mine. "I need you," I murmur. "All of you."

We rip and pull at his clothes until he's naked on top of me. Flipping him, it's my turn to taste the hot skin on the side of his neck, whisper kisses over the planes of his hard chest. I don't have a chance to make it to his cock before he's gripping my hips and aligning me, and I bring myself down, impaling myself onto his thick shaft. We both cry out, the pleasure nearly overtaking me. My thighs tremble as I ride him, and already I feel another orgasm begin to build. His hands wind into my hair. With a gentle tug, he brings me low to meet his mouth.

My own flavor is strong in the kiss as he devours my lips, then flips us again so he's on top. I lose it then. All awareness just fades away save for where our bodies are connected. He takes my hands, the warmth of our connected palms driving my pleasure even higher, and suddenly I'm shattering again, taking Luka with me. I feel him spill hot inside me, whispering my name as he comes, and my eyes tear up with emotion as I wrap my legs tighter around him.

Finally he collapses next to me, pulling me in close.

I run a hand through his hair and let out an exhausted breath.

"You were so right. Waiting was definitely worth it."

My nipples perk as he runs his fingers over them. "I'm glad you enjoyed that, Mrs. Zoric. Because we're just getting started."

BROOKLYN

CHAPTER 28

I have no idea what time it is.

I've been watching Luka sleep for a while now, drinking up the contented, relaxed lines of his handsome face. The past twenty-four hours have been magical, and it's silly, but I'm honestly not sure if this is really my life or if I'm lost in a daydream. This is one of those moments in the movies where people pinch themselves to double-check reality.

Luka is finally sprawled out on the bed after making love to me three times; the last time slowly and from behind so that I could fully appreciate the Eiffel Tower view. Rolling carefully to the edge of the bed, I sit and put my feet on the floor. My pussy and the insides of my thighs ache deliciously in a heady reminder of the incredible honeymoon sex we'd had. I'm already ready for more. And when we decide we've had our fill of sex, there's an entire city waiting to be explored.

Best of all, we're in a good place with each other. A comfortable place. It's time that I open up to Luka a little

THE SHAM

more and allow him to know me—to let him in more than I have in the past. Like real couples do. But I need to take care of something first, before we dive into this honeymoon. I need my guilt out of the way.

Glancing over my shoulder, I make sure he's still sleeping as I rise from the bed, then pause, listening. He doesn't stir. Taking a soft cream-colored throw blanket from the wingback chair near the bed, I pull it around myself and close the bedroom door gently behind me as I quietly pad into the front room where the concierge had left our bags. My purse sits there, tilted toward me as if it knows what I'm after.

I've changed. I know what I want now, and that starts with clearing obstacles from our newly married path.

Opening my purse, I pause to listen again before taking the Elite Image contract from my bag and folding it in my hand. I need to get rid of it, but I'm not sure how. I consider going down to the lobby and dropping it into an obscure garbage can, but that leaves the risk of someone inadvertently finding it. No, it needs to be permanently destroyed.

I don't want this sinister thing hanging over me, not when I've resolved to move forward and enjoy my marriage to Luka, to be present in our union the way a dedicated spouse should be. If things can continue the way they have been lately, I see nothing but happiness ahead for us.

My pulse picks up, the weight of the paper heavy in my palm. I wish I could just snap my fingers and make it disappear—

I make a semi-circle, realizing there's a fireplace in the center of the far wall. Two plush chairs are arranged around it, probably why I didn't notice it before. Going over to it, I inspect the unit while chewing on my bottom lip. I have no idea how to use a fireplace. I realize it's gas, and I have to turn a little knob to get it started. A small basket of long matches sits close by, which seems pretty self-explanatory. I hem and haw for a moment, worried about burning down the Shangri-La.

Finally, I turn the knob and wait until the scent of gas fills in my nose. Shivers go down my spine. What if the smell wakes him? I'll have to tell him I couldn't sleep and wanted some ambiance. There's a hearth rug beneath my feet. I can slip the paper beneath it if I have to. Tight with the urgency to get this over with, I turn back to the fireplace.

Hearing nothing from the bedroom, I strike the match and place it inside the center of the fireplace. It bursts to life and I dial down the knob until the flames reach a soft, steady blaze.

My shoulders sag a little as the heat warms my face and radiates through the blanket. Slowly, quietly, I unfold the contract and look at it one last time. My gut sinks. I can't believe I ever thought about doing this. Infiltrating Danica Rose just to get myself a high-profile campaign. Sure, marrying Luka in order to jumpstart my career might not seem that much better, but at least I wasn't hurting anyone this way. And besides, things are different now. I love him.

The words glare up at me accusingly from the page.

...agreement consists of providing insider information regarding Danica Rose Management (hereafter "DRM") with Elite Image...will act as informant...compensation will be provided in exchange for financial and contractual records obtained directly from DRM...

My throat burns as I crumple the paper and toss it into the fire. It catches immediately, the flames licking at the ball of deceit and lies until it begins to curl into itself and turn black. My palms grow damp, my chest going tight because it's not burning fast enough. I want it gone.

Tears hit my eyes as the last of the contract turns to ash in the grate. Thank God. Thank God it's over. I sit there a while longer, enjoying the heat and the rays of Paris sunlight darting in through the tall, arched windows. I can't wait to take Luka's hand and go explore the city. We'll eat croissants and duck confit and French onion soup and fancy French macarons until we're full to bursting. Have a picnic with amazing cheeses and wine. We'll drink pressed coffees until our hearts are completely pounding, hike the steps up to the top of the Eiffel Tower, visit the Louvre. And then we'll come back here and make love until we can't physically move another inch.

I smile into the flames, the contentment I felt earlier settling over me. I'm so glad the contract is gone. This marriage has so much potential, and I'm finally fully committed. There's not a doubt in my mind that Luka is, too.

Strengthened by what I've just done, I turn off the fireplace and make sure all the ashes have burnt down. Not a trace remains. I peer out the windows on the way back to bed, both excited for the day and exhausted since I haven't slept much.

The double doors to the balcony are still open. Unable to resist, I step outside and am met with the immediate brilliance and warmth of the sun. Cars go by far below, the sounds of the city filtering up to me along with the strong scent of coffee probably coming from the balcony below. I gaze at the Tower and survey the skyline and the city below until the aches in my body remind me that I've barely slept. Luka wore me out so damn good, and I want nothing more than to crawl back into bed with him.

The covers have slipped down his hard body, revealing the firm rise of his ass and the strong lines of his muscular back. I carefully slip back into bed and spoon up against him. He moans and presses against me as if seeking the feel of my skin in his sleep. My arm goes around him, my mind floating off to all the possibilities of Paris and beyond. I trail my fingers lightly along his rigid abs, deciding I'm getting some of that room service coffee as soon as I wake up.

The sound of birds chirping is followed by a honking horn. It sounds far away. As I startle fully awake, I recall cars going by far beneath me when I was out on the balcony. Blinking, I rub my eyes and realize there's a lack of warmth in the bed. I reach for where the comforting heat had been, but it's empty. Luka's gone.

A slow smile crosses my face as everything comes back to me. I wish he was still in bed, but I'm really hoping he's gone to get some coffee, or maybe a whole brunch spread.

I open my eyes and push the hair back from my face. And jump when I find Luka standing beside the bed, looking down at me.

His face is set in stone.

A flicker of alarm makes me sit up and draw the covers over my chest.

"What's wrong?" I reach for him. "Are you okay?"

His eyes shimmer with a blend of outright fury, and something almost like shock...what did my dad call that expression? Awestruck. But not in the good way—not in the amazed, loving sort of way he'd looked at me when I walked down the aisle. He's wearing the kind of confusion that comes with being completely blindsided.

Betrayed.

No. Oh, no.

"Luka?" I say his name slowly, hoping desperately that it's something else.

Anything else.

He looks as if he wants to respond but he either can't, or else he's afraid of what he might do if he does. His bare chest heaves, up and down, up and down, the pace increasing as he struggles with his emotions.

"How could you, Brooklyn? How the fuck could you do this?"

My lips are numb. I touch them, just to be sure they're still there. "How could I what?"

I think I already know. But...how did he find out?

Maybe I'm wrong. It has to be something else. Something's happened with the business, or maybe—

He thrusts his cellphone in my face, gripping it so hard that his fingertips have gone white. There's a message from Monica Shore. My stomach bottoms out when I see her name. She's one of Elite Image's top models, and she's never been shy about her dislike of me.

Hey, old friend. I thought you might like to know what your new bride has been up to. Bonne chance!

My eyes fly to Luka's. I shake my head, but it's a weak attempt. My fingers curl into the sheet covering my breasts as I scramble to think of something. I—I...

He angrily taps the attachment on the text message. I don't need to see it; I know what it is. But the phone is so close to me that I can't look away.

A strangled sound comes from deep in my throat.

It's a copy of the contract from Elite, the same one I just burned, right there for my new husband to see. Outlining in excruciating detail all the ways I intended to betray him.

Even without my signature, I know how this looks to Luka.

This is bad.
It's very, very bad.

~

Brooklyn and Luka's story continues…

Find out what happens in The Contract.

ALSO BY STELLA GRAY

∼

Arranged Series

The Deal

The Secret

The Choice

Convenience Series

The Sham

The Contract

The Ruin

ABOUT STELLA GRAY

Stella Gray is an emerging author of contemporary romance. When she is not writing, Stella loves to read, hike, knit and cuddle with her greyhound.

Made in the USA
Las Vegas, NV
14 February 2021